Champions of Lore

Book One
Roar of the Scourge

Ronald J Brake

Art Contributors
Jennifer Crosby, Map & Axe
Amber Curl, Vile Skull
Austin Morgan, Sihon's Sword
Cassie McCarty, Flower Design
Bone Fire & Silhouettes by the Author & His Wife

My thanks go out to all who were generous with kind and encouraging words. Know that this gave me the confidence to present the book within your hands.

Within these Ancient Lands

Nimeria is the mountain civilization ruled by a people of great size
Haran the old prophet
Lael A leader among the Nimerian's
Argoes A leader and champion among the Nimerian's
Ryn A leader warrior from Nimeria
Amon A champion among the Nimerian's
Colosso A Nimerian warrior
Arnost A Nimerian warrior
Ocean A man who had been taken captive by the Nimerian's in the past
Honora The wife of Argoe's
River ox Enormous plant eating animal with a long neck and tail

The Great City is the capital of an aggressively expanding empire
Mizrahim The ruler of the expanding empire
The Scourge of Mizrahim The most powerful branch of his armies which drives the expansion
Roar Mizrahim's most feared warlord
Commander Roar's second in command
Achaia General of the Scourge's siege weaponry
Bashan Captain of the flying terrors
Flying Terrors Large bat like flying beasts
Gannim Warlord in the service of Mizrahim who leads a large and ruthless band of scouts
The Witchers Sorcerer assassins who spy for Mizrahim
Kedar Leader of the witchers, son of Mizrahim, and half brother of Gannim

Crescent stalker's Furless man sized beasts who walk on two legs and boast a long snout of sharp teeth and a hook claw above each foot

Gannim's wolves A large breed of wolf trained for war

Crow Terror rider under Bashan's command

Elon is the capital city of the giant lords of the west

Bayne Giant king of Elon

Tusks War chieftain of Elon

Arioch is fortress city of considerable size residing within the Land Between the Seas

Arioch Tyrant king of the city bearing his name

Maris Arioch's lead advisor

Wolf Arioch's lead general

Feryn the beautiful and wise daughter of Arioch

The House of Rhone is a fortified village community with an inn; many of its inhabitants are part of an extended family

Gaius A young man of the forest who resides near the settlement

Rhone The strong patriarchal leader of settlement bearing his name

Elon Rhone's son

Elona Rhone's daughter

Mara A young woman who serves in the inn

Gore Monger's Large four legged animal with horns

Rhone's mount Large fury breed of elephant

Walking serpents Big carnivores which reside in a portion of the forests between the House of Rhone and Gull, with a resemblance to the crescent stalkers, but with proportionately larger heads and no hook claw

Gull is a good sized fortress city south of Arioch
Baen King of Gull
Talon Baen's chief general
Armen A leading warrior of Gull who often overseas the guard watches
Ore A leading warrior of Gull and able rider
Hagen Baen's eldest son
Lyon Baen's youngest son

The Port City of Khasar is a city of good size, strategically located along the coast of the East Sea
Un The spokesman for the king of Khasar

The Exiles of Huria is a large tribe of migrating people who have been forced from their homeland and who migrate to the Land Between the Seas during the warm Seasons
Melek King of the exiles

The Land of the Flying Draak consists of a stretch of the coast along the West Sea and some islands
Briain War chieftain who leads those who rider the flying draak
Flying draak Large winged predator with skin wings and a long pointed beak

Iomar is a strong kingdom in the north
Horn Chief among the guards of Iomar
Iomar The sickly king of the city bearing his name
Sihon Iomar's bold and eldest son
Drakon Iomar's younger son
Chaos The vile shield called by this name
Wrath The vile sword called by this name

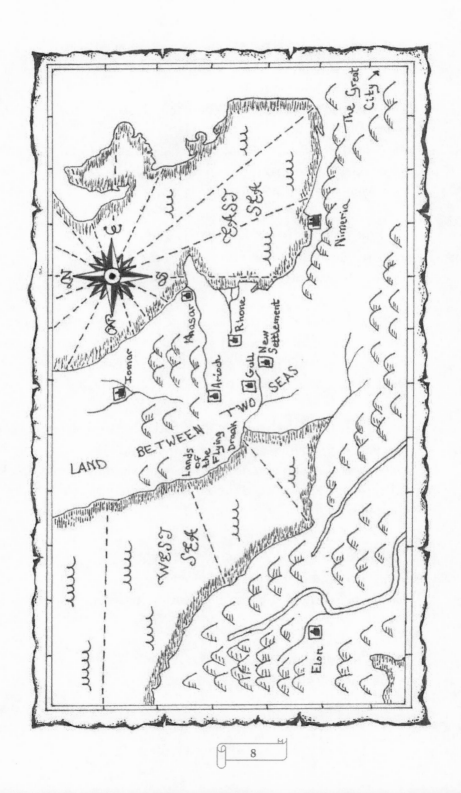

For the Posterity of the King

The burden I the King carry in my last days for those who will follow
I leave you with the telling of what has been
Illumination for the wise and pure of heart
A warning to the wicked
Though Gannim be no more, evil spirits yet seek mastery over others
There are ever two paths before you
Remain children of light and the Maker will guide your steps
But as for the doubters, you have been forewarned

Those of Renown

In the generations after the Great Flood had destroyed the earth, our fathers were divided. When the mountains of ice still stood tall in the north our ancestors spread abroad. As mighty empires arose and the years of man dwindled, it was then that the knowledge of the glowing metal had not yet been lost; that power by which the heavy could be made light and the light heavy. Weapons forged from rocks that permitted a man to bind his will to his surroundings and resist the very force holding him to the ground.

Some say that such weapons were the abandoned remnants from a great battle between the spirits of light and dark; weapons not of human craftsmanship, but forged in another realm. But I know for certain that most were acquired by the clever minds of the past, who through much labor and study of the world had achieved a great discovery.

But whatever, those were days of legend not to be repeated. They were days of renowned where the mighty clashed for supremacy, or in defense of their own. And among these Champions of Lore there was none greater than Roar of the Scourge; this is his tale.

Chapter 1
He Who Foresees Doom

The sun rose over the weary traveler on his journey across what many called the Valley of the Slain. Staff in hand, he stumbled along muttering to himself as if half mad and looking half starved. The great care that had once been taken to weave his garments was barely recognizable in light of the tattered things they had become.

Not far ahead stood the doors to what some believed was the home of gods. It was a grand fortress city hewn from out of a mountain on the southern border of the cold East Sea that lay far north and east of the Mighty Rivers. Here the drying south collided abruptly with the mountainous forests of the north.

But there was no green thing in the valley before him, and as the old man neared the city's towering wall, his mutterings began to centralize on the growing number of the dead surrounding him. Bones and other remnants of would be assailants were everywhere, piled waist high in some places. No one had dared besiege the city in many years, and yet there were fresher corpses, those of slaves who had in more recent times lost favor and usefulness.

Their callous masters had simply tossed them over the walls. "No wonder nothing lives in this valley," he said to himself. "This place is accursed."

As he neared the outer wall, he could see man-like figures engraved upon them, triumphantly standing upon men of smaller stature who looked as though they struggled to bear their weight.

On top of the ramparts upon both sides of its massive doors stood vigilant guards, each bearing a bow, spear and shield, or an orb bow of legend. They were strong and tall, standing at least an arm's length above the average man. Their armament and poise made them appear as proud, beautiful statues, but he knew they were not, though they did not in any way acknowledge his presence. After all, he was but an insect in their eyes, unworthy of acknowledgment.

The little man gazed up into the sky. "And what now," he asked, "shall I just knock?" His tone was bordering on sarcastic.

He stood there a moment, shrugged his shoulders and raised a fist. At this, one of the guards fixed his gaze upon him. "A mortal stretches out his hand," he said to the one nearest him. His comrade drew his bow string back answering with calm, "He is worthy of death."

Before he could release his arrow the old man struck the door with his little fist, causing the whole wall to shake as if rocked by a sudden earthquake. The old man halted, staring at his hand a moment in bewilderment. He then struck it again with the same result, and being encouraged he began to pound away at the massive doors calling, "Open I say! I have words for you, proud men of the mountain!"

The mighty guards of Nimeria who were not used to fear, now suddenly found themselves clinging desperately to anything and everything within reach as the wall shook so violently that the magnificent doors began to break apart. The old man kept on, emboldened by the results until the doors suddenly collapsed altogether. He lifted his arms above his head to protect himself as they crumbled all around him; and yet he was not struck by even a pebble. When the dust had cleared he simply marched over the debris and into the city.

"I have a message for you, oh lords of the mountain!" he announced. His voice was raised and authoritative, "A prophecy of doom!" He fixed his gaze upon those gathering. Soldiers and slaves alike stared in awe at him, but before he could continue a shadow began to loom above him. He turned to see who had come so near, only to be met with the cold stare of a towering soldier. This intimidating warrior glared spitefully from under the protection of his helm which was fashioned after the appearance of a man.

The giant raised an arm and struck the seer with the butt of his short sword, just as he had done to countless other little men and with the same predictable result, and for the old stranger who collapsed to the ground, everything went black.

The old man awoke blindfolded, gagged, and bound. He did not know how much time had passed or where he was, only that it was dark, wet, and foul. There was a strong stench of filth and waste, as well as the smell of death. He could not see them, but there were in fact several rotten corpses lying nearby.

He was not ancient for a man of his generation, but he certainly felt like an old man who had lived for too long and experienced far too many sorrows. But despite the aching of his head, all he could think about was how thirsty he was when suddenly he felt his gag unbind and the sensation of cool water filling his mouth. He was able to gulp it down several times before it was gone and though he could not see anyone, he knew his relief was a gift from the One who had urged him toward the mountain.

This comforted him and kept him from despairing. But as the day lingered on and with no one to unbind his extremities, he was forced to relieve himself in his garment. He laughed aloud at the irony of his situation. Just this morning he had beaten down massive doors with his bare hands and now he was imprisoned, helpless, and wetting himself. "Why," he asked aloud, "does a simple drink of water have to be accompanied with such humiliation?"

He could hear voices approaching and his heart quickened. Footsteps and doors clanged nearer and nearer until he felt the wooden beam he was bound to hoist up. He was being taken away, bumped and jarred about, but before long the air had cleared and the old man knew he was outside again.

He could hear a growing commotion and even discern some of the talk. "Is that him?" A child asked.

"This one is very small, like one of the slaves." A man observed.

"How could an ordinary man break through the doors of the immortal city?" Another countered.

As the crowd grew large, the pole was set into the ground. There was an abrupt silence and then a single voice sounded out clear, "Immortals of Nimeria, clearly this insignificant creature has been strengthened by spirits from the netherworld. We will now put an end to his poisoned words with fire!"

Approval broke out amongst the masses within this open forum where they had gathered and the man who spoke motioned to some guards standing by who were ready with kindling. They began to pile it around their captive's feet. "Am I really to burn alive?" the old man asked aloud, but again there was no answer from the One to whom he spoke.

"I contest you Lael," a new voice called out. The crowd quieted, for this man carried not as much authority as the other man, but something even more influential, a greater respect. "And I will hear his words."

Lael didn't like this challenge at all, "No Argoes, as I am the eldest god among us you have no authority to question me. He will be burned; only now the fire will be lit by your own hand." Lael smiled gleefully relishing the opportunity to place himself above one so esteemed.

"You presume too much," Argoes snapped. "I'll not obey you in this matter."

"Very well then," Lael answered pretending not to care. "If the trickster spirit has already infiltrated your simple mind, then it will be you." He pointed to a younger man standing next to Argoes; his name was Ryn and he was Argoes's closest friend.

They looked at each other a moment and just as it seemed Ryn would step forth, Argoes put an arm in front of him saying, "No Lael, no one but you will go forth. Or are you afraid of this little man?" His words were full of taunt.

Lael approached Argoes coolly and leaned in closely to whisper, "The others may stand divided by your mischief as of now, but after I put an end to him, my word will be law. And for your insolence, the consequences," he paused to consider his words and then finished coldly, "will be severe."

Argoes just looked at him with a smirk, "Why do you tarry? Show us your courage," he mocked loudly for all to hear. "Our valor is renowned," he gestured to Ryn and himself. "What have you ever done?"

The crowd began to murmur and Lael could not hide his displeasure as he cried out, "Has no one the courage but I?" He nearly shouted these words at the crowd in an attempt to silence their doubts, but no one came forward. "Very well then, I will do it myself." He snatched a torch from one of the guards and dragged it along the kindling which immediately began to burn.

The seer, who had held his tongue thus far, began to cry out in desperation, "Stop this! You must hear me! Unless you heed my words there will be no escape!"

Though he had not yet felt the heat, he could hear the sound of the wood popping as it began to quickly catch fire. It had been prepared with oil and the fat of animals; and so the fire raged fast. Strangely though, the man tied to the beam remained quiet even as the entirety of the wood, straw, and even the beam itself began to be furiously consumed.

As the flames rose higher and higher instead of pain the seer felt his bonds being loosed as the flames burned through them. Soon the cloth binding his eyes burned away and he could see the crowd in the open forum staring dumbstruck at this man who did not seem to burn. All at once his bonds were burned completely through and he tumbled out of the fire. The crowd gasped, seeing that not even his clothes were burnt as he stood up and began to brush himself off.

Lael looked at the soldier who had incapacitated the old man earlier that morning and ordered, "Amon, you exercised power over him upon his arrival; do so again! Strike him down!"

Amon stepped forward with a great axe which must have weighed more than the old man himself, but the seer did not act afraid; he just stood still with his eyes closed ready for whatever was to happen next. Without hesitating, Amon raised the axe high and took one big step forward with the intention of splitting him in two.

As the massive weapon slashed down there was an explosive flash as the axe shattered upon the impact of an outstretched hand. For just a moment the crowd caught a glimpse of an illuminated figure which had suddenly materialized for but an instant. It had no mouth, nor ears, but its eyes were blazing, almost blinding; then it was gone.

Amon had been hurled back through the air and crashed into the ground, barely conscious. And the seer, whose confidence was now soaring, addressed the awe-struck crowd, "It is clear to me now, people of Nimeria, that nothing you do will be able to keep me from declaring this message, which is not my own, but comes from on high."

The crowd stood silent watching the old man as the fire behind him blazed so fiercely that he should not have been able to stand so close to it. "Nimeria's time has come; your end is near." Gasps and whispers spread among them as a people who had not known fear for many, many years were now being crushed beneath its waves.

Lael stood indignant, and just when it seemed he was about to speak in protest the seer raised a hand to silence him. Lael held his peace as the old man continued, "I call upon slave and lord alike to be saved from this forthcoming doom. Any who desire life will follow me." He studied the crowd a moment and locked eyes with a frightened slave boy saying, "You are free," and he gestured for him to come to him.

Some of the Nimerian lords began to grumble. "Heed my words!" he shouted. "Unless you do as I say then there is no hope of rescue. Stay behind if you wish to die, but do not stand in the way of any who would live!"

Lael stormed off without a word, and those loyal to him helped Amon to his feet, following behind. Argoes could see the murder in their eyes as they walked away. He and Ryn approached the stranger and Argoes said, "I suspect they will try to stop us old one, but we are with you. What must we do?"

"We cannot return the direction in which I came. Do you have a way out through the north side or even a harbor?"

"There are a few other gates exiting the mountain, but to the north on the far side of the mountain we have a fine harbor."

"Just as I thought," the old man mused. "I dreamt of it. So then," he smacked his hands together with enthusiasm, "let us make haste." He turned and began to trek northward up the mountain calling, "Come all! Yes, even you are of great value," he said locking eyes with a young servant girl.

"We are?" she asked him.

"Of course you are child, but what I meant is that even the ones who had ruled over you are of value." She smiled for they could both see the humor in this.

"Should we gather our belongings?" Argoes asked.

"Only what you must, there is little time. But be sure that every soul has a choice. Believe me when I say that those who stay behind will wish they had listened for by the morrow the sign of their destruction will rise for all to see."

Just then a Nimerian warrior by the name of Arnost came near extending to him his staff. The old man clutched it tight saying, "Thank you for returning this, it is very dear to me. Without a word the giant nodded and carried on.

As the prophet and the growing crowd following him continued in haste, Lael, Amon, and those loyal to them plotted against those who had sided against them. "Let them take anyone they wish without a fight," Lael directed them, "but secretly gather those loyal to us, all but the guardians of the gates, for as they waste their efforts gathering the weak, we will recruit the strong.

"I myself will see to things here while you Amon are to follow them by stealth. Watch and wait for the opportune time to strike!"

"But what of the old one," a soldier interjected. "He has great power."

Amon raised an arm in a gesture to silence him. He wiped some blood from his arm that had been shed when he had crashed into the ground and declared, "But our combined might is a greater power." He looked Lael in the eyes saying, "I will return with their heads."

Argoes led the way as those who had listened to the seer followed through the city's elaborate interior. The crowd grew steadily as they walked along. Most of those who came out to meet them had been slaves, but there were many Nimerian's as well. The seer would repeat his call to join them over and over. And while some Nimerians were reluctant to release their slaves; their pride quickly melted once they looked down the glowing shaft of Ryn's spear.

The old man could not help but notice the city's beauty; its grand structures, orchards, and vineyards that had were spread throughout. "Such a shame," he said to himself, "Such a waste."

They kept on for hours. Some were fearful, but others carried hopeful expectation, believing that wherever this man led them would be better than the cruelty of their masters. Still others had been born into slavery and could hardly fathom what freedom would entail.

Soon they reached the peak of the city which boasted a magnificent view of the north, courtesy of the clear, moonlit sky. "It will not be long, now that we descend," Argoes said to the little man.

"Will there be enough ships?" The seer asked.

"Yes, there are many," he answered confidently.

Argoes and Ryn waited for everyone to pass in order to follow behind. "We're being stalked," Ryn said to Argoes.

"Yes, I know. Make your way through the crowds and tell all of the armed men to be ready. Send some ahead with the sla...," he stopped to correct himself, "the freed men to prepare the ships. Then bring the bulk of the warriors to the rear." Ryn nodded and set out immediately to fulfill the tasks while Argoes jogged back to the front.

"Is everything all right?" the old man asked Argoes with a suspicious glance.

"We will know soon enough," he answered coldly, like a man who had known the calm before the storm of battle many times. "Keep on along this wide path for it will take us to the harbor. Look there," he pointed. "Even now you can see it and if you have need of anything, come find me at the rear." After saying this Argoes returned to the back of the crowds.

They continued on without any threat a few hours more, until finally they had reached the large and elaborate pillars of the Nimerian harbor. The seer was astonished at its grandeur. "Truly there are master builders among you," he proclaimed to no one in particular.

A Nimerian warrior heard him and replied, "Yes, they are worthy vessels."

There were many large ships, yet few of them were in the water. Most sat upon ramps that could be released with levers. An enormous gated wall stood quite some distance away, protruding from out of the water, which, when opened, would only allow a few ships to pass through at a time.

As Argoes came near again the old man said, gazing in awe at the ships, "In all my travels I have never seen their equal."

"Yes," Argoes replied, "they are worthy vessels." He then turned to address the crowds, calling out, "Load up according to families. Get the strongest men on the oars!"

"We must hurry," the old man said. "Dawn cannot be far and I perceive that there is yet much to do before we can depart for the open waters."

"Yes, dawn should be breaking on the far side of the mountain any moment now," Argoes confirmed with some tension beginning to stretch across his brow.

"And their end rises with it," the seer assured, with some sadness.

Argoes wasted no time, "Open the gates!" He ordered some. "Hurry aboard the ships," he called to those who were not armed. He maneuvered his way over to Ryn and said, "Gather some able men to release the ships as soon as everyone's on board, only be watchful for our adversaries."

"No need," Ryn said gravely while pointing towards the mountain passes, "They are here."

Chapter 2
the Scourge of Mizrahim

Dawn had just broken on the south side of the mountain to reveal the approaching formation of a great host. Once the disciplined ranks had come just within a few minutes march from the city's wall, the one leading them halted the advance with a raised fist. He then stepped further out, about a stone's throw ahead of the rest.

As he carefully studied the mountain fortress before him, another man with long reddish brown hair also broke ranks in order to join him. Everyone called him Commander for he was their war leader's favorite general. Commander addressed the men as he walked saying," Behold, men of the Scourge, the mountain of the gods." Laughter erupted among them over his more than apparent mockery, for the city before them was fully expected to be their next conquest. He joined the man in front who they called Roar saying, "Do mine eyes deceive me or has the Nimerian gate been breached? Perhaps they have just suffered an attack?" He smiled, "How fortunate for us."

Roar remained silent and his metal helm began to glow as it stretched around his face. Its power amplified his voice, "Hear me!" he sneered to the growing guard upon the outer wall of the mountain, the echo resounding off the rocks. "You who say you are gods but are not. We are the Scourge and today is your end. Only the ruin of this mountain will forevermore stand monument to your wretched stupidity!" There was a moment's silence and then Roar said without breaking his gaze from the city, "Commander."

"Yes sir?"

"Why do the walls of mine enemies still stand?"

"Oh, right," Commander answered with some embarrassment, then he turned toward the warriors' ranks shouting, "Men! Siege formation!"

Cheers and war chants broke out as the ranks grew wide and siege weapons were pulled to the front lines. They were similar to the ingenuity of the ballista used by the growing kingdoms of the west, only the orb bows, as they called them, were far more destructive being forged from the rocks which had fallen from the skies.

Large metal cylinders of various designs were anchored to carts that could swivel. Some were pushed by men, but the larger ones were carried by large, four-legged beasts which boasted one or more formidable horns, along with armor forged by men to further protect them.

Once in position, one man took aim while his partner would crank the handles that would prepare it to fire. As the metal tube within the cylinder drew back, openings within the exterior would make a sound that resembled inhaling, until it began to hum and glow. Once the tension rope was locked into place they need only let loose a lever to fire. This could all be done by one man, but two was far more efficient. Many among the infantry carried a smaller, less powerful weapon after its likeness. It was after the likeness of the Nimerian Orb Bow which they held vertically like a normal bow. Its benefit over the heavier artillery lay in that it could be fired quickly with a fast pull back and release of its draw string.

Having been alerted to the approaching invaders, Lael joined the guards along the walls. They were already at the defenses which were of the same craftsmanship as the invaders, only mounted to the city's structures. Though it had been a long time since any had dared to attack the mountain, this was far from their first fight. A look of indignation stretched across Lael's face, as he ordered the guards with contempt, "Show these vermin the power of the gods!" Immediately the defenders unleashed a formidable volley from the walls and heights of the city.

Ball-like spheres of green and blue light hummed across the expanse between the contesting warriors. The illumination of the artillery stood out against the dark morning sky and many among the ranks of the Scourge stared in awe, not having expected to encounter their own likeness of artillery on such a grand scale.

Seeing their lack of preparedness, Commander quickly took action, "Intercept the attack fools!" He shouted, jolting his men back to action against the impending danger. Those who had been tempted to take cover responded to his charge, returning fire. Many of the shots collided a short distance away exploding in midair. Several volleys of the Nimerian attack came blazing through, erupting into the ranks with deadly effectiveness.

Roar remained in front holding his glowing axe before him. He waved it from side to side deflecting the enemy fire, causing the orbs to simply explode a safe distance away. Though the invaders could not see exactly how the battle was fairing due to all of the haze and flying debris released from the explosions, the superior number of weapons they boasted were beginning to overpower the defenders.

"Keep firing!" Commander rallied. "Do not relent! Destroy their artillery! Bring down those defenses!"Soon it became apparent that their side was the only one still firing. Roar raised a fist and Commander gave the order, "Halt!" Without hesitation the men obeyed as one.

The air separating the opposing forces held a turquoise tint from all the power that had been unleashed in the air, which was slowly being blown away with the wind. Roar hurled his axe which spiraled forward with a hum. It absorbed much of the excess power within its path before returning to his outstretched hand.

Commander glared contemptibly before chastising them for their reluctance to act at the start, "And what did you think all the rumors of the god's awesome power was supposed to mean? Did we not expect a fight?" The ranks watched closely as he approached their leader and leaned in close to receive instruction. Knowing they had executed poorly at the start, the soldiers waited in anxious anticipation as to how Roar might react, for never had they ever been so taken by surprise.

On the north side of the mountain panic driven women and children scrambled aboard ships in the shadow of the encroaching army. "There is Amon," Argoes gravely motioned with his spear. "I recognize him even with his helm's mask down.

"I will stand with you," the old man assured, "but you will fight the battle."

The human-like metal masks closed over their faces as Argoes shouted to those holding the docks, "Defensive stance! Hold the left!" he ordered Ryn. "Take the right," he shouted to another named Colosso, and standing shield to shield they began to glow.

Some volleys began to be fired from their attacker's orb bows which were also after the likeness of the handheld version belonging to the Scourge. But those who stood with Argoes were prepared and the glowing spheres were merely absorbed into the shields of the defensive line, causing their defensive aura to glow even brighter.

"Well done!" Argoes acclaimed. "We are unbreakable!" he shouted with infectious conviction. Yet Amon and his men were worthy adversaries with fierce determination of their own. They threw themselves into the defensive line, not with a shout, but with the cold, dark stares that had been used to intimidate many enemies of the past.

Some of the attackers recoiled off of the shields with a flash of light, others drove their way through the line, smashing their way onto the docking ramps. Some men even tumbled in a tangle into the waters where they risked drowning as they continued to fight while others scrambled for the shallows beneath the docks. From time to time an attack would flash from underneath before bursting out of the waters and into the night sky, or else shatter the docking boards from underneath, projecting wooden shrapnel everywhere.

Amon was battering the defenders with a war hammer he wielded with both hands. The powerful blows dented shields and caused the men holding them to tumble backwards. Argoes noticed Ryn inching his way over to confront Amon. "Halt, Ryn!" He shouted. He was not at all convinced that his friend could win the fight alone. "Wait for me... wait for me!" he yelled desperately! However, he relented to follow, knowing that if he were to leave his end of the defenses they could easily falter.

Ryn could not hear his friend calling over the noise of battle and hurled his spear as soon as he had an opening. It soared with precision, but Amon was ready, swatting it away with ease. Amon stomped toward the young warrior with powerful swings of his hammer that smashed into those on his left and right, clearing a path for him to reach him. Some of Ryn's allies rallied to him, crowding around Amon in an effort to smother and drag him to the ground. Just when it seemed they would succeed he, smashed his war hammer down with earth shattering power that repelled friend and foe alike with a shockwave.

Ryn scrambled back to his feet as quickly as he could only to find his enemy already within striking distance. Amon swung his hammer with the intention of crushing Ryn's skull, but he sidestepped out of range with a counter slash across Amon's helmet. Unfortunately, it did little more than scratch it and Amon gave a mocking laugh.

Ryn took a step back and raised his sword horizontally alongside his face poised to thrust, when suddenly Amon was blindsided with an orb eruption that slammed him to ground. Though well armored, he lay there motionless as if the life had been knocked right out of him. Ryn looked up to find that his help had come from some of the freed men who had taken hold of the ships artillery and joined in the fight. With this new development Ryn and his allies began to raise their arms in a gesture of victory.

With a few more shots from the ship finding their mark, and with their leader down, it was clear that doubt had invaded the minds of those loyal to Lael. The tide of battle had indeed taken a sudden turn. Argoes raised an unarmed hand, an ancient gesture that they all understood, and nearly all the fighting began to halt. A few moments were taken to extinguish the few existing melees that were still continuing, and as battered men limped or crawled from out of the waters, Argoes addressed them all.

"Flee!" he shouted. "Unless you will join yourselves to us then flee back to Lael and join him in death!"

But what of our families?" one asked.

Hearing this, the old man pushed his way through the crowd of warriors to answer, "We cannot wait. You were unwise to not have joined us from the start. Now your loved ones will suffer the fate of your choice." After a brief pause he added, "Make your decision now for we cannot linger." His voice was stern but his expression betrayed his sadness over the harsh choice they would now have to make.

After a moment of contemplation, men began to make their decisions. Many of them turned and marched dejectedly back through the various paths and staircases leading up mountain; however, others, most of them the wounded, remained with the victors. "Very good," Argoes said to all, "Get them on board, tend to those injured."

"Not all of us made it," Ryn observed as he nodded toward some fallen allies.

"Yes," the old man answered with a little sadness. "Now they return to the One who gave them life, but there is no time for mourning my friends; this mountain is about to become a tomb."

On the south side of the mountain Commander addressed the troops, saying, "Roar is displeased with your cowardice in the wake of the enemy's initial assault, and has therefore decided that you who held the front will now prove your valor by breaking what is left of the enemy, on foot." Commander was pointing to the less than one hundred Nimerian defenders who had gathered within the gap of the shattered gate. Though small in number they held a fiercely glowing defensive aura.

The men sighed in bitter surrender to the command as they stepped forward drawing infantry weapons. "One more thing lads," he added, "Roar will be leading the charge." A cheer broke out among them as Roar's armor began to glow and reform until he resembled less a man and more a monster. Again he amplified his voice, only this time into the battle roar for which he had come to be known.

Lael, though bleeding, had survived the bombardment. He stood as upright as he was able to address the men still holding the gate, "They are men or maybe spirits of evil, but divine they are not. We are the immortals and our mountain stands eternal." He seemed to believe his own words, but if he could have seen the looks upon the faces of his men he would have seen their conviction that they knew the prophet's words were coming to pass; that this fight would indeed be their last.

"You will remain here," Roar said to Commander as calmly as if he were about to sit down for a meal instead of killing. "Their focus must be broken, so as we near their position you will bring their surroundings, the very mountain if you must, crumbling down upon them."

"I understand," Commander answered with resolve.

"And keep Gannim's wretched scouts at the rear and out of the fray. If I look at them, I may be compelled to kill them on the spot," he added just before pointing his axe forward, signaling the march of the final assault.

Nearly everyone had now boarded the ships, even those who had opened the harbor gates. Only Argoes and Ryn remained on the docks releasing the final ship by the lever which would allow it to slide smoothly into the waters. "Once this last ship is released we will make haste and jump aboard at the gate," Argoes said, pointing to the boarding ledges that hung over the water. Ryn nodded in agreement.

The last lever was pulled and Ryn darted off for the boarding point, but Argoes paused. Hearing heavy steps behind him he quickly turned around to find Amon, though battered and bloodied, about to run him through with a spear he had found left behind. Argoes raised an arm to knock the thrust away but his timing was off. Amon drove the long narrow end of the spear through his hand with enough force to pin it to his shoulder.

Argoes gave an involuntary shriek over the sudden pain as he struggled to free his hand, but there was no hope of doing so with Amon, weary as he was, in control of the shaft. Amon drove forward forcing him to the ground. Argoes cried out in angry, painful desperation as he resisted the attack, but once he was to his knees Amon wrenched the spear free for the killing blow. Yet as he stepped forward to thrust at his face, Argoes rolled out of the way. Amon pursued but his concentration was interrupted by a nearby shout. Sprinting back toward them Ryn had let out a battle cry as he hurled his short sword in an attempt to save his friend. The sword spiraled at Amon with a sound that cut the air. Although Amon raised his spear in time to defend the initial impact with a flash, it still carried enough force to whip around and bust him in the face mask with the butt of the hilt, stunning him.

Being fatigued and anxious Ryn had not focused well, and the attack had lost any hope it had of finishing their foe when it was deflected. Now he was unarmed for he had already placed his spear upon the last ship in anticipation of the departure. He seized this brief opportunity of attack to charge ahead, diving full force into Amon as he struggled to clear his head from the swords impact.

The tackle was hard and though Ryn was able to drive him onto his back, Amon began to slowly gain leverage as they returned to their feet. As they struggled over the spear Argoes stumbled over to the short sword. Picking it up he approached Amon from behind and with his good arm swung with all his might.

The blade drove hard into the side of Amon's exposed neck, sinking in until buried to the guard and sticking out the far side. Still struggling with Amon, Ryn could feel his opponent's strength drain with the blood which flowed freely from the fatal wound. Amon resisted a moment longer, but Ryn and Argoes wrestled him to the ground, holding him there until he breathed his last breath, then Ryn quickly stood, and shouted, "Hold the last ship!" but they had already done so. Argoes struggled to his feet but remained partly hunched over. Ryn offered him his arm but he shrugged it off saying proudly, "I will walk." It was slow going but walk they did, side by side to board the last ship, the last hope of escape.

The invaders were closing in on the entrance, and as they neared the gate they began to pick up their pace. Roar was well out in front of the ranks when he stopped abruptly. He began to spin his axe hand over hand and spheres erupted, being hurled out in quick succession. But instead of hitting the defenders they blasted the walls and structures all around them.

Commander followed his lead. "Fire!" he cried out, and as the heavy artillery demolished strategic structures, large chunks of debris began to crumble and fall upon the defenders. In this avalanche of collapsing columns and balconies the Nimerian guards began to lose focus, and as their defensive aura faded the invading infantry smashed into them.

Roar hurled his axe at the Nimerians, who towering above his tallest man, made easy targets. The axe spiraled its way into a wide circle slashing and smashing through several men before returning back to him. He snatched it out of the air and then charged forward slamming the axe into the shield of the first man in his path, splitting it in half.

His men were well trained and poured into the city like frenzied ants, climbing past the wreckage in order to hem the defenders in on every side. The Nimerians were big and strong, but along with being outnumbered, they were simply being outsmarted. One assailant would slash at the legs while another would thrust at the neck. The fighting was fierce, with some Nimerians tossing those they had impaled with their spears high into the air. But such successes were short lived, and did little to prevent the conflict from coming to the sudden and decisive end in favor of the invaders.

"Halt," the eerie voice of Roar amplified by his helm permeated the air almost equally as if he were everywhere at once. The defenders had crowded around Lael in an effort to protect him, yet had all fallen, leaving him alone. The face of Roar's mask peeled away to reveal his sinister countenance. "Are you a god?" he asked with disdain. Lael stared at him, his pride eroding with fear.

"I, I, I...." he stammered as if trying to gather his thoughts. Roar had no patience for it and stepped into a full three-hundred and sixty degree turn which he ended by burying his axe so deep into Lael's side that he nearly spilt him in half. Lael winced in shock, and yelped pitifully before collapsing.

Looking down at him with eyes full of hatred Roar answered his own question with a snarl, "No, you're not!"

With the entrance secured, Commander began to order the rest of the warriors into the city. As soon as he was able, Commander walked towards Roar who was directing men about. Roar met his gaze when he noticed him approaching, "Waste no time seeing that the interior is secured. My ordinances will be upheld or heads will roll; many heads Commander." Roar's voice was emphatic with warning.

"I will see to it. No need to kill anyone just yet," he assured and then he began to address the troops who were crowding into the city. "Come on lads. The quicker we lock down the mountain the faster we get to our rest and our food."

"Aye," they echoed enthusiastically.

"But watch yourselves and don't offend our leader in the way you go about it, or else the Nimerian's won't be the only ones slaughtered today," he added before leading them on. They all understood his meaning. Roar had a strict code of conduct and spared none who tested it.

"Where are my other heads of factions?" Roar asked impatiently.

"Carrying out your standard procedures to be sure," Commander called just before he was out of hearing range.

"Good," Roar grinned with sinister enthusiasm.

But no sooner did the words leave his mouth he saw Commander rushing back toward him with a look of urgency in his eyes saying, "Some of our men have learned from those here who speak the common tongue of the south that a sizable crowd of people has already fled to the far side of the mountain. They claim that they are led by a powerful seer."

"Which means they are led by 'the holy man'," Roar said as if contemplating the significance of this new development. "Get me Bashan and his wretched flying beasts!" he shouted.

"He is at the rear of the ranks sir, where he awaits your orders," a soldier replied.

"Fetch him at once! He is to meet me on my way up the mountain," Roar yelled back as he darted into the interior, racing up the winding pathways of the city, knocking everyone out of his way. He kept a furious pace that few of the others could have matched even if he had ordered them to do so. Within minutes the shadow of one of their large, flying creatures loomed overhead. He recognized the appearance of its shadow and without even an upward glance, raised his axe with both hands. The flying terror, as they called them, swooped down and grabbed hold of it, hoisting him high, clearing the city's grand structures and joining dozens of others.

In order to maintain balance, as Roar changed positions to the saddle, in a well-practiced move, the rider climbed off on the opposite side. Once Roar took hold of the reigns controlling the beast he swooped low above a wide path, and as the rider's armor began to glow, he released the animals belly strap and willed his forward motion slow enough to drop safely to the ground beneath his feet.

Roar and the others pressed on over the highest points of the mountain, ascending high enough to descend in a steeply angled dive in an effort to more swiftly reach those who had fled. Bashan, who led the riders, came along side him and pointed his orb bow ahead with one arm. In the distance they could see several ships already a good distance outside the harbor.

"Something's coming!" someone said, pointing north from the rear ship.

"There are riders upon those beasts," Ryn announced to all. Knowing that Argoes was in no condition to take charge he shouted, "Signal the other ships! Lay hold of the artillery!" A battle horn was sounded, and as the women and children were ushered into the hulls, the men took to the defenses. Almost at once both sides unleashed their attack, but it was clear immediately that the riders, with their much smaller bows, were outmatched by the bombardment of the ships' heavy weapons, as well as the small arms of the numerous Nimerian warriors.

While the superior speed and agility of the riders kept them from getting struck down, neither could they advance. They wisely circled the ships at range and then, following Roar's lead, returned to land on top the harbor gates. Roar dismounted with a leap, twirling his axe furiously into a glow. With an angry sound that barely seemed human he unleashed a powerful orb attack from his axe that screamed toward the rear ship.

Those aboard the ships had thought the danger was over, so when they finally did see the deadly sphere approaching there was little time to react. "Take cover!" Ryn shouted. Gripping his spear tight, Argoes stumbled to his feet. Fighting the pain, he positioned the spear into a throwing hold over his shoulder and with a heavy step he heaved it forward with a jerk but maintained his grip. Power surged along the shaft of the spear and erupted from the end to defend against Roar's attack. The orbs collided about a ships length away from the rear with an explosive shockwave that floored all those who had not taken sufficient cover.

Roar stared on in anger, his attack foiled and his prey escaping. "Shall we give pursuit?" Bashan asked him.

"In time," Roar answered quietly. "For where will they go that is beyond our reach? A day will come when there will no longer be a place for men to hide."

Those on the ships looked on in relief seeing that their adversaries no longer pursued or attacked. "I have never seen flying beasts tamed for a man to ride," the seer said as he looked on.

"So this is what brings mighty Nimeria to an end," Ryn stated with wounded pride.

"Just a remnant of the enemy to be sure," the old man answered.

"Yes, look!" Argoes said pointing weakly. "Smoke rises from the far side of the mountain."

"Then it is as you foretold," Ryn declared with resignation.

"Yes," the old man answered sadly, "so it is." They stared on in solemn quiet for a long time, until eventually the ships carried them out of view and into a new beginning.

Chapter 3
Rivals

Roar wasted no time returning to the front of the city where he and the other riders descended just outside the fallen gates. Men darted out of the way as they landed and Roar leaped off the animal he was riding before it had even come to a full stop.

These flying terrors, as the men called them, had a nature that seemed to cause those who did not ride them to be uncomfortable around them. This was mainly because they had large teeth and claws and tended to stare, not an encouraging combination of characteristics in a creature much larger than a man.

"Secure the signal near the top of the mountain," Roar ordered Achaia who commanded the artillery. "It must be ready to fire by nightfall."

"Shall we secure our own defenses within the strongholds of the city?" Achaia asked.

Roar stopped mid step and turned to look at him, incredulous, saying, "Do we ever secure defenses amongst the rubble of the conquered?"

"Well, no," he answered awkwardly.

"And what do we do to the cities we conquer?" Roar asked.

"We lay them to waste," Achaia replied with disappointed resignation.

"Yes, yes, we lay them to waste," Roar answered gleefully.

"But this magnificent city holds such grandeur and strategic potential. It could be the very pathway from which the rule of Mizrahim controls the north and south," Achaia was almost pleading, something Roar found contemptible.

Roar leaned in close, "It will not be wasted fool! The fear of the Scourge will rise like the smoke of this smoldering ruin." He stepped back and looked Achaia over as if examining his soul. "I'm beginning to question your resolve General. If it is camping and cowering behind walls you seek, perhaps you should crawl back to Mizrahim and grovel at his feet for whatever meager scraps he might so graciously toss at you!"

His words were scathing and Achaia quickly replied, "No sir," and with a respectful bow he rushed away to fulfill his duty.

Though far from being a big man, Roar conjured fear among those around him. It was not just his ruthless war mongering, nor that his control over glow was seen by many to be second to none, not even Mizrahim, the founder of their empire. Nor was it his iron clad insistence of instant and total obedience of his orders and rules. To those he led, Roar seemed to be more than a man and there was a saying among them, "Ever is there hate in his eyes."

Just then Commander hurried to him nervously from inside the city. "Something is wrong," he stated as fact upon seeing his nervousness. "Yes Commander?"

"There is a situation with the scouts. The ones the exalted Mizrahim said would carry word of our progress on to Gannim who scouts ahead of us for lands to conquer.

Roar smiled wide. "I see," he answered in a way that made it seem as though he knew something that Commander did not. "We must hurry then and deal with this, problem. Yes, Commander?"

"Yes," he answered as Roar led the way back into the city to find the scouts huddled among themselves, several dozen of them. Some brandished their weapons as they argued with Roar's infantrymen over treasure and women who had been found hiding within the city.

As Roar approached they all stopped, taking notice. A bearded warrior with long, dark hair who seemed to lead the scouts spoke to Roar saying, "She and these, mine. We take them." He hardly spoke the same tongue of the Scourge, but he pointed to a beautiful Nimerian woman at least a full head taller than himself.

"We tried to explain to them that our ways are different than the other war lords but they hardly understand and I did not want to draw arms against them without your consent. I know not what trouble that would cause with..."

"They understand you fine Commander," Roar calmly interrupted his rambling. For a moment he examined the scene before him and all grew quiet. It began to look as though he was not really looking at the angry warriors at all but rather through them.

The corner of his mouth rose as if he suffered some kind of tick. His fingers on his right hand began to dance frantically along the handle of his axe until they froze wide open like a spider about to pounce. He then smiled and said to the leader of the scouts, "I had surmised all along that I might need to kill you all," shrugging as if the matter were settled and it were a minor issue. "There is no need to wait."

His armor immediately began to illuminate and stretched over the entirety of his body, "Any man who does not wish to die should back away."His voice echoed coldly and his men quickly retreated as one.

The scouts poised themselves for a fight with growls of anger mixed with fear knowing that he meant them violence.

Roar stepped toward the lead man who relinquished the girl's arm and stepped back raising his sword. Roar raised his axe high above his head and, leaping forward with a twist he made an arching swoop toward those enemies closest to him. A shock wave followed, blasting a good number of them right off their feet; thus, clearing a path for him to enter their midst.

Before they could gather themselves defensively he darted in, and with a leap, smashed the base of his axe into the ground. The power he had mastery over immediately bound itself to their wares. All of the scouts were violently hoisted into the air with an impact that snapped the legs of those nearest him.

Suspended in the air, there was no more anger in their eyes, only fear. As Roar began to turn and swing his axe round and round the men began to slowly move in orbiting circles. He transitioned from spinning the axe from his front, to behind his back, and then above his head. Their momentum increased and soon they began bashing into one another and the nearby structures.

Their frightful sounds turned into helpless screams of terror that grew louder the higher they rose. Faster and higher they went until Roar's armor began to glow so bright that his men struggled to see.

"Witness the end of those who cause suffering!" he shouted, his voice echoing off the walls. He then released the axe above him, and yet it still continued to spin on its own. His men were in awe for this was an execution which few of them had seen, or even heard of.

"Now die as one!" he almost shrieked, abruptly reaching a hand up to grab the axe out of the air. The glow faded and men screamed as they plummeted back to the earth. The sound of bodies thudding against the ground and fresh bones snapping was so abhorrent that some of the battle hardened warriors covered their ears and gasped.

Roar's armor began to peel away as he walked past the broken men, being sure to step on the hands and faces of those still clinging to life. "We have a new enemy to kill, oh Scourge," he said with a smile, "and the wretch's name is Gannim." There was surprise on the faces of his men and sighs as well, for he was a formidable war lord in the service of Lord Mizrahim.

"Tonight we signal our victory and tomorrow we hunt our newest prey; and then it's onward to the conquest of the north!" he announced confidently. His enthusiasm garnished cheers, for his men had little doubt that with Roar at the helm, they could indeed over throw Gannim; thus gaining even more influence within the expanding empire for which they fought. However, Roar had plans that he was reluctant to share with them yet, plans he believed they were not ready to hear.

Commander took this opportunity to impress the lesson upon the troops, saying, "Gaze upon the broken and remember the ordinances. Take for yourselves wives from among those with no husband, but any man among the conquered who would join us rather than die will keep his family. Any maiden who wishes to be left alone will have peace. All surviving lads will be recruited for soldiering; those too young will remain with their families. All mediums and the like will be executed without mercy, regardless of age..."

As Commander continued his monologue Roar noticed that nearby, and enrobed in their black attire, stood more than a dozen witchers. They were known as the eyes and ears of Mizrahim. Ever ready to channel what they had witnessed back to their lord, they traveled with those sent out so that their master was ever aware of his armies' progress.

Roar came near and stared into their pale, blank faces, saying, "Quickly puppets, report all that you've seen. Tell your master our quarrel has begun."

He paused a moment before continuing, "Can you see me old one? Do you not perceive the victor? Was there ever any doubt?" He spat at their feet and snarled his words with angry sarcasm.

No one knew what exactly what he was talking about, only that his disdain was obvious. "I should cast you all into the fire," he muttered to the sorcerers as he turned away, but their expressions remained as indifferent as stone.

Roar despised sorcery, as did he despise Mizrahim's prying. According to the laws he had implemented among his men, the witchers should all be executed with the mediums of the mountain; and yet here they were looking over his shoulder.

"And what of these wretches?" Commander asked, motioning to the broken men still writhing and groaning.

"Pile them outside the city and burn them," he answered. Seeing that he who had been the lead man among them was still alive, Roar walked over to him and pulled his head up by the hair saying coldly, "Know that once the fire has devoured your flesh, the Shadow Binders await."

Chapter 4
A New Beginning

By the time darkness had fallen the slain were already piled outside the outer wall burning. The scouts had been mixed with wood to ensure a strong burn and the flames cast eerie flickering shadows which danced upon the walls. There was a hush over the city as the conquered and conquerors alike were haunted by the screams of those still waiting to die within the flames. The horror was deliberate on the part of Roar for he desired both that the slain suffer and that his army fear. He expected that in the days to come they would be tested beyond anything they had yet experienced.

He knew all too well the uncertainty of men and reasoned that if he were the most frightful monster in their world, then their allegiance would be assured, but now it was time to make a much more far-reaching audience fear. With the signal having been secured near the height of the city at the top of the mountain, it was time to tell the world that Nimeria had fallen and whom it was who had conquered the legendary city.

A soldier began to crank the rotating handles on the large metal mechanism. It functioned similarly to the artillery but was anchored to the ground and was much more powerful. Once the crank reached its limit and the shaft's symbols illuminated, it was ready to fire. The man who had prepared it to fire nodded to another who stood nearby ready to aid. He released the lever unleashing a turquoise beam of light that pierced the night sky. Many gazed upon the enigmatic sight, from simple sheep herders in the south camping beneath the stars to those who dwelt in walled cities. Some looked on in wonder, not knowing what they saw; others knowing with fearful certainty. And as for the surviving Nimerian captives, they huddled within the fragile security of their homes in fearful anticipation of what was to come.

The attention of those still awake on the ships was quickly drawn to the south as they too began to notice the turquoise beam in the distance rising from the mountain. Gasps resounded among the vessels. Ryn stood near the Seer and asked," What does this light mean?"

"It means Nimeria is no more."

After a moment of solemn quiet Ryn said, "I am with you old one, but anger burns within me. Some of those who did not come were dear to me; my sister, my uncles, and others." He looked down and clenched a fist, "Someday I hope to meet these men in battle, whoever they are."

"Be careful what you wish for my son."

Saddened and angry, Ryn turned away to be alone as Argoes leaned against one of the ship's sturdy rails saying, "I knew we were not gods."

The old man looked up at him as he stared at the light, but waited quietly for him to continue. "I was young when we settled on the mountain. Our people came there long after our ancestors were divided. We were strong and carried in our possession the sky rocks.

We forged all the weapons we could from them, and quickly became a mighty people. When those weaker passed through looking for a place to revive themselves we would seize them and enslave them. Or we would just take to this sea in search for others. This is how Ocean came to be in our possession." He motioned to an older freedman who was aboard their ship. "Now the Judge of all the earth has brought our evil back upon us."

"His chastisement has done you well," the old man reassured. "He could have offered you no warning at all, but now, by your example, many have escaped to live on. Don't lose heart my friend for I am convinced that we have not escaped the sword only to endure further death and uncertainty upon reaching our destination. And speaking of destinations, where is the lead ship taking us?"

"There is a coastal city not far from here with which we have had some dealings on occasion; it is the Port of Khasar."

"He means it is a place where they have acquired slaves." the freedman Ocean interjected.

"Ah. Well then if it is to this place we travel I can only imagine that it is they who need to be forewarned next." Haran answered before returning his gaze to the light in the north. "I only hope they are as wise as you Argoes."

Back on the mountain Roar sat upon a large open balcony near the signal. As he reflected upon what was to come next, Commander approached from a nearby stairway saying, "There you are. I've been looking all over for you. I wanted to tell you that all is well."

"And the men are content with my will?"

"Agree or not, after what you did to Gannim's scout's they won't so much as murmur in their beds tonight."

Roar smiled, "It was terrible, was it not?"

"Oh, it was, to be sure," Commander agreed grimly, shaking his head at the thought. "I know we can expect opposition from the kings of the lands between the seas," mused Commander, "but I just can't figure out why lord Mizrahim would point you and Gannim both in the same direction."

"Isn't it obvious Commander?" Roar asked, but his friend waited quietly for him to continue. "He has done so in order that only one of us might live. He intends that one of us kill the other, knowing that ultimately there is no room in his reign for the both of us. He knew that to send those scouts to Gannim through us would result in a conflict, and I did not disappoint."

"Oh," he said, as understanding began to flood his mind.

"In fact," Roar continued, "in time there will be no room for him either."

"Who?" Commander asked.

Roar paused before continuing, "My ambition is to rid the world of its oppressors Commander. The world has many tyrants and Mizrahim has become one of them."

"I'll just pretend I didn't hear that," Commander answered nervously.

"Pretending the monsters are not there does not make them any less real my friend," Roar assured. "But fear not faithful Commander, I have much to do before I return to take care of that little matter. Many have seen the light of our victory and deep down they know they can ignore us no longer. Before us lies the kingdoms of the north and with them Gannim's horde.

"South of the Deep Waters are the children of the Nile and their Pharaoh. To the west are the sons of Troy and their formidable allies, the giant lords who were driven out before us. And it is they with whom I am most eager to fight, for they share the likeness of our weapons on a grand scale."

Roar thrust his axe in the direction of the giant capital, Elon, which was several days journey westward. Unbeknownst to them, at that same moment, upon their highest tower stood the giant lords' formidable king. The bearded giant stood with his arms folded as he glared at the distant light with an angry countenance. His name was Bayne and he ruled the giant lords of the west with an iron fist.

Another man, younger but taller, came and joined him. His name was Tusks; he was dark, with long hair fastened in braids, and was amongst the most skilled warriors of their lands. "So, Mizrahim's Scourge has finally found its way north," he said to the King. "Then Mighty Nimeria has fallen," a look of surprise was etched upon his face. "Shall we prepare to meet them?"

"We already are," Bayne's voice was confident. "Our brothers had grown weak sitting idle behind their great wall these many years."

"Should we have gone to their aid?" Tusks asked.

"Ha! We should have taken the city for ourselves," said the king with distain. Mizrahim's power has grown, but so has ours; they will know this soon enough. We will regain the rule of the southeast and then it will be the Great City belonging to Mizrahim which lies beneath our heel."

"This fog seems strange to me," Ryn said. "It does not seem at all natural."

Everyone standing nearby turned to look at the old man who stood with his hands resting upon the ship's railing. He laughed and said, "You may find it difficult to believe but I do not know everything." For the most part, quiet had found its way among the ships. It seemed to grow with the fog that now blocked the moon, stars, and the enemy signal of victory from view.

After only a short time in the fog a commotion could be heard from the lead ship. Seconds later they themselves felt some turbulence from within the waters and then the thump of something that had obviously bumped the ship from underneath. "River Ox!" Someone from another ship shouted and the hearts of all quickened. Though obscured by fog, large heads and long necks could be seen emerging from the water. Everyone knew they had caught the attention of these beasts though one could scarcely see their eyes.

The animals made deep rumbling sounds that warned the ships that they had invaded their space. "Keep the ships together!" a voice called from somewhere unseen.

"Are the River Ox not grass eaters?" asked Colosso, who was standing near the seer.

"Aye," Ocean answered. "But they can chomp a man in half all the same." He looked up at the towering soldier and added somewhat threateningly, "Even a large man like you."

It was apparent from Colosso's posture that he did not like all of the new changes that came with freedmen. It was a tense moment and bad timing for it. Argoes painfully leaned upon his spear to order them, "Quiet all of you! Pay attention!"

There was a brief silence and then a bull male boldly erupted from out of the waters between the ships. He towered over the decks with a fierce glare, blowing water vapor from his nostrils. The challenge had been set and just as quickly met, for a warrior on the upper deck of a sister ship, fired a shot from his orb bow. The blast hit just behind the jaw and the bull swooned a bit before bumping into the side of another ship. It's head and neck smacked the waters with a great splash before disappearing beneath the water.

It was apparent that this had been the lead bull, for only moments later all the others vanished into the fog as well, their groans becoming more and more distant. "Well done warrior," the seer shouted and many others could be heard commending him as well.

"These beasts do not venture far into the deep waters, that can only mean we are near land," Ocean stated as if it were a curious matter.

"But how could that be?" Argoes relied. "We did not chart a course that would so quickly take us to the shallows.

"Could we be nearing islands?" Ryn asked.

"We will know soon enough," Argoes answered. "Let's see if we can't measure our depth."

Ryn walked over to the measurement rigging and cast it over the side. Everyone waited patiently for him to announce his finding. "I don't believe it!" he shouted. "We're not much more than a man deep." As soon he finished saying the words, the lead ship came to a sudden halt.

"We've struck land," a voice called out.

"How can this be?" Ryn asked, and once again all their eyes were fixed on the old man.

He shrugged with a smile, "Patience my friends. Let's just wait and see what daylight brings."

The night seemed to linger on, and few rested well, but eventually dawn arrived. As the sun rose high the haze faded revealing where the ships had come to rest, but to the amazement of all they were wedged between enormous rocks upon a large and heavily wooded hill. "It's not natural," Honora the wife of Argoes mused. "We were in the midst of the sea. Seer, have we passed into the neither world?" She was as beautiful as she was sincere.

The old man laughed, "No, it seems we have simply been placed where we are supposed to be."

"Wherever that is," Ryn thought aloud. "Argoes, we should search out our sur..." he stopped abruptly for his friend's eyes were shut. Alarm took hold of Ryn as he placed his hands upon his friend, "Argoes, Argoes, are you alive!" he nearly shouted. Immediately Argoes opened his eyes and sat upright.

"You're wounds!" Ryn said, "They're healed!" Argoes stood up and examined himself. It was true; he had not so much as a scratch, not even a bruise.

"It is a gift from El Shaddai," the old man declared Now show your thanks by the way you live in this new beginning He has so kindly given you." He smiled and made a large sweeping gesture toward all of the ships. "If we have indeed been placed where we are meant to be, then perhaps we should look around and get settled." His large grin radiated with enthusiasm, for he believed this was going to be a new beginning for him as well.

Chapter 5
Hunting

Commander found Roar standing upon an outcrop along the north side of the mountain; staring intently into the lands that lie ahead. Roar noticed him and said, "Order Bashan to scout for Gannim from the air; however, he is not to engage. He will report to us at once and then we will seek them out on foot."

"I will also prepare men for the hunt, "Commander answered as he bowed his head and turned away.

"Only two hundred," Roar added without looking, "and those vile tracking creatures; we wouldn't want them to see us coming."

It was still morning when Bashan and a dozen of his winged riders scoured north for their quarry. They continued on until midday, but unbeknownst to them, they themselves had begun to be hunted.

From trees and hidden places here and there, Gannim and his horde watched them patiently from near the hill they had encamped for the night. Their number boasted several hundred strong capable killers. Gannim had been trained by Mizrahim himself in the uses of the weapons forged from the sky rocks, among other things. Some of which Roar had not even learned for he did not trust Mizrahim's spirit guides, nor was he willing to practice sorcery for reasons he was not in the habit of sharing.

Smoke from a nearly famished fire had led the riders to a wooded hilltop that had a clearing large enough for two of them to land. Seeing no sign of anyone remaining, they assumed that the camp had been abandoned. So, as most of the riders circled high, Bashan and one other swooped down, landing within the clearing to investigate further. The riders landed facing opposite directions to better cover one another's backs, knowing that many had lost their lives assuming any danger had passed only to be wrong. Their beasts had good hearing but were light sensitive; so their eyes were covered since it was a clear day.

They dismounted looking for confirmation that this was indeed a camp recently bedded by Gannim's horde. The other warrior raised an object to show to Bashan, "Wine skin with lord Mizrahim's crest." The image was that of the silhouette of their capital, the Great City.

"Very good, then we are near," Bashan acknowledged. Just then the large pointy ears of their beasts perked up and they began to utter low grumbling growls of warning. The men's eyes met with a sudden look of intensity, and as one they darted for their beasts. No sooner had they mounted, then a bladed weapon ripped out of the forest and severed the head of one of the terrors. Their comrades circling above could see that a conflict was ensuing as soldiers poured out of hiding to take the riders down.

The Scourge riders began to fire from above, but found that they themselves were under assault as well as a glowing sphere blasted one rider right off his mount, raining some blood down upon those below.

"We are lost," Bashan yelled in anger as they ripped him from his mount and hacked the animal to death. "Fall back!" he commanded them. They wisely obeyed, weaving about skillfully until they were out of range, making haste for the mountain encampment. Once they were gone, a lanky warrior with long white hair pulled the bladed weapon that had severed the beasts head from out of a tree.

Another approached him saying, "Lord Gannim we have them both alive." A smile crept across his face as he turned to join the men who were binding them.

"Where is your master?" Gannim asked them as he lifted his star blade to his lips to lick the blood.

"He awaits news of our conquests at the Great City." Bashan was quick to answer before his comrade.

Gannim laughed, "No fool, your real master."

"We have taken Nimeria and we now prepare for the conquest of the north," Bashan said in an effort to further evade the question.

"Ah, of course," he paused a moment. "And he who leads you?"

"He awaits our scouting report."

"They will have quite a tale to share," Gannim said and he and his men laughed mockingly, "but not you, you're going to die."

"But why?" Bashan asked. "Do we not all fight under the same banner?"

"Come now, I think we all know the Scourge fights under its own banner." Gannim said with amusement. "And besides, the spirits say your master killed my scouts so I am merely responding in kind."

Knowing there would be no way out of this, Bashan smiled, "Yes and you will soon join us." He then spit at Gannim.

"We do not have time to make you suffer properly." Gannim replied and then looked at the men holding him, "hang him by his feet; the forest creatures will dine well tonight!"

"Yes flee coward for the Scourge of Roar will be coming for you!" Bashan shouted as several men began to hoist him up by his feet into a tree where he would dangle upside down from a rope, helpless against any predators.

"I'm counting on it," Gannim answered with a half-glance revealing a sinister grin. "Now drench him with his comrade's blood."

Roar and the men chosen to accompany him gathered at the northeast base of the mountain. There an encampment was emerging from where they would begin their pursuit and in time, the push north. There was a commotion on the far side of the camp and moments later a few men came rushing toward them, "Bashan is within sight!" One called.

"Make room for them to land," Commander shouted. And men began to scatter as the riders soared into view from over the trees. As soon as they landed a dark haired warrior named Crow dismounted and hurried to where Roar and Commander stood waiting. Commander sighed saying to Roar, "This doesn't look good, where is Bashan?"

"You are missing riders," Roar stated flatly, "Where is your captain?"

"We found a camp that appeared deserted," Crow began.

"Ambushed?" Commander asked.

"Aye, "we lost three."

"But why did they attack? How did they know we intended them harm?" Commander asked.

"Gannim is no fool," Roar answered. "We are two lions who have watched each other for a long time, and perhaps Mizrahim has thrown in with him." Commander looked at him with astonishment.

"It will be secret no longer that treachery is in our midst," Roar announced for all to hear. "Mizrahim knows he can control Gannim but I am the beast who has grown much too large for his cage; rightly does he fear me."

"It would seem he would supplant me with Gannim, and here I thought him wise," Roar said, smiling grimly. "Now choose whom you will serve, for neither of us will be merciful, only weigh carefully your decision. You know the quality of my fairness, but Gannim and his horde are they who violate the men, women, and even children among the conquered only to bind them together to be burned. Is this the filth that you wish to rule over all the earth?"

"Not even Mizrahim could cause us to rise up against you," Crow admitted and the others affirmed the same.

"Then prepare yourselves hunters, and keep those vile creatures in the front," Roar said and pointed to several bipedal animals with long noses full of sharp teeth and a large crescent claw above each foot. They were the crescent stalkers; nearly man sized, they were fast, lethal creatures that had been trained for the hunt.

He looked at Crow and said, "You will lead us to the encampment and then fall back unless summoned."

"Commander, you will stay behind and get the men ready for the march northward for I do not intend to be long, but do not let my intentions against Mizrahim be made known to the others for the witchers will make it known to him. I will consider how to proceed and we will deal with his puppets after I return."

"You can count on me," Commander assured. Within minutes the hunting party of about two hundred choice men and more than a dozen crescent stalkers were mobilized and running into the forest, eager for a fight.

Many of the men struggled to keep up with their swift and driven leader, but by midday the riders began to circle above the clearing, causing the carrion birds that had already begun to circle to scatter. Roar stopped a short distance from the clearing and nodded at the beast masters who set the crescent stalkers free to go on ahead. They searched about, sniffing the air and making low grumbling sounds to one another, but finding no trace of a threat they soon returned.

Roar entered the camp first, raising a fist in the air and making a circling motion. This signaled those behind him to surround and scout the perimeter of the clearing. Bashan dangled several feet up from a branch; the slain beasts and his dead comrade lie on the ground nearby. Flies were already feasting on the dead, but by hanging him upside down, Gannim had unwittingly done Bashan a favor; for the birds could not readily perch upon his shoulders to gouge out his eyes.

Roar said to those who stood near, "Unbind him." They quickly set about the task carefully setting Bashan upright. "Did they leave you your tongue, captain?"

"Aye," he answered, relieved that he had been rescued.

"How many were their?" Roar asked.

"As many as you have with you here; perhaps even more, and the large wolves he is renowned for as well."

"Is that so?" Roar asked indifferently.

"It sounded as though they were departing northward, though my back was to them as they went."

"Indeed, their tracks confirm this," Roar replied. "Are you able to hunt?"

"I am well enough. Rather than kill me himself he intended that I be devoured by the forest, thus I am covered in the dead man's blood."

"Give him water and a weapon," Roar ordered some men. "We make haste."

The Nimerian survivors had stayed busy reuniting families, checking their supplies, passing out rationed food and felling timber for the walls they intended to erect upon the very hill they had landed. Metal would be in short supply, and though rock was plentiful they decided it would have to wait until wooden defenses had been secured. But one side in particular needed little in the way of defense, something more like a safety railing for a cliff's edge erupted suddenly a short walk through the trees just south of them, proving once again the impossibility of their landing.

There were times of awkward silence as the giants and newly freed men worked hand in hand. The freedmen were more often than not teaching their former masters the skills that they had robbed themselves of learning through the use of slaves. The old man found himself chuckling often as he observed the former slaves take on the role of teacher again and again throughout the day.

The seer did little in the way of heavy lifting, but was quick to bring water and encouragement. And though not everyone shared his high level of enthusiasm, he smiled enough for them all. They were the first people to have ever heeded his warning. Finally it felt as though he had accomplished something; that all his efforts had not been in vain. His smile was that of great fulfillment.

Argoes approached the old one where he sat watching the people at their labors, but the wise man spoke first, "I think I know what it is you would say, but we will talk at sunset. All of us should gather together then." Argoes merely nodded and returned to the many tasks at hand.

From the ambush site Roar had ordered the riders to retreat unless summoned by horn or signal volley, lest they draw attention to his position and ruin their opportunity to take them with stealth. As he and his hunters followed the tracks, they could not help but notice that it seemed their enemies had taken little care in hiding their way.

"They lead us along," Bashan whispered to Roar at one point.

"Good, that means they intend to fight. Is that not why we're strolling about in the wilderness?" He answered sarcastically.

They continued on unhindered until they descended into a heavily wooded valley that thinned out as they came within view of a slow moving river. The crescent stalkers seemed confused, sniffing the air and moving in circles. "Go on to the river bank and find the location of their crossing," Roar said to those near him. "If that is, they crossed," he mumbled under his breath. Just as soon as he had said this, he noticed that one of the stalkers had frozen in alert and that the others had begun to growl.

Bashan read the change in Roar's posture, but before he could ask what was wrong, Roar said, "On the alert everyone." Only moments later one of the trackers who had gone near the river's edge looked up with alarm. He began swinging his sword above his head in a circle, silently signaling what Roar already knew; Gannim had never crossed the river.

Noticing that some of the stalkers were scratching around the trees, Roar shouted, "Follow my lead!" As his armor enrobed him he stepped toward one of the trees the stalkers were drawn to with an under swing of his axe. The fluid motion continued above his head unleashing a turquoise orb. It exploded high into the tree branches sending an assailant screaming into the air.

All at once the battle ensued; poisoned arrows whistled from the bows of adversaries hidden within the tree heights, while the swift and terrible retaliation of the Scourge's orb archers began to shatter the tops of the trees, raining branches all around. A few of Roar's men were struck fatally in the neck or face, for many had kept their armor light for the chase; however they were quickly overwhelming the hidden enemies.

For a moment it seemed that they had simply stumbled across a small pocket of Gannim's scouts who had attempted to hide themselves, but then the bulk of his forces began to emerge from deeper forest. On opposite sides they attacked, flanking Roar and his men. From the west foot soldiers and dozens of Gannim's wolves fearlessly lead the charge and from the east volley after volley of arrows and even some orbs were fired from the cover of trees.

The stalkers, who had been able to do little else than finish those who had fell from the heights, set their sights on the wolves and sprinted after them. The animals lunged at one another; relentless biting and clawing ensued. Blood and fur were flung in every direction. However there were far more wolves than stalkers and the fierce canines were using coordinated pack attacks to drag down any man or beast that they could isolate.

Gannim himself emerged on the side of the infantry, watching from the hillside. He and several dozen men stood wide open, but more than two hundred warriors stood between them and any of Roar's men. Even from his distant position Gannim hurled his tri-blades across the field of battle; removing an arm here and a head there, only to have the blades return to his grip, ready to be thrown again.

A few wolves found an open path to Roar. With one swipe he split the face of the first at the jaw line and ducked low as the other lunged. As the wolf passed over him he swung around with a back swing and severed the second wolf's spine. Roar looked up to find a warrior charging toward him with a spear. He parried the tip with the flat of his axe and countered with a front kick that audibly cracked the bones in the man's chest. The assailant was thrown back off of his feet and hit the ground with a thud. With two strides Roar closed the distance and slammed his axe down from overhead splitting the man's chest with a pop.

With a glance at the battlefield, he could see that they were outnumbered and the enemy's offence was beginning to settle in with confidence. His men were holding their own. "But for how long he wondered, just as one of his men standing nearby took a fatal blast to the face. This had been a well devised trap.

Roar looked down at his axe and grimaced at what he was about to do. With a few strides he lunged into the air with a twist. As he finished the turn he hurled his axe, which soared straight toward the heart of Gannim's infantry. "Now filth, feel my power!" The words along with the sound of the rotating weapon echoed among the trees. By design, he and the axe struck the ground at the same time with Roar throwing his arms apart as soon as he hit. The powerful weapon exploded upon impact with a powerful shockwave which was permeated with lightning.

Men were launched, nearby trees were shattered, and nearly everyone in the valley was at least knocked to the ground, but not Roar. Though shoved back several feet, he stood alone. His men wearily crawled back to their feet not fully understanding what had occurred. Roar looked to the hillside to see if Gannim had survived even though he had not been the main target. To his disappointment his enemy met his gaze from afar. "Finish them," Roar's voice hissed coldly, permeating the stillness that had followed the blast.

Gannim looked not so much afraid as he was disappointed with disbelief, as if some cruel joke had been played upon him. Now understanding that their leader had dealt the enemy a devastating blow, Roar's men raised their weapons and cheered, confident that victory had just been snatched from the jaws of defeat. With disgust Gannim swung his whip out and with one mighty crack there was a flash and boom that caused a disorientating haze to erupt across the battlefield.

Roar held still a moment to get his bearings. "Clear the air," he ordered his men who raised their weapons to dispel the haze. As the air cleared it was apparent that it had not been an attack at all but an effective diversion allowing Gannim and those standing with him to escape.

"Coward, face me!" Roar screamed with his voice echoing through the forest like thunder, but Gannim had indeed fled, abandoning whoever was left of his men to die, rather than risk seeing how it would all play out. Roar's men quickly turned their combined orb attacks to the east where Gannim's archers had been, but they were already fleeing for their lives.

"Shall we pursue?" Bashan asked Roar.

"Finish those left behind, but this is not the time to chase cowards deeper into the mountains. We will hunt them down soon enough, even if we have to level the entire forest to do so."

Those Gannim had abandoned to their fate were quickly slaughtered, but as Roar's men closed in on a few still holding out behind a cluster of large trees, he shouted, "Keep them alive!" He was hoping to interrogate them.

"Come out and surrender your weapons," one of his men ordered them. The one who held an orb bow looked at his comrade and shook his head no, but his friend thought it wiser to surrender and stepped out from cover. After taking only several steps a blast erupted into his back courtesy of his comrade who then pointed the weapon at his own face, giving himself a fatal blow.

"Can't say I blame him," Bashan muttered to Roar who looked annoyed. Bashan then began to organize the bandaging of the wounded as others stripped the dead of what was valuable. Roar had lost nearly fifty of his own men and many others were injured, more than a few by the sacrifice of his weapon.

As Roar searched the blast site for any fragments of his weapon, the riders who had fallen back returned, descending into the valley. "Could've used your help when we were ambushed," Bashan declared to them.

"You didn't summon us," Crow countered. "We didn't even know about the fighting until we heard an explosion."

"Desperate circumstances call for dire measures," Roar interjected. "Scourer the landscape for fragments of my axe; it must be reformed."

The riders looked puzzled, but then one of them stated, "Something like that?" He pointed to a chunk of metal embedded into a nearby tree.

Roar looked up and replied, "Good, then it was not completely obliterated."

Chapter 6
Haran

By the time the sun had set, those who had escaped the mountain had already stripped many felled trees of their branches. Some of the beams had even been dropped into position; anchored into holes side by side. In the days to come they would construct a matching line across with several feet between. This space would be filled with rock and dirt, making a tall, secure wall, wide enough upon which to walk. It was an old but highly effective defense that could be improved upon later.

The old man waited happily until slowly everyone began to find their way over to him. Eventually a crowd of several hundred had gathered. "Quiet yourselves," Argoes said to them and the voices hushed. He then gestured with a sweep of his arm, signaling to the old man that they were ready to hear his words.

"For the first time in many seasons I am not compelled to press on. Among all those I have warned that destruction was near, you are the first to escape it. Do not take your rescue lightly. He who created all sent me and though I am here with you now, I do not know when I may be called again. You have a new start but how will you govern yourselves? What did our ancestors from the mountains say?" he questioned them as he looked out over the crowd, meeting their eyes.

"To kill the man or beast that kills a man," a freedman from the crowd answered.

"To know no other woman than your own," Argoes said after catching the gaze of his wife from the midst of the crowd.

The old man nodded saying, "These truths and those like them have not been forgotten among your people, so let not the wicked live. Let there be with you no other god than the One who rescued you or else your end may return just as swiftly as your rescue. While I am with you I will help you, but let there be several wise men chosen from among you, Nimerian and freedman alike, who will weigh the matters affecting all. And most of all live in peace with one another, extending the same kindness you wish to receive."

He looked over at Argoes, "You would be foolish indeed if this man is not the first to be chosen as one of those who will govern you. Build your walls, but do not put your trust in them; it is your Creator who will decide whether you rise or fall. The old man paused a moment before concluding, "Rest yourselves and give the sorrow you carry for those you left behind to the One who rescued you. Their fate lies with Him now."

As the crowd began to shuffle in every direction the seer waved Argoes and Ryn over to himself. "The Spirit above all is with you," he assured, "but it would still be wise to post a guard. I do not know for what purpose we have been brought here."

"I'll see to it myself," Ryn answered.

"The food you brought will not last forever," The old man continued. "Tomorrow a scouting party should be sent out to see what provisions this land provides. I think we are farther north and the cold moons are near. It will do you no good to plant until the cold has come and gone."

"You are very wise old one," Argoes said. "What is your name?"

The old man smiled, "I am Haran."

It was early morning and a lad was playing on the outskirts of his village. It was a small settlement of only a few hundred and its inhabitants were already awake and about their tasks, preparing for the cold moons that were only a few months away. Fires burned and animals rustled, but it was the rustling noises at the edge of the forest which garnished the boy's attention. Being more curious than afraid, he approached closer to where he thought the sound was coming from.

Abruptly but quietly a host of men emerged from hiding; Gannim leading the way with a wicked grin. The boy was startled but did not flee and the warlord ruffled his hair as he stepped past him. A woman took notice of them and began to call out in alarm, warning her village that strangers had come. A crowd of men quickly assembled, some carrying the tools in their hands, while others grabbed weapons. They rushed to meet this potential threat but stopped just within several paces of the strangers.

Their leader, who did not look happy to see them, began to speak though Gannim could not understand him.

"What is this dribble?" Gannim asked his men. "I thought the peoples between the seas also spoke something akin to our dialect in the south? Can any of you decipher this angry man's words?"

"Aye," a man answered, "Well enough at least. They must have come from further west like me. His words are different, but similar as those of my own country."

Gannim laughed under his breath saying, "Go on then, tell me what he says."

"He uh, wonders why we've come." The soldier seemed to struggle to translate the words coherently.

Gannim began to laugh out loud and then his eyes and tone grew serious despite his grin. "Tell him we are here for the pleasures of death. Tell him we are going to kill him, and his family, and his village, for we mean to do them great harm." He almost drooled in exuberance and the rest of his men laughed mockingly for they were the type to indulge themselves through cruelty.

Haran awoke early and found himself a quiet spot along the cliff's edge. He made himself comfortable and seemed at ease even though a slip from this precipice would likely plunge him to his death. He sat there breathing in the fresh mountain air and being thankful. After remaining there undisturbed for a good while, at peace, and soaking in the rays of the morning sun, something began to stir within him. He suddenly opened his eyes wide, stood up, and quickly headed for the far side of the settlement which would take him straight into the forests leading north.

Ryn and Argoes were eating when Ryn noticed Haran walk past them. Realizing his route would soon take him out of sight, he tapped Argoes to silently call his attention to the sight of Haran departing. They hurriedly caught up with him and blocked his path; without a word it was clear they wanted to know where he was going in such a rush.

"I am to go into the forest," Haran explained.

"Then we wish to accompany you," Ryn answered without hesitation.

"My friends you need not worry. Have some faith. Perhaps I will return before long."

"Perhaps, but we will accompany you nonetheless," Argoes answered firmly.

Haran sighed resignedly, "Very well, have the freedman Ocean direct affairs while we're away."

They both nodded in agreement and Argoes said, "We will meet you at the forest's edge."

Minutes later they returned, only now they were armed as if ready for a fight. Haran looked at them curiously and then they began to walk. "That's a big spear you're carrying," he commented to them, holding back a grin.

"It's a big forest," Argoes replied.

Roar and his men finally made it back to their encampment, the trek back having been slowed by the wounded. "Finally," Commander said impatiently upon seeing their approach.

"All is well on the mountain Commander?" Roar sought to confirm.

"Aye, as you can see we have already begun to bring the heavy weapons over the mountain," he said, pointing to them in the distance. "Is Gannim's head in the bag?" Commander asked as he motioned to what Roar was carrying.

"He is but a coward," Roar snapped in irritation as he tossed it to the ground for Commander to investigate for himself. "He was compelled to flee, but only at the cost of something most dear to me."

Commander stood back up straight in amazement over the shattered remains of Roar's infamous weapon. "I don't believe it!" he exclaimed, "How did this happen?"

Roar exhaled forcefully, saying, "I will explain later, but now I must think." He snatched up the bag and headed for the city adding, "When the hour is late and most everyone sleeps you will find me in the mountain's heights."

Haran and his friends walked quietly for nearly an hour, though the going was slow. The old man would often stop and look around as though he was seeing things his friends could not, only to begin walking again with purposeful steps. Eventually he came to a pause and then he abruptly sat on the ground. "Is everything all right?" Argoes asked him.

"Yes, I just don't know where to go right now."

Alright then," Argoes said, sitting down beside him. He took a wine skin from around his shoulder and extended it to the old man, "A drink then."

"Thank you my friend," Haran said taking it from his hand and drinking greedily. "I have a bad habit of leaving places without provisions, but not always by choice."

"Will you not sit with us Ryn," Haran asked the younger warrior who was still standing, almost impatiently.

He looked down at them tersely declaring, "I am well," before returning his gaze to the forest.

"He is young and vigilant," Argoes added with a smile that caused Haran to chuckle.

"I am uneasy in this strange forest," Ryn said in his defense.

"I would be surprised if we were to run into anything as fierce as you," Haran surmised with a smile.

"What will happen now?" Ryn asked.

"I don't know," Haran admitted, "but with patience the answer will come."

"Perhaps we have arrived at the place you were meant to go," Ryn mused, wondering if Haran would agree.

"What you say is very wise," Haran said looking genuinely impressed with his perception. "We will know soon enough. Are you still glad you came?"

"We will know soon enough," Ryn answered, and Haran chuckled.

There was a brief silence among them, but then suddenly Ryn held up a hand as if to say, "Pay attention." The others began to listen closely to the sounds of the forest. Soon they too began to hear an echoing, chopping sound. The two comrades in arms removed their helms to better hear.

"It comes from this direction," Argoes said pointing toward the north while looking at Haran for a reaction.

"By all means, let us have a look," Haran said, arising to his feet. He followed his new guardians toward the source of the sound. As they grew louder the three men eventually came to overlook a hill. At the base of that hill was a young man desecrating a wooden idol alongside a wide, well-traveled path. "I wish to speak with him," Haran whispered without hesitation.

Ryn took a step forward, but Haran restrained him by the arm. "My friends," he said, "the mere sight of you will send this young man fleeing for his life. Remain out of sight a moment; it will be fine for me to go alone." He waited a moment for them to respond affirmatively. Finally they looked at each other and nodded to him before backtracking just out of view.

Haran began to slowly make his way down the hill. It was a bit steep, and he tried to be careful, but near the bottom he stumbled, sliding the last several feet until he came to an ungraceful stop on his hands and knees. He looked up to find the young man staring at him warily. The old man held an arm up as if to say he was all right. He then stood up and brushed himself off a bit, though it did little good for his garments, which were filthy even before he slid.

"Greetings," he announced to the young man who was holding the axe at his side. "I am Haran and I have come from afar. Can you enlighten me as to where I am?"

The young man looked at him suspiciously and checked his surroundings to be sure he was not being distracted, only to be ambushed by others. On the hill Ryn said to Argoes, "I do not understand his words. I hear them, but they mean nothing to me." His friend only raised up a finger to signal him to keep listening.

Satisfied that he was not about to come under attack, the young man said, "I am Gaius and you have come to what is known by many as the Land Between the Seas." He watched Haran contemplate his answer a moment, and then added, "Does this not help you?"

"How far are we from Nimeria?" Haran asked.

"Nimeria?" Gaius looked surprised. "The mountain of the so-called gods? Perhaps weeks by land or sea, though I have never been so far south. They say their ships come along the coast from time to time in search of slaves, but that is also days from here if traveled on foot."

There was a moment of awkward silence before Haran decided to ask what he really wanted to know, "Why do you destroy the idol?"

Gaius looked at his axe, suddenly recalling what he had been doing before being interrupted. With a grimace he said, "There is a migrating people who come and go with the seasons and with them comes the deplorable practice of binding their children to such idols to be burned. The people of the forests do not wish to make them their enemies, and neither do the kings. So I take it upon myself to frustrate their purpose any time I come across one of these... things."

"Then whom is it you serve," Haran asked?

"The One who lives," Gaius answered without hesitation. He then slammed his axe down, taking off the idol's head, saying with some anger, "This is not Him, for the One who made us does not require the flesh of children."

"Our meeting is not by chance," Haran assured. "And my companions and I have need of a guide."

"And where are your companions?" Gaius asked, as he again began to scan the forest for others.

"I left them up on the hill. I didn't want to startle you, but I can call them down now." Gaius remained warily silent so Haran continued, "Do not be afraid; you will not be harmed," he assured.

Haran then turned to the hill behind him and called out, "It's all right to come down my friends." Only now Gaius could no longer understand what he was saying. Moments later he noticed two looming figures come into view, armored and well armed. They began their descent down the hillside and Haran could see that Gaius was alarmed. Haran raised both his hands trying to reassure the young man, saying, "Please don't be afraid. They have simply come to watch over me. You mean me no harm and so no harm will come to you."

"They are from the mountain of legend aren't they? That's why you asked!"

As the giants came to stop alongside Haran he answered, "Yes, their city has been crushed and I fear that those who drove them out will soon be coming here as well. I only wish to declare to your countrymen how they can escape the destruction. Won't you help me help you?"

Gaius could not take his eyes off the towering figures whose expressions seemed indifferent. They were accustomed to seeing frightened little men daily in Nimeria. Though Gaius was tall for the men of his land, he still felt small in their presence.

Argoes looked at Haran, stating, "We cannot understand your words when you speak with him."

"Can you hear them?" Haran asked Gaius.

"I hear them fine, but I know not what they say."

Haran felt a tingling in his hands and knew immediately what it meant. "I can help you understand, but you have to trust me. I need only touch you and you will know their words."

Panic flooded Gaius's eyes, and he shouted, "Sorcerer!" He then immediately turned and sprinted for the woods.

"Wait!" Haran called out as his friends gave chase and quickly overtook him. "Don't be afraid." Haran tried with futility to calm him while his friends restrained him. "I wish only to touch you," he slowly reached his hands out toward the young man's face. Gaius turned his head and closed his eyes as if he were about to be hurt, clenching his fists and teeth. Haran laid a hand on his jaw and the young man felt a warm sensation rush to his head. Immediately thereafter he could hear the voices of his captors saying, "Do you hear us now little man?"

"I can hear you," he admitted, seeming to calm down a bit.

"Release him," Haran said, and they did so immediately. "Now please Gaius, do not run. I too serve the One who lives. You may freely go if you must, but please, I ask again, be our guide; help your people by helping us," Haran pleaded.

Gaius sighed in resignation "I will help you."

Gaius lived alone in the forest and, having nothing more pressing to tend to than the opportunity of saving many lives, he agreed to accompany Haran and his friends back to their encampment. The journey was quiet with each man absorbed in his own thoughts. When they arrived the young man's eyes grew wide at the sight as the big and small, young and old, worked side by side at various tasks. The people of the new settlement were equally surprised to see this stranger with blondish hair accompanying their own.

Some stopped their work to watch and whisper, curious, yet Haran and the others did not offer any explanation regarding the newcomer. In fact, almost as soon as they had entered the encampment Argoes said, "Wait here a moment." He then quickly gathered a handful of rocks and set them before Gaius. Taking one from the pile he set it down saying, "If this stone represents our encampment, then where are the nearest settlements?"

"Well there are many smaller ones scattered throughout," Gaius replied, "but the largest one nearby would be here," he said as he set a rock down north and a little west of the first marker, "the City of Arioch, so named after its king. His gates will be open by day, but that does not mean he welcomes strangers. He is a cruel man and would very much like to rule over all the land between the seas. But for now, he lacks the might to make it so.

"Here," he said, as he set another rock down, not so far north as before, but farther west, "is the City of Gull, ruled by the much more sensible King Baen. He seems friendly as far as men of power go. His soldiers are not known to ride about oppressing those who dwell in the forests.

"And here," he placed the rock just a little north and east, "is the great house of Rhone. He is my friend, and though it is not so much a large city as a well fortified village, I think he is assuredly the one most likely to hear you, so long as I speak with him first."

"Any to the south?" Ryn asked.

Before Gaius could answer, Haran interrupted saying, "They are lost. I will not look back." He offered no explanation and none asked him for one. Haran looked Argoes intensely in the eye, saying, "We must leave at once if you wish to accompany me. I am not used to waiting and I feel a sense of urgency."

His large friends nodded and Argoes said, "We will first tell Ocean and the others that we may be gone a few days and what we are up to."

"I will gather provisions" Ryn added.

"Provisions?" Haran said and smiled. "Yes, I guess it would be nice to eat from time to time."

As his friends turned away he looked at Gaius and said, "So, now you see. Here they are... those who fled Nimeria. See how they work side by side with their former slaves who are now freemen. Now that you know we are truthful, can we rely on you to lead us to the places of which you speak?"

"I want to trust you Haran," Gaius said. "But how can I be sure that the Nimerians are not just pushing into the north? After all, with all these ships; it looks as though you are building a fleet."

Seeing that the young man was sincerely concerned Haran said, "We sailed them from Nimeria and this is where they ran aground."

"That's not possible," Gaius contested.

"Tell me Gaius, has anything 'not possible' occurred since you met us?" Haran queried with a wry smirk. He could tell his point was well made though Gaius did not answer. "Well, if it will ease your mind we will start with the difficult king instead of your friend. However you will see; we will earn your trust. But really my boy in light of all you've heard and seen, can you afford not to trust us?"

Gaius looked as though he were silently weighing his words, but assuming he would not back out now Haran further asked, "Will you need to tell your people that you will be away?"

Gaius's expression turned from serious to solemnly bitter as he confessed, "I have no people."

Chapter 7
Hostile Neighbours

Once night had come Commander found Roar as still as a statue sitting on the ledge of the same balcony where he been when the signal was fired. Without opening his eyes Roar said, "You cannot see it but the power within my wares permits me to know you're near. This takes a long time to learn, but perhaps someday I will teach you." Roar opened his eyes and looked at Commander. "I perceive that you are troubled. This can only mean the witchers have not yet been found."

In frustration Commander declared, "We should have just killed them while you were away. But still I don't know how they could have known we meant them harm."

"And you're sure you repeated my words to no one, not even Achaia." Roar asked with a glare.

"I told no one!" Commander was adamant. "But Mizrahim is a powerful sorcerer."

"He is a clever schemer," Roar interrupted. "And surely the witchers that accompany Gannim announced to Mizrahim news of their failure to kill me. But I was wrong in my assessment of Mizrahim's purposes. He did not send us both northward to see who would win out; he has done so in order to secure my death far from his capital. He tries to hide that he has thrown in with Gannim, but thrown in with him he has. He hides it for fear that whatever it is they plan will fail. But I will hide my thoughts on the matter no longer."

Roar paused a moment as he began to recollect the battle. "Believing that we would find ourselves outnumbered once we caught up to them, I had intended to take Gannim by surprise, but it was he who had set the clever ambush. The bulk of his men had carried on along the shallows of the riverside while a good number lay in wait, high in the trees.

"Their plan was to no doubt to engage us from two sides while those above picked us off in secret and I have no doubt it would have worked masterfully, had we not discovered the men above us before the men on the ground had arrived! But still, we were in a dire peril, outnumbered perhaps three to one. So I did what I had to in order to even the odds."

"Bashan says you killed hundreds with the sacrifice of your axe!" Commander said looking for confirmation.

"I didn't count them," Roar answered flatly. "But it was the devastation it wreaked upon their fragile minds which won us the battle, and yet Gannim escaped. Apparently he does not like a difficult fight, but I will say this, Mizrahim has taught him well, for he pulled a whip trick, the likes of which I have never seen before."

"Now what?" Commander asked, throwing his hands up in bewilderment. "I mean what do we do with all these people if we are not marching the bulk of them back to the capital as has ever been our custom?"

"What indeed?" Roar seemed annoyed with this plight. "I have given it thought, and have decided we will leave a small detachment here. It will consist of those who have taken wives and those who have been allowed to keep their families by agreeing to be trained into our army. They will hold this position and act as a supply haven if we should have need of one. The rest of us will press northward, but first my weapon will be restored.

"Well," Commander said with some amusement. "I am surprised. This is very wise."

"Oh?" Roar sounded offended that Commander would be surprised that he was wise.

Commander quickly raised his arms as if to calm him, but still bore a heckling grin, "I'm only surprised by your kindness."

"Bah!" Roar seemed even more annoyed at the thought of him believing him kind. "This is not what I want, but neither will I debase myself with the behavior of Gannim and his like. Oh how I loathe them. And if I could, Commander, if I only had the means to kill them all with one bold stroke I would do whatever it took. If I could find a rock that brimming with the glow ran deep through the heart of the Earth, then I would sink my hatred deep and rip this world asunder."

Commander's smile had faded and he asked, "But why... why do you hate men so?"

Roar paused a moment and stared into the distance before answering, "How could I not?" Commander thought it best not to press him further about the matter. And yet he waited with him as the sounds of the city grew quiet.

"Commander... Commander, you must wake up now," a familiar voice interrupted his sleep. He opened his eyes to find Roar crouched nearby with a peculiar expression. Commander realized that he had accidently dozed off on the balcony and it felt as though he had been asleep for quite some time. He lifted himself up to rest upon one arm, a bit stiff from the hard, stony floor. Then he noticed a cloaked man writhing in anguish just several paces away. A pool of blood was quickly gathering near his head. "Is that one of Mizrahim's...?"

"Puppets," Roar interrupted. "Yes it is," he said smiling, "I just slashed his throat." The man stopped moving and Roar walked over to him, turning the dead man over with a foot to reveal his face. "He is dead now, but I believe the others are near. See the knife?" he said pointing to a long dagger lying on the ground. "He thought he would kill me all cunning like, but to his surprise I had mortally wounded him before he even knew what was going on."

A look of alarm crept over Commander's face as Roar continued; "Now they stalk us from the shadows." Commander stood reaching for the horn slung around his waist to summon aid but Roar took hold of his arm. "No, they might flee. Let us kill them together, you and I," he said with what seemed like the excitement of a boy about to pierce his first deer.

"Why do you put me through these things?" Commander whispered in frustration.

"Oh come now Commander, it will be fun." The faint sound of a bow string releasing echoed from somewhere unseen. Roar raised a glowing gauntlet in front of his friend's face freezing the projectile just before it was able to strike him. "He's mine," Roar snarled as he released his hold on the arrow which fell like a rock. With his short sword already drawn, he darted off, leaping across the expanse separating the balcony from the shadows where the attack had come, disappearing from sight.

Commander drew his sword, "I need a shield," he murmured nervously. He surveyed his surroundings carefully and walked toward the stairway leading down. But standing at the foot of them was another hooded witcher. They stared at each other a moment, and though Commander could not see his eyes, he could see the witcher's blades slowly emerging at his sides from beneath the cloak. Immediately his fear was replaced with a rush of battle fury. "Then let's get on with it!" he yelled, charging down the steps with a downward slash of his sword.

The assassin side-stepped out of harm's way with a counter swing, but Commander was able to duck his head in time to avoid the cut. He quickly turned to face his foe with a wide arcing attack, and yet the witcher easily avoided injury by simply gliding gracefully up to the balcony as if he were riding the wind. There was another sudden twang of a bowstring and the witcher looked toward the shadows just in time to receive an arrow to the face. It burst out the far side of his hood and he dropped.

The bowstring sounded again and Commander heard the arrow plant just behind him. He turned to find another cloaked figure mortally wounded in the neck. Commander stepped into a swing that opened the man's chest finishing him off. As soon as the sorcerer hit the ground Commander spat on him. "Ha!" he mocked. Suddenly there was the sound of someone rushing towards him from the balcony. Commander immediately turned ready to attack only to find that it was Roar who said, "Go ahead and blow your little horn for I cannot both hunt and keep you alive any longer!"

Commander wasted no time. He blew the horn and shouted, "The puppets of Mizrahim seek to kill us in our sleep! Let none escape! Let none live!" He would blow the horn and repeat this again and again until soldiers were up running about in a frenzy. "Go ahead and lead the men," Roar ordered him. But he himself remained where he was, and moments later it was only he who was left on the balcony. Roar set the bow and quiver that he had taken from the slain down, took up his own sword again, and listened carefully as the sounds of commotion grew distant. He waited patiently for what he knew would come. As he stood in the quiet darkness near the center of the balcony a cloaked figure silently emerged from the shadows behind him, inching his way close.

Just as the witcher was about to take hold of him and thrust his dagger Roar took one large step forward and turned with a backslash. The assassin slid out of range as if pulled by an invisible rope. Roar rushed in but his adversary raised an armored hand that released a shockwave which checked Roar's forward momentum.

They eyed each other and circled slowly, each waiting for the other to make the next move. Just as it seemed like no one would attack Roar hurled his sword at the witcher who dropped his blade in order to catch the rotating sword with a clap of his hands. But Roar had already followed the throw with a lunging kick that smashed into his enemy's forearms nearly shoving the blade into his face.

The witcher tilted his head out of the way of the blade just in time as he stumbled backward. He recovered his balance only to find Roar nearly on top of him throwing heavy punches with his own armored fists in an effort to smash one through his skull.

The assassin back-pedaled, blocking blow after blow with the sword, but could not find the slightest opportunity to counter. With a lunging uppercut Roar sent the sword soaring out of his hands. He then stepped forward for the finish but his foe dashed out of the way, fleeing for the balcony edge. He leaped over the half wall, falling a distance that should have broken his legs, but instead of being shattered he hit the ground running.

Rather than follow him over, Roar hurried to the bow and quiver he had discarded and raced back to the balcony edge. The witcher was leaping about here and there in an effort to escape, and Roar knew he would soon again vanish back into the shadows if he did not hurry. He held his aim for the strategic moment and fired just as the sorcerer was leaping over an expanse between two porticoes. The arrow looked as though it would strike him as he was midway across. Just as it was about to pierce him the witcher turned in midair, catching it with one hand. He tumbled to the ground on the far side only to roll immediately back to his feet.

He stopped to look at Roar from afar and raised the arrow high above his head like a trophy. He then cast it down despitefully to the ground before disappearing into the darkness. "Very interesting," Roar murmured coldly as he stared into the darkness where his opponent had disappeared. "Very interesting indeed."

Gaius and his new companions pressed on late into the night before taking any time to rest. As they made themselves comfortable under the clear starry sky, Ryn pulled out a pouch full of nuts. "Dinner as well as breakfast should I assume?" Haran asked lightheartedly.

Argoes pulled out a wine skin and held it up saying, "To strength for our journey."

"Hear, hear," Haran agreed and they all took turns drinking. After receiving his, Haran looked at Gaius asking, "How long before we reach Arioch?"

"Hmmm...," he thought for a moment. "We can reach the city tomorrow if we're not delayed."

"Excellent! Well, then I will rest while the resting is good," said Haran. Grabbing a few more nuts, he then laid back on a patch of clover and looked up at the stars. After a moments silence he said to his large companions, "Thank you for not letting me travel alone. It is good to have friends again." A tear ran out one of his eyes, though he made sure they could not see.

At first light Roar summoned all his men to the lower heights of the city where they had defeated the last of the Nimerian guard. He came and stood just in front of the fallen gate declaring, "As you must all know by now, Mizrahim ordered his sorcerers to slay me in the middle of the night like a coward. Clearly, since I stand before you, they failed. The heads of those we killed testify to this as well." He motioned to several heads piled not far from him that had belonged to the witchers. There were four, for his men had managed to corner and kill one as well.

Roar raised a foot and placed it upon the pile, leaning one arm upon his thigh before continuing. "We are surrounded by enemies, Scourge of the south, and what are we to do?" He asked, but the men remained silent. "Some of you have families for whom you care still residing in the shadow of the Great City. If you wish to go to them and lick the heel of the dog king who ordered this attack on me, then leave at once, for I will permit no other opportunity. But before you take this first step, listen closely.

"For years we have crushed every obstacle in our path and here we stand on the brink of owning the world for ourselves. Who would you have at your lead, Mizrahim who elevates himself above you and hides behind his walls while you die in his service, or I, who has taken more risk than any of you can boast? I cannot say what he will do to your families should you remain with me, but what I do offer you is the opportunity to never again have those you value leveraged against you. But count well the cost of your decision now, for in turning back you will only one day raise your eyes to see the Scourge of Roar returning with terrible retribution."

Finished, he walked past them following the main route up the mountain. "Whom do you serve?" a warrior called out from the crowd. "Roar of the Scourge!" someone answered. Suddenly the men began to chant, "Roar of the Scourge! Roar of the Scourge!" until they all shouted it as one. In the light of such a united resolve, not even one of them was willing to depart.

"We are getting close," Gaius said to his companions. "Just ahead is the broad and well traveled path that will lead us to the city." No sooner had the words left his mouth then a man steering a horse-drawn cart came into view, heading their way. The man approaching was gripped with panic at the mere sight of the large warriors and he immediately turned around whacking the rear of his animal to hasten it.

"I imagine we can expect a lot of that kind of reaction," Gaius all but mumbled. Soon he was proven right as the few who were willing to pass by them did so warily, staying on the far side of the path, but just as many returned the way they had come. Eventually the forest thinned and the walled city of Arioch came into view. The gate stood open, but dozens of mounted lancers had gathered outside seemingly ready for something. "Oh good, it looks as though news of our coming has already reached them," Haran said so optimistically that the others could not tell if he was serious or not.

"Allow me to approach unarmed first," Gaius suggested, handing them his axe. "We would not want to accidently provoke them."

"Very well," Haran answered.

Gaius approached the guards casually, and though the distance was not far it was still just out of his companions hearing.

"If we are able to enter, we would also like to know what is being said. Can you make it so we can hear their words?" Ryn asked Haran.

"Sorry my friends, but I do not feel it in my hands right now," Haran replied. Ryn did not fully understand this response, but he did not press the matter.

They watched Gaius and though his back was to them it was apparent that their conversation had begun. He looked back and pointed to them briefly before turning back to talk further. The soldier discussing the matter with him sent one of their number back into the city as Gaius returned to them to report on his conversation. "Many of those who turned back along the road told them about the approaching giants," he said. "We now await word as to whether or not we will gain an audience with the King Arioch himself."

"What if they will not see us?" Argoes asked Haran.

"Then maybe they have it coming to them and we will leave them to their fate," he answered.

Soon the guard returned from inside and spoke to the lead man among them, who then turned to bid them welcome. "Well, well," Haran said with a smile.

As they neared the gate the guards gathered around the four of them, not threateningly but it was clear that they would not be walking about freely inside the city. The guards also remained on horseback, no doubt to appear larger, but even then Argoes and Ryn stood tall enough to peer down at some of them. "At least they cannot understand us either," Ryn muttered to Argoes.

A guard on Argoes' side was staring at the two of them boldly and Ryn took offence, causing his helm's face cover to slowly fall and the metal around his eyes to glow. The intimidation was working on the guard, but Argoes soon noticed and shook his head at him, so he let it fade back to normal. They were led to a large stone stronghold with twin wooden doors that were opened by sentries as soon as they came near. The horsemen leading in front moved out of the way and it was apparent that they were to go inside. Haran entered in without hesitation, the giants shrugged at one another, and followed.

Once inside they found themselves alone. There were some windows up high, but the room was not otherwise well lit. There was also an elevated walkway protected by a half-wall which was even out of reach of the Nimerian's spears. They could see a doorway on the walkway leading to somewhere out of view, but had no idea of knowing to where it led. As they reached the center of the room the door leading out was shut abruptly and they could hear it being secured from the outside. "I don't like this," Ryn declared, looking as though he were ready to fight.

"Just remain calm everyone," Haran advised as if he had been in this exact situation a dozen times before.

"What do you say Gaius," Ryn asked. "You know the way of this people better than we?"

Gaius breathed deeply before answering, "I think I would be far more afraid if you were not here with me, but still, I had rather not be locked inside any building of Arioch."

Ryn looked at Argoes, appearing as if he were about to rage, but Argoes assured him, "You know as well as I that we can leave this room any time we choose, but the time is not now." His words were both reassuring and firm.

"What manner of room is this?" Gaius asked.

A serious expression crept over Haran's face, "It looks like a hall of judgment to me." Just then a man entered in through the door which led to the walkway.

He was mostly armored save for his bearded head, and his hair was long and black with some grey throughout. He had a cold, hard look to him as he stared down at them. A procession of soldiers with bows followed after him, filing in until they filled the walkway on all sides. "I stand corrected. This is the place where the condemned come to die," Haran murmured but his tone was such that his friends did not become anymore alarmed then they already were.

"The one who led them in, he is Arioch, the king," Gaius whispered.

"So," Arioch said, "you have come to spy out our fortifications and know our strength. Does it feel secure enough for you in here?" His men laughed at this, for his tone was mocking as they looked down upon them.

Gaius whispered the words to his large companions as Haran began to speak, "We are not spies, but we have come to warn you of a very real and dire threat."

"Oh?" Answered Arioch with a look of amusement that deliberately showed his unbelief.

"Yes," Haran continued, "I wish to warn you and help you, just as I have done for my companions who have traveled from afar."

"Nimerian's eh?" The king looked unimpressed. "My guards have told me."

"Yes, that's correct," Haran confirmed.

"And how is it that this ragged forest dweller is leading you about?" Arioch said motioning to Gaius. "Is he not just the first of what is to become many slaves?"

"No, King Arioch," Gaius began.

"Silence dog!" the king shouted him down.

"The real enemies will soon come oh king," Haran said firmly but maintaining his calm in the face of the king's cruel arrogance. "And you will fall unless you heed my words."

"Tell me the location of the other invaders or you will be the ones who soon fall unless you heed my words," Arioch declared emphatically with no lie in his eyes.

As soon as Gaius related these words to Argoes, the giant said to Haran, "Tell him we are leaving now and he would do well to let us go peacefully."

"What's that large one?" Arioch asked mockingly. "I do not speak the exalted dialect of the mountain."

"He says we will be taking our leave now." Haran answered.

"Take aim!" The king shouted and his men drew their bows. Without hesitation Argoes thrust his spear high unleashing a blinding glow of power that pinned all the soldiers to the walls.

Some of their arrows were loosed but they too were immediately repelled and pinned alongside them. The king had been standing in front of the open doorway and was abruptly thrust out. He tried to re-enter the room, but the closer he came to entering the more resistance he felt. Ryn stepped forward with a thrust of his spear towards the entrance. An orb erupted from the shaft, cruising across the room until it hit the door, causing it to explode outward.

"Move them along," Argoes ordered Ryn, taking up the rear as they exited. He kept the men above pinned as best he could until they were all out of the room. Ryn took the left and Argoes the right, their face masks down, shields up, spears ready, and keeping their little friends sandwiched in between them. Power radiated from them furiously and all who gazed upon them fled or hid, continuing to watch from cover.

As they made their way toward the gate which had yet to be closed, the guards circled far out of their way until they exited. But once they were out the guards began to clump near the entrance, immediately shutting the gates fast behind them. Once they were a good ways out Haran pushed his way to the rear saying, "Let me address them once more from here."

His guardians stepped out of the way and calmed themselves to a degree so as to not garner so much attention. By this time Arioch had also found his way to the wall, along with what looked as though it could be half the city.

"You have erred greatly this day King Arioch," Haran warned. "I pity your people. Weep and fast all of you, for the day of mourning is near." Haran waited a moment for a reply, but seeing that the king was making no effort to do so the four of them backed away until they were out of view, and then they hurried on their way.

Chapter 8
Forged Anew

The sun had just gone down when Gannim noticed a sudden alarm come over some of his troops. Startled, they had quickly drawn their weapons as several silent figures entered the encampment.

"And I thought I was the scary one," Gannim said without looking up. Realizing that he did not share their fear; his men stood aside as these cloaked figures came near to his fire.

"So, is he dead Kedar?" Gannim asked, seemingly enamored with the task of making a necklace from the teeth of those he had slain. The one who had fled from Roar came forward and pulled back his black hood. He had a small build and, though young, he had white hair that was straight like Gannim's. He looked around the camp, taking notice of several impaled skeletons sticking out of the ground here and there. Some were large and others quite small. Due to the black scorch marks, it was apparent that the flesh of whoever they had belonged to had been burned away. Gannim had allowed few from this village to survive and those who did were young and being kept for servitude.

"No, he is not," Kedar answered. But now he knows we have allied against him so my father will aid you openly. You need only watch yourself and stay alive until he sends you more soldiers in the weeks to come."

Gannim took a bite of something sitting within arm's reach saying with some dejection, "Then neither of us has proved able to kill him." He gestured toward an arm roasting on the fire, "Hungry?" But seeing that it was human flesh, Kedar did not answer him. "Come now," Gannim said almost daring him, "by eating the flesh of the conquered their strength becomes ours and we have mastery over them even in death!"

"I know you did not receive this teaching from my father," the sorcerer replied, unconvinced.

"The spirits tell me," Gannim almost muttered while adding another tooth to his necklace. "They also say we are brothers you and I, but what do you say? If anyone knows the truth would it not be you?"

"That is a question to ask Lord Mizrahim himself," Kedar replied, but Gannim only smiled at this answer as if amused by his avoidance of the matter. "We must continue on." Kedar said, changing the subject.

"Oh?" Gannim pretended to be surprised.

"We travel northward to conquer through diplomacy, at least this is the plan," Kedar added as if he were not sure it would work.

"And what is it your men carry within the cloths?" Gannim asked. He then closed his eyes hard, and began tapping his forehead with bloody fingers, "I hear them speaking to those who speak to me... inside my head."

"We bring very special gifts to the sons of Iomar that will aid in securing what we desire," Kedar admitted. He could see that Gannim thought this was a curious answer, but he did not deign to clarify. "How many of the witchers remain yet with you?"

"They all live," Gannim answered indifferently, "for none of them were in the battle. You did hear about the battle, eh?"

"Yes, Roar is a formidable adversary, but just a man nonetheless. His day will come, you will see. And speaking of such, are you ready to become the new lord of the Scourge?"

Gannim stood holding out his finished necklace and smiled, declaring, "On the day I take the reins, the earth will writhe in anguish!"

Arioch gathered several of his choice men into his great hall. Everyone else was promptly ordered out. It was dark, but they had gathered near a great hearth which cast more than enough light for them to see.

"Such power... the likes of which I have never seen," the king mused with his back to his men as he looked intently into the flames. "What do you think, were these strangers truthful or false?"

A robed man with a shaved head answered first, "It would seem that if they had meant us harm we would not be standing here my king."

"I think you are right Maris," the king answered with some regret. "But what manner of kingdom could threaten all from here to the mountain of legend?"

"Perhaps the fractured tribes of the west have been united under the banner of the giant lords?" his war chieftain Wolf suggested. He was so named because he was a fierce and burly man.

"If they came to us, then they will go to others as well," Maris pointed out.

"Yes, you're right," the king said, turning to face them with renewed hope.

"But we do not know to whom they will go or even if they came to us first, last, or somewhere in between," Wolf interjected.

"It matter not," Arioch said to them all. "I will send emissaries to Baen under a peaceful banner, ready to hear their words. And if they have already come to him then it is from King Baen himself that we will learn more.

"The two of you," he continued, pointing to Maris and Wolf, "will be going along with our most precious and influential jewel." The king smiled with confidence that his plan was flawless. "Now go! You will have everything ready to depart by first light."

The hour was late and the moon was high. Roar stood upon the same large balcony where he had fought the witcher with the shattered pieces of what was left of his axe laid out before him. Achaia, Commander, and Bashan approached from the nearby stairwell together and gathered round. "We have all that you asked for and more," Commander said to him. They presented to him various Nimerian artifacts, as well as some from their own stores. Roar looked them over carefully, holding his hand above them and seeming to sense the power within. After the inspection he turned to them and said, "The scepter will not work; it has been polluted with gold. But I will take the longer of the two Nimerian daggers. Combined with the arrows left over from the witchers it will be enough."

"Why only these?" Commander asked, curious to understand; Achaia rolled his eyes, annoyed at his ignorance.

Noticing, Roar addressed Achaia, "Go ahead general of the war machines, inform him."

Achaia sighed before he began, saying, "The dagger and the arrows are just like his axe, being forged from the rocks that fell from the sky."

"I knew that," Commander almost snapped, acutely aware of Achaia's condescending look, "but why does it matter if it's mixed with gold?"

"The heaven's metal is lighter, stronger," Roar answered. "It does not *feel* the same when it's mixed with other metals, so naturally the heaven's metal holds much more power when not bound to those materials that do not hold power as well.

"Oh," Commander answered, surprised at his own ignorance concerning such things.

"You are the top-ranking man among us three and you did not know this?" Bashan chuckled.

"Shut-up," Commander muttered, embarrassed.

"Who among you, other than Achaia, has ever performed the Metal Smith's Secret" Roar asked them, but Bashan and Commander remained silent.

"I was afraid of that," Achaia answered with a look of genuine anxiety.

"Well there is a first time for everything, right artillery captain?" Roar jabbed, and Achaia ran his hands nervously through his hair, looking up so as not to make eye contact, but unwilling to speak his mind. Roar continued, "The only way to forge the heaven's metal is to use the glow to mold it; however, even then it is a delicate process, dangerous even. And once it is fashioned it tends to hold that given form.

"You must remain focused throughout the process so as to not cause sharp, pointy pieces of the metal to spiral about. I will do the actual forging, while the three of you channel the glow from your own weapons, providing me with even more power with which to work. Any questions?"

After a moment's silence Achaia answered, "No, but we should all armor up."

"Very well, coward," Roar seemed to be joking but he really could not tell. They all placed their helmets on and held a shield in the hand not holding their weapon with which they were to channel through. "Weapons at the ready," prompted Roar, and they all pointed their swords at the shattered pieces of the axe placed on the ground. "Now let your powers permeate among them, but slowly."

Their swords gradually began to glow and soon the fragments on the ground did as well. "Good, very good," Roar said, praising them.

"Now steady your power and let no distracting thought enter your mind." Roar began to lean in intently as the metals started to run like metallic water until the various little pools rolled into one, gathering together to resemble his axe. The axe began to rise off the ground a bit as he began to mold the various shapes that he might use in battle. As they watched, the shaft would lengthen and then shorten; the reverse pike would grow longer and then shorter until it was blunt like a hammer.

"So that's how you're able to do it!" Achaia said in amazement.

"Focus!" Roar ordered sharply without looking up. "We are nearly finished." Soon the weapon came to once again resemble its familiar form. "Enough!" Roar snapped. They stopped immediately and watched as he took hold of it, causing it to run the series of shapes that it had while they were reforming it. Once he was satisfied with his examination Roar smiled, "Well done."

"So that's how you do it," Achaia said excitedly. "It must go through all the forms you want during the forging."

"That is correct," Roar answered, "and in so doing I will now be able to make it transform smoothly in battles to better suit the needs of the moment."

Commander seemed bewildered, asking, "If this is how they are so formed, then how do they get their power?"

"It's inherent in the rocks from which they came," Roar answered him. "The nature of such weapons is to draw its strength from the world around us, yet not all are equal in ability. But this is a fine weapon, perhaps even superior to the original."

Achaia looked at Commander shaking his head as he asked, "How is it that you know so little of such things and yet are in authority over us?"

"Trust," he answered defensively.

They all looked at Roar who shrugged and nodded in agreement, "His loyalty is without question." He then raised his axe proudly, declaring, "And now that what was shattered has been remade, all I need to do now is add some things," he paused a moment and smiled sinisterly, "like lightning."

Chapter 9
The House of Rhone

After escaping Arioch, Haran and his companions agreed to travel next to the house of Rhone. They trekked throughout the night and on into the next day, stopping little. It was almost dark again before they neared their destination. Just before they came into view of the main door to the little, but well-fortified settlement, Gaius said to them, "Let me approach by myself again, only this time I think you should wait just out of view."

No one argued to the contrary, so he ventured just into view of the entrance. A heavy wooden door, which was also gated, bared the way into this portion of the settlement. This door led straight into a building which regularly served as an inn for those who traveled between the seas. Above the door, on the roof of this guest house was Elon, Rhone's son, who was keeping watch from a large wooden bench.

"Gaius!" He stood upon seeing him. "It's been a few weeks, good to see you man. I'll raise the gate at once.

"Wait my friend," Gaius answered. "I'm not alone."

"Oh," Elon said with curiosity. "Where are those who accompany you?"

"Please do not be alarmed," Gaius warned, in an attempt to prepare him for whom he was about to meet. "I have only brought them since they bring dire news."

"All right then," Elon said. "Bring them forth."

"Come out now," Gaius called in the direction where his companions were hiding out. As they approached Elon's eyes grew large, "I'll call for my father at once," he said, and left immediately.

"Is all well?" Argoes asked.

"I think so," Gaius answered. "I know them well, they will not harm us. They may not let us in, but they will not harm us. You will find that Rhone and many others within these lands speak similar to those in the south." He looked at Argoes as he continued, "How is it that Haran knows my words, and yet you do not?"

"Where we come from it was unlawful to speak any dialect but that of the mountain," Argoes admitted. "It was one of our many prideful customs, and though Haran is not from the mountain, it seems he is able to speak to anyone he has need to."

"And Haran says he cannot give us understanding of your words in the same way he gave you understanding of ours," Ryn added.

"It is not mine to give," Haran interjected. Just then, Elon returned with his father Rhone, a large bearded, but balding man wearing sleeveless furs. "What is the meaning of this Gaius? Who are these strangers?" he almost demanded.

"This is Haran a messenger of the God above all and his friends who have escaped the destruction of Nimeria."

"The destruction of Nimeria?!" Rhone repeated with surprise.

"Yes, and they come bearing bad tidings, for the threat that came to their land is also destined to come to ours. He wishes to speak to you concerning these matters."

Rhone looked at them a long moment, weighing his next decision carefully. "I will trust your friends to enter so long as they entrust their weapons to me until they leave."

Gaius repeated Elon's words in the hearing of his tall friends. "It is not that simple," Argoes said. "You cannot just grasp such weapons untrained without the danger of unleashing their power."

"We could just drive them through a tree." Ryn suggested. "None of these little men could hope to pull them out."

"I think driving them through a tree might send the wrong message." Haran suggested.

Gaius held up a finger as if to say wait and then turned back to face Rhone who had been watching their conversation with great curiosity. "Their weapons are not safe to touch. The stories about the power of the Nimerian's are true, at least some of them."

"Show me." Rhone replied with his arms folded.

"He asks to see the power of your weapons," Gaius said to Argoes and Ryn.

"Very well," Argoes answered, stepping passed them. He raised his shield up and slammed it into the earth, with the result of a blinding flash. When he released his hold of the shield it remained upright on its own. Stepping forward the giant drove his spear straight through a tree that was as thick as a man. With both hands he gave the glowing shaft a hard twist and the trunk of the tree snapped in two, crashing down in the direction away from the walls.

Gaius' companions then all looked up at Rhone and Elon to see their reaction. With a serious and troubled look Rhone admitted, "I think that if your friends wanted inside my house they could have entered easily enough. So, they may enter with their arms, for I'll not be handling such things."

"Open the gate," he ordered his son who began to crank the wheel that raised it up. He and his father then hurried down to unlock the door. Once it opened Argoes and Ryn ducked their heads as they entered and found themselves within a large cabin-like room with plenty of wooden tables. There were many travelers within as well and all their eyes were fixed upon these large strangers.

Rhone was by no means a small man and yet he appeared so as he stood next to these newcomers. "Come with me," he said, "We'll talk on the roof where we won't draw so much attention." As they passed by a woman who was serving the guests, Rhone said to her, "Mara, bring some food and drink to the roof." She gave a nod of her head and the men continued on to the far side of the room, turning a corner which led them to the steps which brought them back to the guard post. Rhone gestured for them to sit, but only Haran and Gaius accepted. Argoes stood and Ryn slung his shield around to his back kneeling on one knee, supporting himself with his spear.

"So who is this threat that boasts such a long reach?" Rhone asked.

Gaius looked at Haran, nodding for him speak, so the old man began, "Well, of that I can tell you very little, except they are a fierce and powerful army from the south."

"A powerful army you say?" Rhone repeated with some alarm.

"Powerful enough to take the Mountain of Legend within a day." Haran added.

"How long...," Elon began, "How long before they come this way?"

Haran shrugged, "Who can say, but it will be soon enough, and this is why I have come; to warn any who will listen. To let people know that the only way to be saved is to is to..." Haran paused a moment, as if he did not know what to say, then, as if a sudden realization dawned on him, he confidently announced, "You will be safe here so long as you remember the Eternal One in all your ways and do not ally yourselves to those whose end has come."

"You mean by way of alliances?" Elon asked.

"Yes by any similar means of friendship. The tribe that Gaius told us of, those who bind their children to be burned, have you befriended them?"

"No!" Rhone looked almost offended. "But neither do I seek a quarrel with them. In fact, by this time they should be moving farther south for warmth; that has ever been their custom. They are exiles from Huria in the distant south. "

Haran looked at Gaius, "There is no danger here; we should go"

"And where will you go now?" Elon asked.

"To Gull," Gaius answered. "We hope to find an audience with Baen. We first went to Arioch, but that meeting did not go so well."

"I see," Rhone replied as if contemplating something, "I'm not surprised. Arioch is a hard man. But perhaps I should go with you to Gull, for Baen and I are friends."

"That would be excellent!" Gaius almost shouted and then looked at Haran. "Isn't it?"

"I see no reason why not. If Rhone is of the same mind as we, then this can only encourage his friend, this King Baen, to be wise."

Rhone looked at his son, "Tell Elona to go to the stables at once. I want our finest animals sattled and ready.

"What kind of beast can our large friends possibly ride?" Haran asked.

Gaius smiled, "You will see."

Chapter 10
The Jewel of Arioch

The sun had not long set when a delegation of more than twenty riders approached the city of Gull on horseback. Armen, who was in charge of those standing guard that evening was the first to notice them. "Those dark saddle blankets of blue and red are the colors of Arioch royalty. Send for the king immediately," he ordered a guard.

The guard hurried off as Armen began to clear the way of any who was standing idle near the entry, for he believed it prudent to show these visitors a respectful deference. The riders were permitted to enter without so much as being halted to give up their armament, for relations between the two little kingdoms was cold at best, but it was King Baen who most earnestly sought after peace.

"We bring a message of urgency to your king," Maris said to Armen, who immediately led them toward the king's hall. They were followed by guards, but they kept some distance, being careful not to offend, or make them feel threatened. About the time they reached their destination King Baen himself was already coming out to greet them. He was an older man who was a little heavy around the waist, and by his informal appearance, it was evident he was not expecting guests. Even so, he was unwilling to make them wait until he was properly attired.

"Peace and fortune to you my friends," he said. "You have come at mealtime. Come in and tell me what good news brings you to my city?"

A white horse, smaller than the others came forth from the middle of the pack. Its rider was small and wearing a dark blue, hooded cloak with dark red trim. Delicate hands reached up to remove the hood to reveal Arioch's daughter; the beautiful Feryn.

"You are most gracious to us King of Gull," and following her lead, all those with her began to dismount.

"Formalities aside Feryn, you know you can call me by name. But right this way," he gestured. "My servants will feed and water your horses and we will dine well."

As they entered his hall and returned to his table, the king waited for them all to be seated before he and those dining with him sat back down. Without being asked, the king's leading general Talon, gave up his seat at the King's right hand and offered it to Feryn who accepted with a bow of her head. He then moved to an open space further down the table. "Forgive my impatience Feryn," Baen began, "but I am anxious to know why exactly you've come."

"Recently strangers visited our city with a dire warning. But, you know how my father can be, and being offended, they departed before all could be heard. Since that time my father has come to regret his inhospitality and wishes to make amends."

Baen looked nervous upon hearing these words, being almost afraid to ask, "And how is it that I can help you?"

"Have these strangers not come to you?" Feryn asked.

"No, I know not of whom you speak."

"They came to us and they will surely come to you as well," she assured. "So I humbly ask that we be permitted to await their arrival so that I may hear their words."

"They will be coming here?" the king sought to confirm. "Are you certain of this?"

"My father was quite certain."

"But of course Feryn," the king answered nervously. "Now tell me more about these strangers."

Upon reaching the stables even Argoes and Ryn were amazed at the sight of the enormous beasts which they were expected to ride. Rhone smiled at their reaction. He kept more than a dozen various four legged animals and any one of them was a sight to behold.

"This is how I've maintained my independence from the kings and all the other would be rulers," Rhone said to them as he patted a large horned beast on the jaw. Not many have mastered the training of such powerful animals and certainly not on the same scale as I. It's a lot of work, but its work we gladly perform in order to govern ourselves."

Gaius repeated his words to his friends and Ryn asked, "How do we mount them?"

"What does your friend say? "Rhone asked Haran.

"He asks the proper way to climb on."

"Tell him they are well trained and will not respond in fear so long as he does not act afraid of them."

Haran communicated the message and Ryn smiled at Rhone and nodded. "I'll go first and demonstrate," Rhone said as he unbound a little rope latter which he then used to climb high enough to mount. Gaius and Haran did the same while the larger two needed only to grab a firm hold of the saddle's pommel and hoist themselves up.

Those who tended the stables opened a large gate that led directly outside the village into the surrounding forest and Rhone led the way. The beasts walked slowly by nature but their large steps carried them faster than they would have walked had they been on foot.

The one that Rhone rode was hairy with two enormous tusks. Haran and Gaius sat upon enormous black bulls with large black horns to match. They stood taller at the shoulder than either of them could reach. The giant's beasts each had three horns and what reminded them of a shield at the back of their skulls. They traveled along a path that was at times only wide enough for them to ride single file; however the tri-horned beasts which they called gore mongers, would often refuse to follow the leader, aggressively plowing through some of the rocks and trees in their way instead of going around them.

Rhone looked back with a smile saying, "Tell your friends not to be alarmed, it is just their way. But if they don't like defending themselves against falling braches, the beasts will obey a firm hand."

Gaius related the words to Ryn, who then steered his alongside Argoes saying, "I don't like this. These creatures are stronger than us."

Argoes laughed, "The little men seem at ease enough. Have no fear of them, only do not fall off!"

The mere expanse of their formation, due to the size of the beasts, provided them with little opportunity for conversation, but the journey was full of scenic views and enough opportunities for lighthearted exchanges to keep them entertained. For hours they kept on until, all at once, the animals began to be agitated. Rhone looked back and, realizing that it was not only his beast, shouted, "Halt! Keep a firm hand on your reigns." He kept quiet a moment, carefully watching the surrounding forest.

After a moment's silence they could hear quiet but heavy footsteps, as if something large was trying to remain unnoticed. "Draw arms my friends." Rhone called to them.

"What is it?" Ryn asked Gaius.

"This is the hunting ground of the walking serpents. They are very large beasts which have a long snout full of dagger sized teeth. I believe Rhone thinks some may be sizing us up. One of our animals would certainly score a large meal for them. They probably think we are a herd. However, they are known to commonly attack men as well." Ryn was disturbed by this news. They did not have large predators on their mountain, and he was offended at the thought of one trying to eat him.

A good distance straight ahead a large creature burst abruptly out of the trees and stopped just on the path. It was hairless, red and brown in color, and seemed to be sniffing the air as if it had not yet seen them. "Ignore him and keep your eyes to the trees," Rhone ordered. "It seeks to distract us from its mate. We should slowly begin to circle in so that the rears of our animals face one another."

Gaius was quick to repeat all of what was said, but just as they began to slowly change their formation Argoes pointed his spear toward the trees nearest Ryn shouting, "There!"

No sooner had the words left his mouth than another of these large creatures, which was crouching behind the trees, lunged at Ryn who barely had time to raise his defense as it clamped its massive jaws over the top and bottom of the shield. The force nearly shoved Ryn off the far side of the saddle, but then it backed up hard, forcing Ryn to release his shield lest his arm be ripped off as the beast cast it aside.

Argoes blasted it on the side of the head with a shot from his spear as Ryn raised his spear in front of him with one hand, while turning his gore monger to face it head on. After wincing briefly, the walking serpent crouched low again, holding its ground. On the trail the other had begun to rush at Rhone's beast, but the tusks of his animal kept it at bay. Ryn fired an orb, striking the creature nearest him right in the front of its nose. The attack drew blood and the beast made an angry noise, bearing its teeth as it began to back up into the forest. Its mate soon followed, convinced that this meal had proven too resilient to eat.

Ryn and Argoes fired a few more shots into the forest after them for good measure, urging them on their way. Then they all waited quietly for the sounds of their heavy steps to grow faint with distance.

"They hunted us," Ryn said, dismounting to pick his shield up off the ground.

After Haran had shared his words, Rhone answered, "They hoped to scare us and scatter us as you would separate an animal from its herd."

Haran related the answer back to them, and then smiled as he declared further in their hearing, "Well, that was exciting," and they looked at him in disbelief.

Late in the evening the travelers came within view of Gull. "We are here," Gaius announced to his friends. Seeing gulls fluttering about the heights of the city Haran muttered, "And so it is thus named."

"It's only Rhone," the guards upon the wall said to one another. A visit from him would usually have caused quite a stir, but they were anxiously awaiting the strangers they had heard so much about. After looking closely at those approaching with Rhone, Armen declared, "Look at the size of those men upon the beasts. Surely this must be them!"

Without any comments to Rhone regarding his traveling companions, the guards allowed them through the gate. Single file they entered almost out of necessity, and just as soon as they did, King Baen was already rushing to meet them. "Welcome my friend! I see you have met the strangers who are new to these lands."

Rhone looked surprised, asking, "You know of their coming?"

"All will be explained in private," Baen answered. The travelers dismounted, allowing the king's servants to lead Rhone's pets away. "Can a horse not carry you from here to there, Rhone?" the king asked, shaking his head at the size of the beasts and just imagining all the things that could go wrong with creatures of such size.

"You know how I like to make an entrance," Rhone said jokingly. "And besides, their presence makes it more difficult to be eaten." The travelers dismounted and began to follow Baen toward the hall where he had been discussing matters with the emissaries from Arioch.

"Oh, encountered some of those wretched beasts did you?"

"Aye," Rhone answered.

"You know we should mount a hunting expedition, you and I, rid ourselves of those vile creatures once and for all..."

As the king rambled on, Gaius drew close to Rhone saying, "Look there, do you see those men on horseback, heading toward the gate, as if avoiding us?"

"Yes, I see them," Rhone answered.

"Notice the dark red and blue colors blanketing their horses' backs? They are from Arioch." It was obvious that Gaius was troubled by this.

"Fear not lad. Baen can be trusted and I will not hesitate to ask the significance of their presence here."

As if on cue the doors to his dining hall were opened and waiting therein was Feryn. "It is good to see you Rhone," she said warmly as she approached them.

"Expecting me were you daughter of Arioch." Rhone said, giving the king an annoyed glare.

"No, actually I have come in the hope of meeting your companions."

"Then you are not to be disappointed," Rhone answered her.

There was an awkward silence that was too uncomfortable for Baen, which prompted him to admonish them cheerfully, "Come now everyone. Be seated. We are among friends." He tried to sound lighthearted despite the tension, and though his words fell a bit empty, everyone played along well enough.

Argoes and Ryn struggled to sit at the table, and feeling quite silly once they did manage to squeeze themselves in, with a glance at one another they got back up, and pulled other tables over which they used as seats. Now, even while seated they towered over the others, but were comfortable at least.

The king looked at them wearily and then gestured for Feryn to begin speaking. She looked at them all and asked, "To whom shall I speak?"

Haran met her gaze saying, "It is I who brings these grave matters to the attention of all who will listen."

She wasted no time as she began, "My father Arioch deeply regrets offending you with his inhospitality."

"You mean hostility," Haran interrupted.

She smiled, accepting his pointed correction gracefully and nodded, "I have come in peace to hear you out and return your words of warning to my people."

"And what of the soldiers who departed on our arrival," Rhone interrupted.

"Out of concern for me, my father insists on being informed of all the significant comings and goings while I am here."

Rhone did not answer her, but it was clear, just by his look, that he found her answer less than adequate.

"I am happy to have another opportunity to share this message of hope with you dear girl," Haran said, diffusing the tension. "In the days soon to be, an army from the south will come to these lands, brining destruction upon all who practice cruelty, divination, and other vices."

"If your father does not want to die in the wake of their onslaught, then clearly he has much to change. For those who desire life will return themselves to the One who gave it. He is whom our fathers served when they survived the waters that covered the earth."

She waited a moment for him to continue before confirming, "And this is all?"

Haran laughed, "Yes, it is a simple message I know, and yet few have taken heed." His smile quickly faded as the sadness of that truth resonated within him.

"And now that we have received this message, you and your powerful companions will ally with us and aid in our protection if we have need," she stated confidently.

"If your people truly receive these words, then you will not need any protection, for you will have changed your countenance to match your Maker's. That is the point, and we ourselves will be soon leaving from here to continue warning others."

"I see," she said with a look of disappointment. "Then I must send word to my father at once."

"Will you be taking your leave then Feryn?" Baen asked hopefully.

"No, I need only write it down and send envoys," she answered. "I wish to reside a few days more before returning home, if that is acceptable."

"I will have rooms prepared for all, as well as the materials you need sent to your room at once," Baen assured her.

"Thank you," she said, and as she began to stand, they all stood respectfully as well. "Thank you all. I will look to speak with you more on the morrow."

"Very good," the king said lightheartedly.

They waited for her to leave and then returned to their seats. Baen looked at Gaius saying in a friendly manner, "I have seen you before, have I not, young man?"

"I have visited your city a few times, but I did not know you had taken notice of me," he answered.

"A wise king notices the newcomers," Baen advised. "And where is your village?"

"I have long resided in the forests near Rhone's people."

"Who can blame you?" Baen said graciously, not looking down upon his humble circumstances, knowing that perhaps in doing so he had avoided the troubles that come with kingdoms.

"I have a special warning for you King of Gull," Haran's tone was almost grim and Baen leaned in close, listening intently.

"If Arioch proves to be unchanging in his evils, you would do well to keep yourself from him, unless you wish to share in his fate." The table grew silent and a troubled look came over the king, for there was no misunderstanding the intention of these words.

By sunrise, the exiles from Huria were beginning the third day of their migration south. They would encamp within the region just bordering their homeland so as to avoid the bitterly cold months ahead. Their king was a dark haired man named Melek. He led the long procession at the front along with his leading warriors. At midday, those leading encountered a gangly white haired man blocking their route.

Though menacing, the sight of this one man did not cause them alarm. Soon, however, Gannim's men began to slowly emerge from the forests surrounding the wide path on which they traveled and Melek's warriors began to take battle stances. Most of the exiles were barefoot, the men wearing masculine flowing skirts with their hair long and black, usually in ponytails. Their weapons mainly consisted of wooden shields and spears or bows, though some carried metal swords.

Gannim addressed them in the common tongue of the south saying, "Calmness, calmness... I only wish to speak with you. My name is Gannim, and I am the fist of the Lord Mizrahim. My master knows your comings and goings and says there is no need to travel south when he can give you cities between the seas in which to dwell."

He waited a moment as the leading men exchanged words in hushed tones, but Gannim really did not like to be kept waiting. "You should really hurry up with your answer, for my offer soon expires." Gannim's friendly act was quickly fading, his tone betraying his impatience. He glared at them almost contemptuously as he began to pat one of his infamous throwing blades into the other hand.

It did not take long for those discussing the matter to come to a decision, and Melek came forward bold but cautious, saying, "We know the reputation of your king and we will hear more of his offer."

Gannim grinned, though the sinister nature of his gaze remained, "Good."

Chapter 11
Smitten

The king had given Gaius and his friends among the finest of his guest rooms in which to rest. The weary travelers slept long into the day, exhausted by the last few days lack of quality rest. They intended to return home soon after getting up, yet relented to remain when King Baen urged them to stay just a bit longer. As the day grew late, it became apparent that the king intended to hold a feast in the honor of his many guests. While the men of Nimeria kept mostly to themselves, getting their questions about the land answered by Gaius, Baen filled his hall with food and music, preparing the same outside for those who would not be permitted in.

By sun set he even sent food, drink, and music makers to the guards on duty. After the men inside the banquet hall had their fill, they began a time honored tradition amongst their inhabitants, throwing weapons at wooden targets fashioned after the shape of men for sport. Secured to these targets were shields and helmets. The game was simple enough, choose your throwing weapon, and hit what would be vital in battle to score; hit a shield or helm and you do not.

Eventually Gaius disappeared from the table only to find his way into one of the three lines to attempt to earn his turn against Talon who was crushing all the competition. As the game wore on, scores of men were forced out. This carried on for more than an hour until, to the surprise of all, it was only Talon and Gaius left. The young man had proven resilient and talented. This had not escaped the notice of Feryn who had seemed to grow more interested in the outcome the longer he remained. Though Gaius was aware of her attention, he pretended not to notice.

After taking a long drink from his cup Talon turned around to find the young man waiting patiently. He could not hide his surprise as his brow raised and his drink dripped from his beard.

"All right boy, it's just you and me now, eh? Ha!" Talon jabbed lightheartedly, but also hoping the pressure would to get to the younger man. "You'll not be beating me tonight lad!" The room roared with laughter as he carried on with his taunts and they both chose their weapons. Gaius went with throwing axes and Talon chose spears. "Ladies first," Talon shouted over the noise as he stepped out of the way.

Gaius laughed and shook his head. Pouring with sweat, he gathered his concentration and the room began to quiet down a bit. He stepped into his throw; and the axe hit the chest center. "Ahhhhhh!" the crowd chimed with sounds of impressed approval.

The second throw hit at the shoulder and the onlookers debated the value of the blow. As Gaius prepared for his last try Talon said to him, "Don't worry lad, it's only your last attempt and all the ladies are watching."Laugher broke out, but Gaius did not wait for the noise to fade as he tossed the weapon which rotated into a direct hit to the face.

As the crowd began to stand, shouting with applause, the blade, not having had enough force to stick deep into the target, slowly lost its hold and dropped to the ground. Moans instantly followed and Gaius shook his head with a grin knowing that he had probably just lost. "That wee little arm just cost ya boy," Talon jeered and the room roared. "My turn," he said stepping up to throw with a confident grin. His throws all came quickly, one after another. The first and second hit the chest and the last landed at the jaw line. His triumphant swagger earned him both cheers and boos as he waved a victorious fist, growling.

He gave Gaius a slap on the back, saying, "Well played woodsman, well played." Many others nearby did the same.

"How about your friends? They look fierce enough," a man in the crowd called out.

Ryn and Argoes noticed that all eyes were suddenly on them. "They're talking about us aren't they?" Ryn said to Haran.

"Yes," Haran confirmed, "they want to see your throwing prowess."

"Very well," Ryn said. As he suddenly stood the room shook as the men began to stomp and pound the tables in anticipation and approval. Ryn stepped up to the throwing line with his spear. As he took aim the room grew still. He took two steps and, without using the weapons real potential, he hurled the spear hard and fast. It hit the center of the shield of the target and ran through the back side, the spear end embedding itself into the wall behind.

The room remained quiet in awe as he uttered something. Haran stood up to translate, "My friend says that had the target been a real man, he still would have died." With this declaration the room lost it. Cheers and laughter erupted as Ryn wrenched his weapon free, tearing the target in two. He then returned to his seat.

After Ryn's display, Gaius, decided to cool off from the exertion of the very long competition. He headed for one of the twin stairways leading to the walkway above, exiting onto a large open balcony. Once there, he was surprised to find that it was not more crowded, but then he realized why. The few men who were present were standing guard over Feryn who had also apparently decided to step out.

Not wanting to intrude and seeing that the guards were giving him hard stares, he began to turn around and depart. "It's all right, you may refresh yourself here as well," she said.

"Thank you," he replied and walked to the edge to look below at how the people outside were celebrating, though He was careful to keep his distance from her.

"You did well in the game," she said to him.

He smiled, "Better than I thought I would, to be sure. At the end I was just very tired, while the king's man remained strong."

She remained quiet, yet looked at him beneath her hood. Being very beautiful her regard made Gaius a bit uncomfortable, so he returned to looking at the activity below.

"Talon is a warrior of renown. There is no shame in losing to him." She paused a moment before continuing, "How is it that you have gained such powerful friends like Rhone and the men from the mountain?"

Gaius considered her words a moment before explaining, "I often sleep under the stars near the house of Rhone. He befriended me in a time of distress, and I have proven to be a faithful friend in return. As for the Nimerians, well that's a strange story. As formidable as they may look, they are very agreeable." She looked at him as if waiting for more explanation so he kept on, "It would seem our paths crossed by the hand of the One Creator and so I have agreed to be their guide, not by force of course," he was quick to point out.

"I think that we have in common the suffering that has changed us." He stopped himself, turning red and feeling as though he had said too much, yet Feryn still seemed to be listening closely.

"Will you be leaving soon?" She asked.

"By sunrise to be sure. Haran, the old one, does not seem to stay anywhere for very long."

"We will be departing tomorrow as well," she replied. So then, we will dine together in the morning before departing, you and I." She declared this as if he had no choice in the matter, and then turned to depart with her guards falling close behind.

"I will see you then princess," is all that Gaius could think of to answer her.

Late into the evening after Melek's people had settled for the night, he and his leading men gathered to meet with Gannim. Melek spoke first, "Your master, he is one and the same as he who drove the giant lords out of the east?"

"He is, and now he sets his eyes on the north; these lands will soon be ours." Gannim's words were emphatic with the certainty that what he said would surely come to pass. "But he is not the only one to have set his eyes here. An enemy of ours contends for it as well. For this reason I have come in search of allies who wish to have a place here once our rule begins."

Melek's gaze fell upon Gannim's necklace, knowing that the teeth were human. Some of them were so small that they had surely belonged to children. Taking notice, Gannim grinned holding it out for him to see better, "Not all are given the opportunity to rule and what I offer you is a great privilege. If you refuse us now, you will have no place here once it is ours."

"How is it you know things about us?" Melek asked.

"My mother was from your homeland," Gannim answered flatly. "Huria has grown into a formidable nation and so even if she was not, I would still find it necessary to know some of the ways of those we will in time conquer. And further, my witchers tell me that you are only a vagabond king who will never gain an allotment among the people of your homeland. Is this not why you wonder about so?"

Melek's expression revealed that, true or not, he was offended by this candid expression of his lot in life, but Gannim did not care. "Two paths have been presented to you. The first path leads to further exile and humiliation for you and your people, but the second will secure your future. Ally yourself to us, secure your place here and you will have your own country, and the days of wandering will be no more."

"If you refuse, you must move along, never to return, for we will tolerate none who rejected the kindness of our outstretched hand. In time no one will be safe from our ultimate grip, not even those of Huria. Wouldn't it be nice to one day return to your ancestral home as their conqueror?"

Melek exhaled heavily as he considered Gannim's words, filled with conflicting emotions and thoughts. He and his chieftains stepped away and discussed the matter quietly. It did not take them long to come to a decision, and when he returned to where Gannim waited he proudly declared, "Your enemies are now our enemies."

Late into the night, after the festivities had wound down, Gaius and his companions departed for their rooms. Rhone remained in discussion with the king, making up for lost time, for they were good friends who did not often make the journey to see one another.

Tonight they would rest in the king's own house, deeper within the city. Haran was amazed by the many stone and wood houses built right into the walls of the city. "Thousands must reside here," he mused for all to hear.

"Yes, more than a few thousand to be sure," the attendant leading them confirmed.

Their rooms were all in the same hall a few stories up. There was one for Gaius and Haran to share, and another, even more spacious, for their much larger friends.

"I see now why Rhone and Baen are friends. He is very generous and hospitable," Gaius said, as they examined one another's rooms. The attendant had stepped away, but quickly returned with a set of clean garments. He brought them to Gaius saying, "Just as you requested."

"Our many thanks to you and your most generous king," Gaius replied.

"You even receive cloths," Haran stated with surprise.

"They are not for me," Gaius answered with a smile. "These are for you. I asked for them as soon as I learned our rooms had a bath." Gaius walked into the room pointing to a filled tub. "See, it's ready and they have provided salts with oils of lavender and even a scrubbing brush."

Haran looked perplexed and Gaius smiled, setting a gentle hand on the old man's shoulder saying, "How can I say this gently my friend? You smell bad, and coming from a man of the forest, that's really saying something."

Haran's mouth opened, but he was at a loss as to what to say. He looked at his tall friends for support. Argoes shrugged, "It is true Haran, a bath and change of clothes would do you good."

"Very well," Haran said defensively. He snatched the clothes and ushered them out. "I do bathe you know; I've just been busy!" he snapped and then abruptly shut the door.

Chapter 12
Hate

Roar had kept to himself after addressing his troops, contemplating the manner in which they should proceed, for this had indeed become a complicated game. Near sunrise he summoned his generals, for he was unwilling to wait any longer, knowing full well that his enemies were busy with their own schemes. The three of them found him on what had quickly become his favorite balcony where the blood of the slain witchers still stained the stones here and there. "So, my wise men of war," he said emphatically, "what are we to do?"

They all looked at each other, "You don't usually ask us what we think," Commander said a bit surprised. "At least not when we're all together."

No one seemed to want the floor so Achaia took this opportunity to say, "We have learned some things in these recent days."

"Do tell," Roar replied.

"The conquered all agree that the refugees departed with the old one upon the ships that you chased after. But we have also learned that the Nimerians did have dealings with the Port City."

"So you presume that this is to where they fled," Roar said, as if a great mystery had been solved. He remained silent a moment considering his words before continuing, "Believe it or not captain of war machines, this does influence my decisions. For as much as I would like to march upon Mizrahim now, perhaps it would be more prudent to hold this position until we can be sure that Gannim will not return to nip at our heels. We cannot have him building alliances with the inhabitants of the land ahead, nor with those who escaped."

"But does he foresee this?" Bashan asked. "Mizrahim is very crafty."

"With the witchers no longer with us, his insights will be limited," Achaia interjected.

"Then we will cut off the arm before we sever the head," Roar declared resolutely. "Agreed?" They all nodded their affirmation. "And I am not at all convinced it matters if he does know our comings and goings," Roar added with indifference.

"How many Flying Terrors do you command Bashan?"

"Nearly forty."

"You will lead the majority of them in search of Gannim, as well as gain insights into the geography of the Land Between the Seas. But several will remain here in case Achaia must reach us quickly. Meanwhile, Commander and I will march the majority of the Scourge along the coast to conquer this Port City."

Roar looked at Achaia, "You will hold the mountain, but be vigilant and do not think yourself safe here; we could be gone for weeks. You will turn the subjugated into our warriors and the men will behave as though I was here or else your body will be missing its head when I return."

"Understood," he said without hesitation.

He now looked at Commander, "Gather the bulk of the Scourge to the foot of the mountain. I want them ready to move on by midday. That is all," he finished with a wave of his hand. Bashan and Achaia hurried to the stairs however he noticed that Commander had not yet departed. "Something is on your mind... yes, Commander?"

His most trusted soldier seemed to weigh his words carefully before proceeding. "For the few years I have been under your command we have conquered many and yet never have I served under anyone who treats those conquered so... so... kindly."

"Oh," Roar seemed surprised and perhaps even insulted.

"Don't get me wrong," Commander continued, "you kill a lot of people and all, but the others I've fought under were more like Gannim. Not only did they permit the rape and the torture and pillaging, but more often than not they were leading the unrestrained brutality."

"Missing the old days are we?" Roar asked with sarcasm seasoned with contempt.

"No, well, that's not what I meant," his friend struggled frustratingly to find the right words.

"Oh, I see," Roar said. "This is another way of asking me why I hate men so, isn't it?" Commander remained quiet, but this was indeed what he wanted to know.

"Very well then, since you are dying to know, and obviously do not believe the rumors circulating among the men, that I crawled up from out of the burning depths of the earth." Roar had said this with a smile but it quickly faded as he began to recall events from his past.

He stared at the moon a moment before he began. "When I was a young man, I was not at all like I am today. In fact, I was better at swinging hoe than I was an axe. I knew nothing of the weapons of power, nor had I ever killed a man. I had..." he seemed to struggle to speak the words and he looked as though his mind was beginning to get lost in the world of thought.

"I had a family once," he admitted, "long ago. A precious young wife who became great with child. She was..." he swallowed hard, "perfect... but the violators of Gomorrah raided my ancestral home." Immediately a grim look of intense hatred crept across his brow, "They came swiftly upon horse and camel; the fight did not go well for us."

He gripped his axe tight which began to glow bright, but he quickly reigned in his emotion and it faded just as swiftly. "I was knocked senseless by a horse and hit my head upon a stone. They must have believed me dead already for when I awoke they had taken no prisoners."

Roar looked Commander in the eyes and ran his finger silently along his own throat, signaling that they had all been slain. "They had taken everything of value with them, save for human life. It was then, Commander that something changed within me. It was as if I buried my heart along with my dead. So I departed to live in the wild, and never again did I ever lose a battle with man or beast. Therefore my infamy grew with my victories, and in time the runaway, the outlaw, and the outcast sought me out. These became my army."

"Once my numbers grew strong we marched toward the city of the violators to put an end to them. But as we looked down upon the valley in which the city was known to lie, all we found was a smoldering wasteland of smoke and death. It was said that He who made us had purged them from the earth for all their evils. And though their end had come, it was not by my hand and neither could their death bring back those who were so dear to me. Now within me burns an unquenchable fire, and I will kill, and I will hack, and I will hate, for this is all that remains."

The two of them remained quiet a moment before Commander was willing to break the silence. "You may kill men such as them in war, but you are not the same as they. You are amongst the finest men I have ever known."

"Then this is indeed a lost and hopeless world," Roar mused more solemnly than angrily. "But all this talk reminds me of something I should add to my weapon."

Roar raised his axe and held it out before him firmly with both hands. As it began to glow bright he released the grip of his left hand and elongated the metal attached to the fingers of his glove into claws. He began to engrave symbols upon the shaft and once he had finished he said, "There, that's better."

"I do not understand those markings," Commander said. "What do they mean?"

Roar looked at him as if his heart were cold and answered, "Hate."

Haran arose just after sunrise to find that his friends had already left their rooms. He wandered about the enormous house of Baen until a servant showed him the way to their whereabouts. They all sat in the king's private dining hall which was very similar in size to the massive hall from the night before, though much more formal. Many were already seated and eating, but seeing him, his friends waved him over. As he came near they began to clap in recognition of how well he had cleaned up. "Oh, shut up," he muttered and laughter broke out.

As he took his seat next to Gaius the king said to him, "So, will you be soon departing? Your friends tell me you are the one who decides."

"Yes, well I'm sure my friends would like to get back to their people, but I may yet have others to warn."

"Well," Baen began, "the winter can be harsh here. We can send you some grain if we know how to find you."

The table grew quiet as Haran spoke briefly with his friends and then he looked to the king, "My friends say they appreciate your kindness, and will give Gaius permission to tell you, so long as you can be trusted not to share this with any other than the few trusted servants who will make the journey."

"But of course," Baen assured.

"And what of us?" Wolf the chief general of Arioch asked. "Will we also be able to come and bring you some supplies?"

Haran didn't hesitate in his answer or even bother to ask his friends, "No, you will not." He gave no explanation and though Wolf seemed a bit irritated by this blunt rejection, he did not ask why.

Feryn quickly sought to smooth over the awkward exchange saying, "We are truly thankful for your willingness to speak to me, and I have sent your words to my father, confident that he will heed your warning."

"I will pray the same," Haran answered.

As other conversations began again Feryn quietly stood from the table only to pass beside Gaius and whisper, "Walk with me." Without hesitation, he stood and followed her outside and though some took notice, none asked them where they were going, as if her guards had been forewarned not to interfere.

Once they had departed outside into the warm morning sun, Feryn leaned nearer to him saying as if for his hearing only, "My father is a difficult man, but I am not my father."

"I understand," Gaius assured her. "I am very different from my parents as well. But perhaps as a princess, in time, you will have the opportunity to do things differently."

"I don't think so," she lamented. The people of my homeland do not take kindly to the idea of lady heirs. But, the differences of which you speak are they the reasons why you live in the forest?"

"Yes," Gaius admitted. "I live alone, but there is some peace in that. And by residing near the house of Rhone I am not without friends or help if I should need it. But really, the unsavory kind tends to keep a good distance from his settlement; he is a good man but does not hesitate to drive away any he does not trust."

"Had you ever been to Arioch before coming with your friends?" she asked.

"No, I am not so bold as to venture there," he smiled as if jesting, but was actually being truthful.

She did not need to ask why, for she knew full well both the reputation of her father and the vile acts of his men when roaming the countryside. They continued to stroll among the busy people of Gull, talking about ordinary things. She seemed to ask many questions about he and his friends, but not to the extent that it was intrusive or awkward. Gaius found it odd that she would take the time to get to know him, for when does a man of the forest get to speak leisurely with a princess. He wondered if she was simply putting on a clever act in order to gain more insight into his friends, and yet she talked to him as though she did not see him beneath herself in the least, and this too surprised Gaius.

Eventually his giant comrades caught up with them, "Are you ready my friend or will you also be returning to Arioch?" Ryn teased. Gaius laughed and Feryn's eyes revealed her curiosity as to what they were saying, but he was thankful that she could not understand.

"I would like to speak with you more sometime Gaius. When shall I see you again?" she asked.

He could not hide his surprise. "I wish I knew, but perhaps the next time you travel here, you could ask the king to send word to their settlement. It is not far from here and I may yet be aiding them for a time."

It was then that Rhone approached to bid them farewell. He was accompanied by several of Baen's soldiers who were there to ensure his safe return. Rhone gave Gaius a pat on the shoulder saying, "I look forward to getting to know your friends better Gaius, and once it gets cold, you know you are welcome to warm yourself by my hearth."

"Thank you Rhone, you are a faithful friend," he replied with sincere thanks.

After taking time to privately explain to Baen how to reach their settlement, the four departed. For the journey home the king gave them two work horses that were nearly as large as Rhone's bulls, large enough to carry Argoes and Ryn. This burden they carried with ease in comparison to their normal daily workloads. One was male and the other female so that his new neighbors would have some breeding stock. Gaius and Haran didn't leave empty handed either, as they were gifted with smaller horses.

"Tell your big friends to be careful on the work horses," Baen warned, as they trotted off. "They are used to being steered more than they are ridden, but may they aid you in your quest to help others."

"These are truly better to ride than those horned monsters, "Ryn said to Argoes as they exited the city.

"Your home is not far from here," Gaius said to them, "especially on horseback. We should reach your settlement about the time the sun is at its highest."

"Excellent," Haran sounded optimistic. It felt good to be clean and well fed; to have friends and success in his endeavors. But alas such times do not last forever; they fade just as surely as the warmth of summer, when the cold moons arrive."

It was still morning when the Scourge of Roar had begun to move. He led the strong, seasoned force of more than a thousand by horseback. With all the siege weapons, the going was slow as scouts checked ahead for threats and clearer routes.

As the day dragged on Roar felt a growing sense of foreboding that seemed unreasonable, unnatural even. It was as if he could feel invisible enemies watching and plotting against him. "You look angry," Commander said to him at one point.

"I will feel better once my axe is buried within Gannim's skull."

"Hopefully Bashan will return with news and you will be able to return to your cheerful self," Commander joked.

But Roar grew quiet, withdrawing even more into himself as the day waned on. His friend knew that if his wrath was not soon poured out upon Gannim, then the Port City would receive the blows that were being stored up for another.

Gaius and the others rode out of the forests leading to the high, rocky encampment overlooking the wooded hills. Excitement quickly spread throughout the settlement as they entered through a newly built wooden gate. Haran dismounted as soon as he entered. "You have been busy!" he declared being amazed by their progress. The people gathered around them, examining the newly acquired animals with great interest and even a little fear; for they did not have horses in Nimeria, and even those who had seen horses had never witnessed the likes of the larger two.

Argoes found Honora and his children within the crowd and embraced them. "I was afraid for you," she said.

"There were a few times I was afraid for myself," he answered for all to hear. "We have some exciting tales to share with you to be sure."

Ocean came near to Haran, "Good to have you back."

"It's good to be back. Was all well in our absence?" Haran asked.

"There was peace among us. The people were anxious for you all to return, but we distracted ourselves with work."

"I can tell," Haran exclaimed, smiling broadly at the progress and their pride in their accomplishments. Then, seeing that Gaius was remaining to himself, Haran said to him. "Come Gaius. Let us find a place for these animals of ours. Since they were good enough to carry us all here, I would say we owe them a drink. What say you?" Gaius returned his smile and nodded. The two friends set about the task with a growing crowd of children following from a safe distance behind.

Chapter 13
Signs of Trouble

Day turned into night and everyone save the guards of the new settlement had gathered around Argoes to be entertained by the story of their journey, though Gaius seemed to watch things more than be a part of them. As the hour grew late and the tale had finished, people began to wander off to their various places of rest. Haran came near to Gaius and asked, "What's troubling you lad?"

He shook his head as if it were nothing, but offered a question of his own, "Will you be needing my help any longer?"

Haran was surprised that he asked this, but it also explained the distance he had kept since they'd arrived. "Well son, what is it you want? Do you wish to return to your life in the woods?" Gaius remained quiet so Haran continued, "You know, I'm sure there is a place for you here should you like one Gaius."

Gaius looked down as he replied, "I remember your words Haran, how you said when we first met that you did not think our meeting was by accident. I never travel this far away from the hills belonging to Rhone, and yet for some reason I had felt compelled to continue hiking for hours this way. I think you were right, but how could I belong here?"

"Think about it at least my young friend," Haran said, giving him a pat on the arm. "Can I find you a shelter for the evening?"

"No, I will sleep under the stars tonight," Gaius answered without hesitation. Haran nodded and then went his own way, leaving Gaius to his thoughts.

As he went his way the old man noticed Ryn standing upon an enormous rock overlooking the south. He climbed his way up beside him and then said, "I think our young friend does not want to leave, but is concerned as to whether or not he belongs."

"I find no fault in him," Ryn answered without breaking his gaze into the moon lit distance.

"Then perhaps you would involve him in whatever it is you're planning to do tomorrow," Haran suggested.

Ryn looked down at him with a stern, almost troubled gaze, "That would be good for I would like to travel south tomorrow." Haran's eyebrows rose, but he waited for him to continue. "You do not approve."

"If I were meant to search out the people south of here then when the fog had lifted we would have found ourselves somewhere else."

Ryn's expression let Haran know that he found the answer lacking of substance, yet he was not willing to say so. "Ocean says that they saw much smoke rising just south of here," Ryn explained. "He said it did not look as though it were a simple fire."

"And why should that concern you?" Haran asked as if challenging his faith in all that he had learned, but the seer could tell that he had not fully persuaded the young warrior. "Well, I will not disappear in the middle of the night so long as you don't," Haran added with a lighthearted smile.

Feryn and her guardians made haste for Arioch, reaching the city during the night. Upon entering the city she was immediately ushered directly to her father's chambers. There, in private, she shared all that she had seen and heard in Gull.

"So then, you do not believe them a threat?" the king asked her from across a sturdy wooden table.

"No father, you taught me long ago many ways in which to recognize deceivers and there were no lies in them."

There was a brief look of relief upon his brow which was quickly replaced with angry annoyance. "Long have we worshipped the celestial entities; am I now to just cast aside the gods of my fathers who secured my throne?" He smacked the table with his fist and stood.

"No, there must be another way, a way in which I can further expand my rule until this Land Between the Seas is fully within my grip."

"Be reasonable father!" Feryn countered. She knew her father to be a stubborn and unyielding man, but this was something she had not expected, an obstinacy that was maddening.

He seemed indifferent to her protest as he surmised, "There must be a way to ally ourselves with them, to learn their secrets, to gain their power. The young man of the forests you mentioned, he was reasonable you say." She nodded. "And quite taken with you to be sure," he grinned as if a brilliant idea had just been forged within his mind.

"It was not hard to get him to speak," Feryn affirmed. "He is eager to trust."

"Good, then you are to return to Gull at once."

"But I just arrived!" Feryn contested.

"Very well then, go to bed. But on the morrow you will return to Gull and you will send for your friend, and you will do all that I instruct you."

"But why do you not just heed their words?" she pleaded, but he turned away. With a silent wave of his hand she knew that he had brushed her aside. Quietly she took her leave. Though exhausted from the journey, Feryn could hardly sleep, distraught over whatever schemes her father intended to use her for next.

In the morning Haran arose to find many within the settlement already awake and about. As he entered the largest stretch of the open forum a woman said to him, "There is food prepared over there." pointing across the way to where several people seemed to be roasting grain.

"Thank you," he said, rewarding her with a smile. As he approached, he found his friends in a seemingly important discussion. He walked up just in time to hear someone asking Gaius, "And what provisions does the forest provide?"

"Mostly meat this time of year though there are many fruit bearing trees. It would be difficult to forage for this many people. You will have to plant and Baen will give you seed, but it will do you no good for now."

"When spring returns you can show us more of what grows in the wild here and where to forage" Argoes said to him.

"Of course, I would be happy to," Gaius answered without any hesitation.

Argoes looked at Ryn but said to all, "Some have gone foraging already without incident but I think it wise that any who go out should be accompanied by those armed," and all gave their approval.

Just then Argoes noticed Haran and said with a smile, "It's good to find that you were not called away during the night."

Haran just smiled and shook his head. He then took Ryn and Gaius aside asking quietly, "Are you still going to proceed with what we discussed last night?"

"Yes," Ryn confirmed. "Gaius said he would lead me to the place."

Haran looked mildly disappointed, "Well, be careful my friends."

"Don't worry we will move swiftly, especially since you will not be with us," Ryn said in an effort to lighten the moment and Haran gave a little laugh.

"Though I must admit you do not do so bad for a man so well advanced in years," Gaius added. Haran just shook his head.

Ryn turned to Gaius saying, "Come, my friend, I have something to show you. He led him over to a ship that the giants seemed to enter often. Once they crossed the ramp that took them onboard, Ryn led him into the hull.

There, Gaius found himself in a room full of armament; swords, bows, shields among other things, the likes he had never seen before. Ryn watched him to see where his eyes would go and noticed that he fixed them upon a bow. Ryn took hold of one near it, holding it out for him to see. You already have excellent aim but with this you can hardly miss. He held out the bow saying, "Go on; it's safe. The bow and the quiver of arrows to match have been polluted by other metals, so their power is such you will hardly notice, and even more importantly you'll not hurt yourself."

"Very funny," Gaius answered.

"You can use them for our journey today."

Gaius's eyes grew wide as he took hold of the weapon and Ryn added, "After all it is a child's bow."

Gaius shook his head, smiling, as if to say you got me, "I thought it looked a little small for you, but it's incredible none the less."

They began to exit and Gaius asked him, "Is everyone going to laugh at me, a grown man for wielding a child's bow?"

"Oh, to be sure," Ryn assured.

The two of them left alone traveling on foot and though many would have gladly gone with them, Ryn did not accept. Gaius estimated that it would only take a few hours for them to reach the location and as they got a good ways out they began to come across an increasingly amount of human tracks.

"An army perhaps," Ryn surmised.

"I have seen a few imprints from smaller feet, but still, you could be right," Gaius answered. A short while later they came across the kind of well-traveled trails that so commonly lead to and from villages.

They followed one of them quietly until it led them into the ruin of a village. Immediately they knew this had been the location of recent horrors for not only had the settlement been burned, but many of its people still dangled upside down from trees. By the looks of them, they had been used as targets. "Could this be the doing of those from whom you fled?" Gaius asked in horror.

"If it were, then surely my people would have seen the light of their victory."

"Their light?" Gaius had no idea what he was talking about.

"They announce their victories to the world by way of a ray of light that pierces the night sky."

Gaius looked down and then back at the devastation around him, "No, I don't suppose they could have missed that."

"He was right, of course," Ryn seemed disappointed.

"Who?" Gaius asked.

"Haran foretold as much." Ryn exhaled a heavy sigh, "But come, we will search quickly for survivors and then return with haste."

Alarmed voices caught the attention of Argoes as some sort of commotion had begun near the gate. As he hurried over, other warriors joined him and they quickly ascended the ramp and ladders leading to the top of the wall which faced the north. Just near the tree line stood a lanky white haired warrior with a piercing stare. It looked as though he was alone but Argoes did not like the looks of him at all. He spoke to them, but only some of the former slaves who had come from south of their former home could understand his words. "Call for Haran!" Argoes shouted, but the old man was already on his way. Without asking, large men took hold of him and hoisted him up to where he could stand upon the rampart and look over the defensive half wall.

"Is there none among you who hears my words," Gannim shouted coarsely.

"I understand you fine," Haran answered him flatly.

"Good," Gannim's demeanor lightened immediately. "My name is Gannim and I bring ill news of an approaching threat. Like so many others, I have been driven from my homelands by a ruthless enemy that sets its sight on the north. It is a mighty host who will do the same to you as well! So I implore you to join us who would stand against this evil and together we will secure our safety." He finished optimistically as if he expected the gate would be opened wide for him to be welcomed in.

But it was not to be. "Is that blood spattered across you boots and leggings or have you just come from a wine press?" Haran asked with harsh sarcasm.

Gannim smiled and began laughing darkly for it was indeed blood. "So does this mean you will not talk with me further concerning this grave danger?" his smile vanished as he tried to sound sincere.

"There is no threat to us here unless you have brought it with you." Haran said standing firm in his gaze. Gannim sort of shrugged with indifference before disappearing into the forest."

"What did he want?" Argoes asked him.

Haran answered them all, saying, "Remain vigilant, brave men from the mountain." And before he could say any more a loud tumult of men shouted from somewhere in the woods.

"Ready the artillery!" Argoes shouted for a few of the large orb bows from the ships had already been mounted to the wall. But as they waited with baited breath, the sounds faded and no attack came.

Inside the forest a puzzled Melek questioned Gannim, "Why do you not order the attack?"

Gannim sighed saying, "Because, by the look of them these are the people my wise men told me escaped the Scourge's grip. You could not see their might up close but I could. I'm not sure that we can take them yet, but so long as we don't attack them now, then we are not their enemies. Perhaps in time they will yet prove to become the enemy of our enemy."

Melek remained silent but was evidently satisfied with this explanation. "We will continue to search for more to rally to our cause," Gannim added. "And once fresh troops from my master arrive we will have all that we require to defeat our enemies and bring settlements such as this beneath our heel."

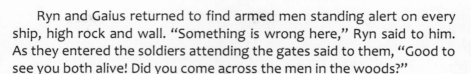

Ryn and Gaius returned to find armed men standing alert on every ship, high rock and wall. "Something is wrong here," Ryn said to him. As they entered the soldiers attending the gates said to them, "Good to see you both alive! Did you come across the men in the woods?"

"What men?" Ryn asked perplexed.

From the wall another said, "Argoes is waving for you to come to him." They looked up to see him in the distance standing with Haran.

They hurried over to them, with Ryn saying, as they came near, "What has happened?"

Haran spoke first, "An army of some kind has discovered us. The one who spoke for them offered to make an alliance."

"What did you find in the forest? "Argoes asked wandering whether or not there was a connection.

Ryn looked down at Haran and quietly admitted, "It was just as you foretold. We found a village of moderate size, burned; its people mutilated."

"Is this not one and the same as they who besieged the mountain?" Argoes asked Haran.

"We have not seen their light," Haran countered.

"Unless it is a scouting party," Gaius proposed.

"Yes," Argoes said as if realization had just flooded his mind. "Everyone knew of our mountain, but what if they are unfamiliar with this territory."

Haran breathed deeply, "Patience my friends. Remain vigilant today, but at dawn search out our surroundings to learn if they have truly moved on or not. But until then just have some faith."

"And we should send word of this to Rhone and the other kings," Gaius added and Argoes and Ryn nodded silent approval.

As the day lingered on, so also did the tension of the village, yet they saw no more of this man or those with him as they kept a quiet, vigilant watch.

Near sunset a guard came hurriedly to Baen as he was returning to his banquet hall for the evening meal, "Sir, Arioch's daughter has returned."

The king's jovial demeanor quickly changed to that of sudden anxiety, "Oh dear, what now?"

Chapter 14
The Port City

The Scourge had rested little as they marched along the coast towards the Port of Khasar. By midday a cry rang out, "In the air; it's Bashan!" Three riders soon came into full view gliding to a stop near the front of the troops just a short distance from Roar and Commander. Bashan's beast began to squeal, a bit irritated by how little it had been permitted to rest the past few days. Roar reached out his left hand and with a firm grip closed its mouth saying, "Shhhh." With the beast settled down he addressed Bashan with seething irritation, "I expected you sooner, Captain of the air. What is your report?"

"I had not come sooner, for I had nothing to report. We've searched far and wide, but so far, nothing."

A look of disgust that screamed that he thought him incompetent stretched across Roar's face, "Are hundreds of filthy, wretched swine really so hard to find?"

"I don't know," Bashan said, seeming a bit humiliated by his failure, "but perhaps some of the others will soon bring better news. They know that if they cannot find me that they are to search for you along the coast."

"Perhaps he is very careful so as to not be found just yet," Commander reflected. "That is, until he has more help or time to set another trap."

Roar clenched his teeth angrily and looked at Bashan, "And what of the mountain?"

"All is well there. Achaia seems to have a good handle on things."

"And what of the Port City, have you seen it," Roar asked?

"Seen it," Bashan laughed. "You're practically on top of it! Do you not see the ships?" He pointed past them to a few distant specks upon the water.

Roar glared at him in annoyance and snatched him by his breastplate pulling him close, "Rest your sickly animal for you will soon be expanding your search," he snarled. The beast took offence at the way its master was being treated but Bashan kept the terror calm, for he did not want it to be slain on the spot.

"But you should know sir that as we flew over the city yesterday, there was no sign of the Nimerian ships."

"What? Ugh," Roar growled before releasing him to contemplate this new development. Bashan respectfully bowed his head and moved his beast aside.

"It is curious, but perhaps they did not travel there after all." Commander suggested.

Disgusted Roar turned to face his men, "I'm sure this news has not escaped your hearing and is therefore spreading among you already. Prepare yourselves men of war, for we are near." And in his voice was the harshness that they had grown accustomed to when the time to kill had come. He looked at Commander, "Whether Nimerians are here or not, this city falls!"

Ryn had led one of several groups of men into the surrounding territory but found no one, only the traces of where the strangers and their various sub-packs had trekked on further north. Gaius, knowing the terrain better than any had led a group of men of his own, but during the heat of the day everyone had returned, satisfied that the threat had passed.

Once all were accounted for, a council was called together consisting of those who had led each tracking party, men like Gaius, Ryn, Colosso, as well as those who had been embraced as leaders such as Argoes, Ocean, and Haran. Gathering inside of one of the ships they seated themselves wherever they could find a place to sit. The right to speak was first given to Haran who took a moment to consider his words before he began, "My friends I know you have been through much, but my council to you is simple; have some faith."

"You are a new people, a changed people, and the One who delivered your mountain into the hands of assailants is also able to rescue you from their hand."

"Now the same holds true for all those you have warned as well. Is this not why we went to them? Our Creator does not tell me everything, even when I ask, so I cannot explain what all of this means. But if you want to go and warn those who have embraced our message about the dangers they may encounter within the forests, then I see no harm in that. But it is Gaius who knows the way."

There was a brief silence, but then Ryn spoke, "I know the Maker allows you to know the language of strangers, but does He also give you understanding of their writing?"

Haran considered this for a moment, "I would understand them already for their speech is akin to my own however the engravings might prove more difficult. I need something to write with... a knife, or some kind of tool." Argoes handed him a knife that by the look on Haran's face was larger than what he was hoping for, but he accepted it anyway.

He walked over to the ramp leading to the deck where the light was better and began to carve markings on one of the steps. He made three, all different from one another.

"The first one is of our nation," Colosso pointed out.

Haran nodded saying, "The next is of my own people and the last is of this land. It is not so different than that of the south, but the differences have been given to me. I have it up here," he pointed to his head. "I can feel it," he said confidently.

"Then you record the message and I will go to Baen," Ryn volunteered. The way is not hard. It is but a few hours travel through the woodland before you hit the well traveled path leading to his city."

"Then you will take one of the large horses and one of our well trained men will ride with you," Argoes said.

"And perhaps from there Baen can send word to Arioch," Gaius added and Haran rolled his eyes, but did not protest.

"Then it is for me to lead the way to Rhone," Gaius mused as a statement of fact.

"Is there no other way? Argoes asked, "I have reason for you to remain here with me."

Gaius looked surprised, but spoke the only other idea that came to mind, "Baen could also send word to Rhone without losing much time, so long as they are able to ride along the well traveled routes. But there is the matter of these marauders. They continued north and could block the way."

"I've said it before," Haran interjected, "Rhone is in no danger and I'm sure that the men of Gull can come up with their own clever route if they think it necessary."

After a quiet moment of contemplation it was clear that the matter was settled. "Then I will leave at once," Ryn declared.

The battle lines of the Scourge were drawn up along a large sandy expanse bordered by the East Sea on their right and the forest on their left. The city before them had a high, smooth, tan colored wall that stretched out into the sea with only one gate of moderate size facing them. Their main entrance by land was on the west, but by following the coast the Scourge had approached from the south.

A crowd was beginning to gather along the heights of the wall, watching carefully the mighty army before them. Roar, having already dismounted, as was his custom, walked out ahead of his men a ways. Once his armor crept over him he announced in his projected voice, "Hear me port of vermin. We are the Scourge and today your reign over the seas comes to a violent and bitter end!"

"Men," Commander called, "Siege formation!" but just as soon as the battle cries began they were silenced by the halt signaled by Roar's raised fist. He had noticed a man squeezing out the gate which had just barely been opened enough for him to do so. Nervously he scurried toward them. Commander came along side him saying, "You do know that since we are this far north, I don't even know if all the people will any longer even understand what you're saying. Only some among the slaves could understand us on the mountain."

Roar slowly turned toward him, his armored face resembling a large fanged beast. "It scares them anyway," he said flatly.

As the shaven, unarmed man attired in a fine robe, came near he said, "I bring word from our king who wishes to surrender peaceably."

"I stand corrected," Commander murmured.

The man stopped several paces away, unable to bring himself any closer to the fiercely armored foe staring him down. "Word of your long victorious marches has reached our ears. We were assured of your coming when we witnessed your light piercing the night sky. Our king wishes to open wide our gates to you as long as you will treat kindly with us. Otherwise, he says we will be forced to flee by way of the sea."

"Oh, like that's never happened before, "Commander mumbled.

Roar's face reemerged from behind the monstrous image, "You mean to say that your king will not fight to defend his people?"

"We have an army, but the king wishes only to surrender," the timid man assured.

A look of disbelief quickly turned into angry disdain, "Bah! Roar stepped forward with a swing of his axe that released a shockwave that forced the man to stumble back.

"His head!" Roar shouted. Go now! Announce to your people that if the head of this weak and pathetic king of straw is not immediately tossed over the wall, then we will unleash a hail of wrathful devastation upon your city!"

The man scurried off in a panic and soon disappeared inside. Roar looked at Commander and nodded. "Ready the onslaught!" Commander ordered the men who prepared to open fire, yet again Roar halted them. A growing sound of violent tumult could be heard from inside the city. The invaders watched and listened with great curiosity for a few minutes when suddenly a head missing its body was hurled over the wall.

Roar smiled at Commander and raised a victorious fist into the air declaring, "Justice!"

Colosso meant large in the Nimerian tongue. This was not the name given to the giant man at birth; it was given to him by the warriors of the mountain for he had grown in to a broad, strong man. Eager to see the city of their neighbors he volunteered to ride with Ryn. The two men departed just as soon as their craftsmen had done what they could to give the horses more protection, and to make them more comfortable to ride as well.

Though the men were much lighter than many of the animals' workloads, they still struggled to keep a fast pace, not having been bred for speed. Despite this fact, the men pressed them on, with a message in hand and watchful eyes.

Meanwhile, at the settlement Argoes led Gaius back to the armory where he had received his bow. "You are handy with an axe, skilled in throwing, and apparently capable with a bow, but how would you like to begin learning to fight like us?"

Gaius remained quiet a moment and looked down without answering a word. "You are welcome here Gaius..." Argoes assured, "should you choose to remain with us. And if you choose to return to your forests then you would be all the more capable of keeping yourself safe." Gaius nodded in agreement and Argoes smiled, giving him a firm pat to the arm. "Now then, go to the washing tent on the southwest corner. No one is there; I've made sure of it. Therein is a gift for you. Wash yourself, put it on and then I have something else for you to see." Gaius looked as though he wanted to say something, but departed instead with a look of contentment and curiosity. Argoes watched him go, happy for the opportunity to return his friend some kindness.

Once inside the tent, Gaius found a new set of clothes sitting on top of a wooden stool. They were similar in appearance to his own, but of a much finer quality. In front of the stool was a chest, he carefully opened it and inside there was a complete set of the Nimerian armor that was used to train boys while they were yet young and learning to control the legendary metal. He breathed deeply, a bit overwhelmed with Argoes' kindness, saying, "If only Feryn could see me in this."

He wasted no time cleaning up, as he was in such a rush to try on his new armor. He knew that not even the kings of the Land Between the Seas boasted its quality. He carefully put it on over his new clothes taking great care to be sure that every piece was secure. He saved the helmet for last; studying it carefully and noticing that engraved upon each side were what resembled the likeness of he and his new friends riding the horses they had received from Baen.

Gaius knew that this had been engraved especially for him and that there was not another helmet like this in all the world. He crouched down and touched the front of the helm to his brow. In awe he just held it there a moment, rocking slightly back and forth. After taking several deep breaths he arose, placing it carefully upon his head with both hands.

In this attire he felt different than he had ever felt before. After mustering up his courage, he let himself out of the tent, determined to go thank Argoes. A freed woman noticed him and stopped what she was doing, only to begin clapping. Soon many others joined in doing the same. Hearing this, Argoes came out of one of the ships and as he came near to Gaius he smiled with pride for his friend saying, "It suits you."

Gaius was at a loss for words, "I... I... don't know what to say."

"How about, thank you," Argoes answered.

"Thank you, thank you," Gaius declared to all who came near him knowing that this was their way of accepting him as one of their own.

Argoes gestured with an outstretched arm, "Now come with me."

Shortly after Ryn and Colosso had reached the main road, they encountered a host of ten riders headed toward them. "I recognize these as men of Gull," Ryn said to his companion. The riders stopped a respectful distance from the towering warriors, but said nothing at first, knowing they did not speak their language. Ryn wasted no time, holding out the rolled up parchment that Haran had written the message upon.

Ore, the leading man among them, pointed to himself to silently ask, "For me?"

Ryn nodded and led his enormous horse over. Towering over them he handed the message down saying about the only thing he could, "Baen, Baen."

Ore took hold of it and in return extended a message up to Ryn saying, "Gaius." Ryn nodded and then both sides turned around to head back from whence they came.

Carrying a sheathed sword by a belt, Argoes led Gaius just outside the main gate. They took no one with them and though some guards stood watch upon the various ledges and rocky lookout positions, it seemed as though they were making it a point not to pay much attention. Argoes unsheathed the magnificent weapon and raised it up, "This here is the real thing Gaius, unpolluted. You are able to focus well or else you would not be able to hit your targets so accurately. That is exactly what it takes to wield such a weapon, a strong, undistracted mind. "

"But just like in the game you played in Gull; fatigue will prevent you from using it to its full potential, as will a distracted mind. Just before we left the mountain we fought against those who would prevent our escape. Ryn had the chance to strike our strongest advisory with a killing blow but it failed to glow because he was tired and in fear of my plight. He did not discipline his mind before he made the attack. Though he did still managed to save my life," he added with a smile.

"But I've brought you out here so that no one would be accidently harmed if you should like to see if you are able handle such a weapon, for it is a very powerful sword."

"I am not afraid to try," Gaius answered confidently.

Argoes smiled and nodded, "Remove it slowly," he said, offering him the hilt.

Gaius took hold of it and began to draw it out. "Do not let it glow," Argoes warned. "It may feel as though it is alive, but it has no will of its own. What you feel will be somewhat of a reflection of yourself."

"I understand I think," Gaius said as he took his eyes off the weapon only long enough to glance up at him.

All was calm until the weapon was nearly half removed and then Gaius felt a surge run from his hand to his head. Gripping the sword tight he took a step back, turned to face the forest, and hurled the weapon with gnashed teeth. It soared fast and bright imbedding into a tree up to the hilt with a pop that nearly split the trunk from the branches to roots. The guards could not help but stare now as even some of the people inside the walls were a bit alarmed by the sound it made.

Breathing hard he looked up at Argoes who's expression seemed almost perplexed, saying "If you were afraid you could have just let go and left it inside the sheath."

"I wasn't afraid," Gaius shook his head. "I was exhilarated!"

Argoes paused a moment before saying, "Well then, let's try once more. Only this time remain calm. When you feel the surge just let go if you don't think you can control it." Gaius nodded and walked to the tree while Argoes waited where he stood.

Gaius looked back at him once he reached the sword, but Argoes only nodded. He took hold of the hilt and, staying calm, wrenched it free. Gaius looked down at the weapon. He could feel it vibrating within his hand, though now it did not glow. Slowly he allowed the power to emanate and then subside.

"Good," Argoes commended him, "now keep going." So again and again he repeated this exercise and confident that he had some basic control, Argoes picked up some stones saying, "Now prepare to defend against this barrage."Gaius faced his friend in a wide ready stance, with the sword held out before him. It was only a one handed weapon for the men of great size, but there was plenty of room for both of Gaius's hands, so he used both his hands to grip it tight.

"Ready?" Argoes asked.

"I am ready," Gaius confirmed and so Argoes pitched the first stone underhanded. As it came near Gaius took one step forward and with a sudden surge smacked it with the flat of the blade. The stone immediately shattered almost to dust.

"Impressive," Argoes exclaimed with a nod of his head. They practiced the same move a few more times successfully and then Argoes said, "Now, when I cast these all at once, point the blade up. As they descend toward you try to keep them from falling. Just have the conviction of what you are seeking to accomplish; the sword will do the rest." Argoes pitched four stones at once and as they came down at an angle Gaius extended the blade toward them.

Just beyond the reach of the blade the stones came to a halt as if sitting upon invisible ground. Gaius smiled wide as he held them there, "I did it!"

"Now toss them aside from where they are," Argoes ordered.

Gaius's smile disappeared as he focused. With a side-step and a sweep of the blade he sent the stones hurling a good distance toward the hillside leading to the valley east of their settlement. "Remember the way it felt to suspend the stones Gaius, for this is how you can defend yourself against a variety of attacks." Argoes approached him extending the sheath, "That's good for now." Gaius carefully inserted the blade and Argoes said, "This too is now yours, only for now you may not wield it or even take it out of its sheath unless you do so with me in training."

"I understand," Gaius answered as he wrapped the belted sword around his waist.

"I think in time you will be able to handle the full power of a pure armored set," Argoes commended him optimistically.

Gaius laughed, "I'm in no hurry. In fact I am a bit overwhelmed as it is now."

"Let's at least find you a shield," Argoes said and with a hand on his smaller friend's shoulder the two returned to the confines of the settlement.

"We've rounded up all who will be condemned and await your command," Commander said to Roar after finding him alone within the dead king's lounging room which overlooked the midst of the city.

He sat alongside a window ledge as if relaxing in deep thought, but did not hesitate to answer, "Good. I do not like this... this taking a city without a fight, but we can at least make a lasting impression upon those who live. I will meet you down below."

As soon as he finished, Roar rolled out of the window making himself light enough to land safely. It was a distance that would have killed anyone not able to repel that which pulled them to the earth. Soldiers and the conquered moved out of his way as he crossed over to the ramp that would take him atop the rampart of the outer wall. There, waiting, were many men bound with a rope around their neck which was tied to any stone or wooden beam capable of holding them. Roar looked down at more than a thousand people who his soldiers had rounded up to be forced to watch the end of those he would not accept.

He came to the first, and kicked the frightened man off the outside city wall where he would die with a snap of his neck if his head was not ripped off altogether once the line jolted stiff. Roar did not bother to look and see the outcome; for he knew the result; he would be dead either way. Instead he addressed the crowd declaring, "Here are those who lived among you as mediums and diviners and the like." The people gasped as another yelped as he was kicked off the rampart to his death.

"Understand that none such as these will be permitted to live. For the spirits are deceivers and even if He who made us bothers to look down upon us at all, then He has surely given you into my grip." Roar motioned for soldiers to carry out the rest of the executions and then he leaped to the ground below, again making himself light enough to land with little effort. As he landed he noticed a young boy, not quite a man, who was looking down. Roar came along side him and grabbed hold the back of his neck, forcing him to watch the executions.

Pointing to the wall with the free hand he said to the boy loud enough for others to hear, "Look upon the cruelty of men and the end of those who trust in sorcery as a means to manipulate their own kind. There are two kinds of men in this world boy, the conquerors, and those who are conquered." Releasing him he turned to address the crowd saying, "Remember what you've witnessed today and listen to my men who will carefully explain to you how to live under my rule or else you will join them."

As he stomped away Bashan leaned over to Commander and whispered, "He's really in a mood today, eh?"

"Aye," Commander answered, "And it's liable to last a while, so I'd better go prepare the signal, and you my friend had better get back on your winged beasty and go find the whereabouts of the cause of his ire."

Chapter 15
The council of the wise

To the surprise of those guarding the wall, Ryn and Colosso came riding out of the forest at sunset. Arnost was on watch and gave the order, "Open the gate!"

They rode in single file, ducking with just enough overhead room to let them pass while mounted. A crowd quickly began to gather, so Ryn announced, "Worry not, we simply came across some soldiers of Gull who were on their way here. So it seemed expedient to just exchange messages." He scanned the crowd, "Where is Gaius?"

"Right here," the voice came from almost beside him. Ryn looked down to find his friend in his new attire.

"Ha! I thought you were one of the lads, but it suits you." The crowd giggled at this for they agreed that he could pass for one of the boys in training.

Ryn handed the message down to him and as Gaius took it he admitted, "I will need to have Haran read it to me."

Hearing this, the crowd immediately began to look around for him. "He comes this way even now," a woman said. As he and Argoes approached together Gaius met them in eagerness to find out if it was from whom he hoped. "I have received a note from the king, I didn't bother to open it for I cannot read it," he admitted.

Haran took it from his hand, humbly admitting, "Nor could I if not granted help from above. Breaking the wax seal he began to examine the contents. "Oh well this is recorded in both the local dialect as well as that of the south, which I knew already. Wise man, really thinks ahead," Haran observed as he studied its contents.

As he read further he shot Gaius a peculiar look, "Come with me, we have some things to discuss." The two of them, along with Argoes, moved away from the crowd to the rocky outlook where Haran had visited with Ryn some nights before. Upon the rock he announced, "This, my friend is a message from Feryn. She has returned to Gull and requests that you again visit the city."

"Really?!" he could not hide his excitement.

Haran sighed, "Listen my boy, she is beautiful, charming, but has been so groomed by her father for the purpose of coercion. Do you not understand this?"

Gaius's smile immediately melted away, "So you believe she calls for me only to do the bidding of her father."

Haran placed a hand on his shoulder, "I am saying be careful. Maybe she is not like her father, but it doesn't altogether matter, for if she remains in his service then her fate may very well be bound to his."

"Do you not want me to go to her?" Gaius said with obvious disappointment, as if Haran had suddenly just trampled all of his hopes to dust.

"I do not presume to order you at all, but if you are determined to know what this is about, then I would urge you not to go alone. You may need some wise council, yes?"

Gaius nodded with a smile admitting, "Yes."

"It is a trait of greatness to listen to the council of the wise Gaius," Argoes said to him. "If only I had acted upon what I knew to be true at your age, perhaps the mountain would still be our home."

Just then they heard the growing sound of a fretful commotion near the gate of the city as people began to crowd to the heights for a better view of the eastern sky. "Now what?" Argoes blurted coarsely with thoughts that invaders might have returned, but as they looked to the east and saw a familiar distant light soaring into the heights he could not help but feel that this was much worse. This familiar sight caused some of his anger to be replaced with alarm.

"How far?" He said to Gaius, but he did not know that Argoes was speaking to him.

"Is that the sign that Ryn described to me?" Gaius asked.

Argoes placed a firm hand on his shoulder to get his attention and turned Gaius to face him, "How far is that light from here?"

Seeing the concern in his expression, Gaius quickly answered him, "Not far enough. Several days march perhaps, though it is difficult to know for sure."

"Are there any large settlements to the east?" Haran asked.

"There is the port of the East Sea. Yes, I am sure that this must be from where it comes."

Argoes looked down at Haran with a troubled brow observing, "Then we are not so far from home after all."

"I do not share your alarm." Haran countered. "For what reason would we have for concern? No, this trouble is meant for others not us," he spoke his words with unwavering confidence, and it was evident in Argoes' face that these words were of comfort to him.

"Will you tell the people?" Argoes asked. "It will mean a great deal more if comes from you."

"You underestimate your influence but very well," Haran answered. "However once I've finished reassuring them, you should lead your people in entreating He who saved you. For whether I am slain by the sword, or my body just turns to dust, I'll not always be here."

Argoes seized this as an opportunity to lighten the moment, "Yes, you are very old and I'm sure you could die at any moment. Would you need me to carry you back down?"

Haran began to laugh so hard a tear came to his eye but Gaius remained stoic and with his gaze fixed to the east said, "It is to purge this land of Idolatrous, murderous, oppressors, this is why they come."

Haran thought this was a curious thing to say but answered, "They will execute justice upon those who are evil, but I don't think that means they are necessarily good themselves. Given they attacked us when we fled the mountain. I doubt that they even know they are executing the Living One's justice."

Gaius looked at them with eyes ready to burst with tears, "It is good that they come. Is this not why I live in the woods? Is it not because the men of my youth were weak, allowing the ways of the exiled wanderers to defile them?"

His tone quickly turned from grief to anger as his friends listened quietly, "Oh how my people were quick to make friends with these numerous strangers from the south and adopt their ways to maintain peace. In time it was my own young brother and sister who were bound to their cursed engravings and burnt alive!" His friends waited patiently for him to continue as he gathered his calm, "When I learned it would be them that were dear to me... I fled. I was not yet a man but still I fled."

He looked at Argoes and motioned to his new armament, "I am not worthy of such things. It would have been better that I had been killed trying to save them than for me to flee into the wilderness and abandon them to die alone."

"You were just a boy," Argoes countered, "and even Ryn and I abandoned our people to their fate."

"As did I when the voice of the Spirit first came to me," Haran added.

Gaius just shook his head, "It is good that they come, these men of violence. It is good that they purge the world of these evils."

Knowing sometimes that there are no words that can comfort, Haran placed a gentle hand upon his shoulder, "Yes, but it would be even better if all who are evil were to change."

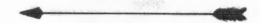

The king's riders approached Gull in a gallop encountering the curious site of the outer wall lined with people looking toward the east. As they rode through the gate, Ore said to Armen who was again in charge of the watch, "I have a message for the King."

"He watches the skies from the height of the common hall." He pointed to the balcony where Baen was easily recognizable standing alongside Feryn and Talon, all focused on the skies.

"What is everyone looking at?" Ore asked him.

"Once you reach their vantage you will see," Armen's expression betrayed his concern as Ore continued on his way. After tying down his horse he entered in, finding the king and his companions as still as statues looking into the distant skies. It was then that he too saw the bluish green pillar of light.

Ore gathered his thoughts and stepped to just behind the king saying, "I have received a message for you sire."

"A message you say?" the king replied, not really seeming to be paying attention. "Good."

"It is from the hand of the giant Ryn," Ore added, hoping this would get his attention.

"Ryn," Baen mumbled beneath his breath and then recognition captured his thoughts, "Oh yes, Ryn! I must read it at once!" He quickly took the letter and untied the thread binding it. Talon and Feryn watched him as he read silently in order to determine from his expression if it were good news or bad.

"They say that many invaders trek north and they believe this may be the first sign of the approaching doom. They advise that we should remember to heed their warning and also to be careful about traveling abroad."

Feryn's eyes lit up with a thought, "Then perhaps this light is also a sign."

"We encountered no outsiders along the road save the ones who gave us this letter and they in turn received ours," Ore said.

"When the young man Gaius answers my summons surely he will know more," Feryn said, seeming certain he would come.

"I hope you're right my dear," the king answered her. "And if he does not come to us within a day I will send Ore to them again. They have entrusted us to warn others as well, therefore I will pass their message along to Rhone, and you can send some of your guards to tell your father."

"But of course," she answered him. "I will send them at once." With a bow she immediately departed.

The king looked at Ore and Talon saying, "Double the guard and tell the people to rest easy for we have received word from our powerful friends. It is well but they should only travel toward the West Sea to do business until the dangers have passed." With a bow the two men made haste to fulfill their duties, leaving king Baen to wrestle with his thoughts.

Gannim removed himself from the crowd to the outskirts of the encampment, summoning the remaining witchers to him saying, "I wish to speak with lord Mizrahim."

One of the hooded sorcerer nodded his head answering, "He has been awaiting you." The medium began to stiffen as if in contorted paralysis as his master took control of his body. Moments later Mizrahim began to speak through his puppet saying, "So, you have seen the sign of the Scourge's triumph again."

"I have gained a sizeable army through an alliance, but these warriors will be swept away in a real fight," Gannim reported. He did not grin at the thought of this and how it would affect his goal of defeating Roar. "I need real troops, skilled warriors, and soon."

The puppet medium moaned as if the experience was excruciating before answering, "My spies within the walls of Elon tell me that they are gathering their strength now that the sign of the Scourge's coming has reached their view. If they only knew that my most seasoned and powerful army had turned against then they might try their might against the Great City."

A look of disbelief came over Gannim's face, "Are you saying I will not receive aid?"

"Kedar will bring strength from the north but it will take time. You are not to wait for him. The spirits that guide me say the king of Arioch is ripe for an alliance. See to it and await my command. Fan out and you will find his city in a day as you march westward toward the setting sun."

Chapter 16
Deceivers

"Ryn!" A quiet voice called from nearby. The large warrior was resting atop a ship deck shared with many other sleeping men. "Ryn! I will be leaving soon with or without you."

The sleeping giant opened his eyes to find Gaius looking down at him impatiently, "Can you not wait for the rising sun?" He asked, trying to rouse himself as he sat up and yawned. "My friend, to rush after her on a whim will not make you appear strong." Gaius just looked at him impatiently and Ryn shook his head in resignation, "Fine." He leaned over and shook the man lying next to him saying, "Colosso, we are leaving, do you still wish to come with us and visit the city of Gull?"

"Follow the rabbits into the bushes," he mumbled.

Both men chuckled at this, "He's dreaming," Ryn said with a smile. He shook him again repeating the same words but this time consciousness found his friend. "Yes, I'm coming. But why are we leaving so early?"

At first light Roar summoned Commander to the room where he had exited from the window. As he entered in, Commander was surprised to find a table laden ready with food. "Eat," Roar said to him as he looked out the window.

"You know I don't remember ever seeing you eat; is this just for me?" Commander asked jokingly.

Ignoring the question as he continued his gaze, Roar asked one himself, "What do you report?"

Commander fumbled through the food answering, "Well, we now have another thousand soldiers happy to fight for us... and live that is. They are trained soldiers which means we'll just have to retrain them of course."

"Of course," Roar murmured.

Commander continued, "The uh spokesman, Un, has been most helpful. He has been trained in several dialects so as to better serve the king whom he had served, for this is a port often visited by strangers. Interestingly, among those with which they have had many dealings in the past, is a wise man who became great, one Mizrahim of the north."

Commander was watching for Roar's reaction to this news and it was apparent without even seeing his face that this had caught his attention. Roar turned to face him, "Indeed this was the name by which he was known before he gave himself the title Lord Mizrahim."

Roar walked towards the table saying, "More and more I feel that we have been playing an elaborate game, that my own ambitions have blinded me from seeing what was coming sooner. Don't you see Commander?"

"See what?" He looked confused while Roar looked as though he had just solved a great mystery.

"He is connecting the north and the south. When he came to the south years ago, he was not so much a ruler as he was one who gave council. Apparently he never lost sight of his homeland and now he prepares to take it back. He will control the north, south, and all in between. We hold the mountain," Roar mused, "and now this strategic port. If we take but one more important city to the west then we sever whatever hope he has of connecting north and south between the seas. Thus we shall thwart him until we can finish him."

Commander raised his brow as something came to mind, "Un tells me that there are two kingdoms not far to the west of here, before you reach the west coasts: an agreeable man and just north of him a tyrant."

"Good, learn the way and we will march upon this tyrant first and then the other. And within the web of these positions we will no doubt find the fiend Gannim."

Commander had a sudden look of optimism, "This empire building is going to take some figuring out, we're so used to others handling it for us."

"If by figuring out," Roar began, "you mean we kill those who dissent, then no, it will not take long. I would rather destroy than build, but we must do what we must to win." Roar said, seeming to lament his predicament.

Commander took a bite of an apple and smiled, saying, "Well I kind of like it. It's much more comfortable than sleeping in the rain." Upon hearing this Roar gave him a contemptuous glare.

Far to the north, Kedar and his witchers had finally reached the lands of Iomar. Here the cold had already begun to take its toll on the leaves of plants and trees. The sky was dark and grey and the clouds blotted out the sun. It appeared as though a cold rain could pour down at any moment as they approached the Tower of the Iron Gate which was the main entrance into the capital city.

Looking down upon them from a guard post was the commanding sentry. He was known as Horn, so called because the dark helmet he wore boasted only one, while the other horn was broken in half. This had occurred in a great battle long ago but he kept it the way it was as an emblem of honor.

"State your business outlanders," he demanded harshly. Long had he been the master of the gate, honing his talent for recognizing strangers over the years. Besides, there was something about these hooded men that the guards found unnerving. It seemed that every time he blinked, more of them appeared until there were twelve of them standing below.

Kedar came forth and removed his hood, "We have come from afar bearing gifts of renown for your lords."

Gaius and his friends reached the city of Gull by midday. The gate was closed due to the news they had received from Haran but opened immediately upon the sight of them. Word reached the king fast as he walked with Feryn along one of his exquisite garden passes.

"Gaius and his friends have come my king," the messenger sent to find him declared. Feryn looked at him and grinned as if to say I told you so. "Well let's not keep them waiting," Baen said to her.

As they came to greet them, Baen and Feryn found them handing their horses over to attendants. Happy to see that his horses he had given them were being useful the king said, "I trust the animals are serving your needs."

"Yes, to be sure. We are most thankful for your kindness," Gaius answered. "We would have been hiking well into the night without them!"

"Good, good," Baen answered. "Would your friends like something to eat? He recognized Ryn, but looked warily at Colosso.

Gaius smiled wide, "Would they ever? You needn't even ask."

"I would as well," the king said gesturing for them to follow. "Come, we will dine in my home. I will call for my sons. They have just returned from the West Sea and are eager to meet you."

Feryn placed a gentle hand on Gaius's arm, "We will be there shortly. I wish to speak with Gaius a moment."

"Very well," the king said, looking surprised, but carried on.

Ryn looked at Gaius before following and said to him, "Whatever it is she wants, don't be hasty."

Gaius smiled and gave a nod. Feryn waited for the meal procession to move away just out of ear shot before declaring, "I hardly recognized you in this new attire. It suits you."

She looked sincerely impressed and Gaius laughed, saying, "That's what I keep hearing. My friends are very kind to me."

"Thank you for coming so quickly Gaius," she said warmly.

"It is good to see you again," he replied, "but I am anxious to know why you have returned so soon to send for me."

"My father requests an audience with you."

"With me?" Gaius could not hide his surprise.

"Yes, he has heard all concerning my time here with you and your companions and he wishes to speak with you in particular. If you accept this invitation, we will ride out together as soon as you're ready." Her words seemed generous with time, but behind her poise there seemed to be a desire for an immediate answer.

Gaius looked down, clearly uncomfortable at the thought of again traveling to Arioch. He shook his head looking as though he were about to answer, but fearing it would be no, Feryn quickly raised a hand as if to stop him with a gesture, "You needn't rush, only think about it for a time."

She smiled and held out her arm. He smiled and nodded as he took her arm in his. Together they strolled towards the king's home and Gaius felt both as anxious and happy as one could imagine.

Even after they had eaten their fill, Baen and his guests continued talking late into the afternoon. Much of the discussion stemmed from the king's sons, who were nearly grown, but not quite fully recognized as men in their tradition. This was done at twenty, and the eldest of the two by a few years was yet a year from this. The eldest was named Hagen and the younger by a year was named Lyon. Although they were in a hurry to receive full recognition as men, today they seemed more like boys as they asked a great deal of questions through Gaius, concerning his friends.

They seemed friendly enough, but had been indulged their whole lives. Few believed they would walk in the humble steps of their father. Hagen who had been keeping an annoying eye on Feryn almost the entire meal finally spoke his mind in front of everyone. "You are very beautiful," he said to her from across the table, but Feryn did not in any way acknowledge his compliment and being embarrassed by his son's bold and untimely remark the king gave him a mild rebuke, "No need to state the obvious boy."

A sudden awkward silence came over the table as Hagen turned red, but Ryn seized this opportunity, saying, "Gaius, Argoes asked me to train you some more if we had an opportunity. This way it is Gull and not our city that is destroyed." Colosso tilted his head down just in time to spit his wine out on the floor rather than the table. He had been so tickled by the comment which Ryn had given with a straight face.

Gaius laughed as well and, as all the eyes turned toward him he explained, "My friends are making fun of me for I am learning their ways in combat. So if you'll excuse us, we would like to step outside the city for just a bit where we can practice safely."

"Would it be all right if we watched from the wall?" Baen asked as interested as a child.

"A better question would be is it safe to watch from the wall, for I am very new to such weapons," Gaius answered.

"We'll keep a good distance," the king insisted. "You will find some open spaces on the south side of the city.

"Then it is to the south side we will go," Gaius replied. Everyone arose with them, but departed to follow the king to where he would choose to watch while they themselves veered away to exit the main gates.

Gaius took this opportunity to ask Ryn, "Are you not curious as to what the princess had to say in private?"

"You can tell me about it after you have focused on something else for a while." He looked at Colosso changing the subject, "So what do you think he should learn next?"

Without hesitation Colosso answered, "The wind."

Ryn nodded his approval, "The wind it is."

Soon after turning the corner that brought them south of the city they found an open field that had already been harvested. "This will do nicely," Ryn announced. "Watch me carefully Gaius." Ryn raised his spear and down slashed like a sword toward the forest across the way. What looked like turquoise windy haze emerged with enough force to carry dust and debris in its wake, only to fade by the time it reached the trees, pushing the leaves like a gentle breeze.

"You're weapon is perfect for this," Colosso said to him. "But you'll have to see it in your mind." He pulled out his shield and stood several strides away from Gaius. "Take a step and slash towards me, don't worry I'll not be harmed."

Gaius drew out his sword and focused. Once his sword began to glow bright, even in the light of the afternoon sun, he stepped forward and slashed the blade downward. The blast was much greater than the one Ryn had demonstrated and Colosso raised his shield, effectively bracing himself as it passed his way. He peaked over the top admonishing, "Well done Gaius. You're a natural. Now again!"

Gaius didn't hesitate and this time it was just a little stronger, but instead of bracing Colosso countered with the same attack, only with a more narrow blast range. His counter move cut through Gaius's wind attack with enough force left for Gaius to be pushed back a step.

"Do you understand what he did," Ryn asked?

"I think so."

Ryn nodded at Colosso and stepped into a full turn before slamming his spear down. With two hands Gaius counter swung, severing a space through which he could safely remain as the gust passed by. A crowd had begun to grow upon the wall but Ryn was right, this was a good distraction for the exercises were requiring Gaius's complete attention and he had yet to notice them.

"All right then, it's time for a little game," Ryn said to them and Colosso nodded. "We'll fan out a bit and blast one another relentlessly, seeing who can remain standing." After giving each other plenty of space Ryn shouted, "The last man standing wins. Ready?" Gaius looked nervous as he took his shield from his back and tossed it to the ground. He again gripped his sword tightly with both hands, giving an affirmative nod.

Ryn glanced at them both, "Begin!"

The giants attacked each other first, one blast neutralizing the other as the debris swirled around about half way between them. Having prepared himself to defend, Gaius had lost the opportunity to attack and take advantage of them focusing on each other. He soon found himself on the defense as his friends would look at each other only to deceptively send a blast surging his way. During the course of several minutes he managed to be offensive a few times, but was soon overwhelmed when attacks from each of them whooshed at him, one after the other.

He barely stayed on his feet against the first while the other knocked him into a spin that sent him to the ground.

"It's just you and I now skinny," Colosso teased, but Ryn wasted no time and with both hands now on his spear he sent wave after wave with short rapid swings.

With the constant pressure Colosso was not finding any opportunity to counter. He powered through the onslaught with the blunt of his shield and heaved forward making enough space to slam his spear down. Ryn was ready for this and sliced up with a strong leap that carried him through the wave and then he down slammed with his fall. Colosso braced for the first but was blasted off his feet by the second landing upon his back.

He lay there for a moment in disappointed disbelief and then sat up tossing some dirt at Ryn, "You set me up with those pestering little attacks, didn't you?" Ryn just smiled in a way that acknowledged that this was the truth. They trained a while longer, working hard on Gaius's ability to summon defense. For a reason Ryn could not ascertain, he had a feeling that such training was important to impart to Gaius. These lessons he reinforced with the words, "Attack may win a fight, but good defense allows you to remain in the battle long enough to find your attack."

Chapter 17
The influential hands of Mizrahim

The witchers had waited patiently for an answer to their request for an audience with the rulers of Iomar, and by nightfall the massive Iron Gate was raised. Horn approached them with dozens of armed soldiers. The soldier's clothing was dark and grey, and the look in their eyes, as warm as the weather. "You have been granted an audience with the sons of Iomar, but you will give up your arms," Horn demanded.

"Very well," Kedar seemed indifferent. "A few of my companions will await our return here and so they will be left with them." Horn did not protest so they began to disarm. They left a sizable pile of various weapons at the feet of the two who would wait behind, but purposefully kept their gauntlets, arm bands, and the like on. Horn did not protest for they were defensive items but then again he did not know with whom he was dealing.

The witchers raised their cloaks, allowing the guards to search them, and satisfied with the results, Horn ordered them to follow him. After they passed through the enormous gate they found themselves entering into a large wooden side door. It soon became apparent that Horn was deliberately leading them through a series of dark pathways and doors that would make it difficult for them to keep their bearings.

Eventually they entered a large wood and stone room with a vaulted ceiling. There they found themselves before the steely glare of the sons of Iomar. The young rulers sat upon twin thrones and three times as many guards as there were witchers stood on either side of the room, not threateningly, but at the ready.

The eldest son, Sihon, who was a strong and formidable man addressed them first saying, "A curious sight this is; strangers from afar bearing gifts. My men tell me you have come by order of one Lord Mizrahim, ruler of a vast and growing empire in the south."

"Yes, this is correct." Kedar replied respectfully.

The younger son, Drakon, glared at them suspiciously, then said, "Is this Mizrahim not one and the same as he who left our father's court so long only never to return?"

"Indeed he is," Kedar answered them calmly. "And now that he has forged the most powerful empire of all, he desires to make inroads to the north. In fact, he has already begun to do so. A war amongst the kingdoms between the seas has begun and Nimeria has fallen."

As he spoke a growing look of surprise, anger, and even alarm was taking hold of the princes. Sihon stood and looked down at them coldly, "Did you really think that in hearing such bold words our hearts would simply melt in fear? Mizrahim was nothing, a mere advisor when he was here, nothing more, nor shall he ever be more than this. And as it is now, only your heads will return to him."

Kedar raised his hands as if to signal calm and stated as a matter of fact, "Dear princes, we only gave up our arms knowing full well that we did not need them if we wanted you all dead, but it needn't be this way."

"We've heard enough from the likes of you," Sihon shouted. "Cut them down!" he ordered his men. The guards immediately drew their swords as did the princes themselves, but as the soldiers stepped toward the strangers with the intention of killing them where they stood, the witchers raised glowing gauntlets which blasted the encroaching soldiers back a few steps.

The guards paused a moment, trying to come to grips with what had just happened to them as almost inhuman groans began to echo from the dark clad sorcerers. Abruptly the torches illuminating the room blew out with sudden violent gusts.

"I cannot see them," one guard called with alarm.

"Where did they go?" another shouted.

"Calm yourselves!" Sihon ordered, but no sooner had the words left his mouth than a body of a dead soldier dropped from above, collapsing on the steps before them. They all looked up and the windows provided just enough light for them to discover that these hooded men were silently crawling along the walls and ceilings as if they were insects.

"We've got to get out of here!" Drakon said to his brother as fear gripped him. They turned toward the door only to find two of the hooded figures blocking the way.

Sihon's anger burned brighter than his fear at the reality of being accosted within his own thrown room. He leaped at them with a shout swinging boldly. This was far from what the witchers were expecting him to do. However, they simply dashed just out of reach of his attack in the same manner in which Kedar had done on the mountain.

As Sihon continued to swing wildly, Drakon flung the door open wide and they defensively backed their way out into a long indoor walkway that overlooked a large room beneath. The brothers could see little going on through the doorway but they could hear a soldier cry out, "They're on the walls!"

Inside the throne room the men grew quiet as they watched for haunting shapes moving about here and there.

They could see a man just coming into view of the door to escape when an arrow suddenly burst from out of his neck. He stumbled out and collapsed at the feet of the princes. The witchers were now using the weapons of the slain against them.

"Come on," Drakon pleaded with his brother.

"I'll not flee from the likes of them. You call for aid!"

Drakon looked at his brother with frustrated disbelief but knew he was a stubborn man and that there would be no changing his mind. "Stay alive," he called as he darted off.

Inside the throne room the soldiers had crowded together in a circle with everyone facing out. "Where is everyone?" a soldier whispered, noticing that most of their comrades were nowhere to be found. There was a long moment of tense quiet when the clank and thud of impact sounded just behind them within their circle.

They jumped and turned as one discovering that the sound was made by the collapse of the dead having been dropped from above. "Make for the door!" a man shouted, but as they began to flee the witchers seemed to emerge from behind every pillar to run them through and cut them down with the swords taken from their fallen comrades.

The piercing death cries of the soldiers echoed throughout the chamber and then there was silence. Sihon stood his ground outside the chamber, afraid but unwilling to flee. The voice of Kedar echoed from out of the darkness, "Are you ready to be reasonable son of Iomar, or do we have nothing left to discuss?"

Sihon could hear the growing sound of his brother returning with troops as he stared intently into the darkness. He paused a moment weighing his options. In truth he was intrigued by these men of mystery and the power they possessed.

As soon as his brother came bursting into the room below followed by dozens of soldiers, Sihon glanced down at them. "Hold your position!" He ordered before peering back into the darkness of the throne room. "You who speak for the others, what is your name?"

"Kedar." Somehow his voice, which seemed little more than a whisper, was heard even by many of those in the room below Sihon.

"You and I Kedar," the prince said with his sword still high, "we alone will talk."

Gannim and his growing hoard reached Arioch not long after dark. He did not attempt to hide their numbers as he had with the settlement of the Nimerians, but instead approached the outer walls boldly. The slow, deliberate pounding of the exiles deep sounding war drums could be heard even before any of them could be seen.

Arioch rushed to the exterior wall to join his men, and many others followed to strengthen the outer walls. Soon the masses of approaching foreign warriors began to emerge from the forests. The moon provided just enough light to reveal their fierce appearance. Many of Melek's men wore wooden helms of sorts covered with the pelt heads of wolves, bears, and large cats. This adornment along with their numbers, and silence aside from the beating drums was intimidating indeed, though Arioch could not fathom a way this vagrant tribe could pose a real threat.

"The exiles" he muttered with disdain. "They are bold to believe they can threaten us."

"But still, this is bad timing considering the message from your daughter," Maris counseled.

"Look there," Wolf pointed toward a cluster of men gathering together near the center. "It is hard to say from this distance in the dark, but they do not look like the wanderers. Is that not the gleam of metal about them?"

After more than a thousand warriors had emerged from the forest the drumming abruptly stopped. Gannim and Melek walked boldly to the front in full range of Arioch's archers.

"And you're sure they will know the words of the south?" Gannim asked Melek.

"Yes. Their ancestors are also from the south and we have been sojourning these forests every warm season for nearly a generation. Most of those residing here have found it prudent to know many of the subtle differences between our cultures words."

Gannim did not answer him, but considered the strength of the warriors upon the wall before calling out loud enough to be heard clearly on top of the walls, "I will have words with the king of Arioch. He should come forth unless he wants me to come find him."

Arioch growled with contempt at being addressed so by this stranger, but answered none the less, "And who is it that presumes to summon me? Are you not the herald of the south scouting ahead for the coming threat? Is that the meaning of the light we've witnessed in the skies?"

"My name is Gannim and I am the herald of Lord Mizrahim, the only power that will ultimately matter. But the light you saw is the sign of our enemy. I come forging alliances, in order that those of us who bind together will put an end to the infamous Roar of the Scourge.

"See, here with me stands Melek, lord of a vast and brave army. Will you not discuss the matter with us and see why he has seen the wisdom of an alliance? Believe me when I tell you that I am your only hope of survival, for without our aid the army that follows, led by the merciless Roar, will crush you!"

"Then perhaps it is he that I should be building an alliance with," Arioch replied, his tone smug.

Gannim's voice grew cold, "Be certain king of Arioch that this uncompromising murderer will seek your death above all others."

"Ask him why we should believe he can succeed when the power of the Nimerians failed them my king," Maris advised. Arioch looked at Wolf who nodded his agreement.

"And what do you possess that the Nimerian's did not that could possibly be of help to me?" Arioch asked in the pompous and condescending manner that was his nature.

No sooner had the words left his mouth then one of Gannim's tri blades was already in the air arcing along a course that would take it right over the heads of many of those standing along the walls. Panic escalated as this glowing weapon spiraled by them, severing the tops off of spears that fearful soldiers clung to while ducking for cover.

The blade returned to Gannim's hand and he said, "Should I remove some heads with my next display of power?

Arioch smiled shrewdly, "Let us discuss what manner of alliance will prove useful for us all."

Gaius and Feryn spent much of evening walking about the cities quiet places talking about things that seemed common and little in significance. He knew that she had come by order of her father, yet he could not help but believe that she sincerely enjoyed her time spent with him.

As the hour grew late they returned to the king's house to part ways for the night. "I will have an answer for you in the morning," he assured her as he began to ascend the stairs that would lead him towards his room. She responded quietly with a smile and a nod.

He found his door open with his friends sitting comfortably inside drinking a little wine. Though tired, upon seeing them Gaius said, "I'm glad you are here."

"You've seemed happy, but troubled today Gaius," Ryn mused. "Tell us the whole matter."

Gaius sighed as he sat down, almost collapsing into the chair until he slouched before admitting, "I have been asked to return with the princess to meet with her father."

Ryn clenched his fists and squinted as if he were about to attack a foe who was not there, "And what did you answer her?"

"I said I would tell her in the morning, though I already know I will not refuse her."

"Gaius…" Ryn said his name as he leaned back with both disbelief and resignation, "be reasonable. This man cannot be trusted. At best he will only seek to use you just as he uses his own daughter."

"I know, I know, but I don't know at the same time," Gaius replied, looking down into the palms of his hands, resting his elbows on his knees. "Maybe with the warning and the distant light this man grows fearful and will now himself listen to reason."

Colosso looked down at him saying, "But isn't it strange he would ask for you and not Haran?" Gaius remained quiet so Colosso continued. "If it's a woman you want, then are the daughters of my people not beautiful enough? Are they not without equal?"

Ryn watched him closely for a response, but he was to be disappointed. "You and the others have already given me more than I could ever ask. And besides I don't know if my pride could handle me being weaker than the woman I would take for a wife," Gaius grinned and though he was trying to lighten the moment, there was some conviction to his words.

Colosso could not resist the opportunity to add a jab of his own. "Oh it'd be great she could carry you around whenever you were tired."

Ryn cracked a half smile before dragging them back to the matter at hand. "If you have determined this in your heart and there is nothing we can say or do short of binding you, then we will be at your side. Haran has said it himself that our home is not in danger and they can go a few more days without hearing from us."

Gaius looked comforted upon hearing this, "I would not have asked this of you, but neither will I refuse your company. Arioch will no doubt be encouraged to behave himself with you there."

It took some convincing, but eventually Sihon was able to get his brother Drakon to relent and to allow him to escort Kedar and his men to the front of the city where he and Kedar stood before one another. Upon the wall Drakon, Horn, and many guards watched with bows at the ready. All of the witchers save Kedar retrieved their weapons and disappeared into the darkness of night.

On the ground, covered in fine dark cloth, were several objects of various shapes. "Are these the gifts of which my gatekeeper spoke?" Sihon asked with great curiosity.

"Some of these will be yours should we come to an agreement," Kedar affirmed while reaching down and picking up the longest of them. He removed its cloth to reveal a large, magnificent sword. A vile skull connected the blade to the hilt with metal horns protruding to form the hand guard. The hilt had more than enough room for two hands yet Kedar held it with one as if it were light.

"How is it that you can hold such a large weapon with one hand?" Sihon asked in awe.

"It has been forged from the rocks which fell from the skies and thus is capable of many... unusual things, depending upon he who wields it." Kedar thrust the blade into the ground causing the onlookers upon the wall to grow a bit agitated. "Restrain yourselves!" Sihon shouted with a glance.

The sorcerer next laid hold of a good sized circular object and unveiled a shield which also boasted a vile skull protruding from the front. "The sword is called Wrath and the shield is Chaos and with them you can be more than just a man."

"With these I will share in your power," Sihon stated with some hesitancy in his voice.

"In time," Kedar answered, "but you must be a willing student." Kedar offered him the shield, "Try it on."

Sihon slowly slid his arm through its straps until he laid hold of its grip. As soon as he had done so the bindings closed fast on their own. He looked up at Kedar with alarm, "Don't be afraid. It has accepted you," Kedar said with calm.

"You say it as though it were alive," Sihon watched him with suspicion.

"Did I?" Kedar made it sound as if it were nothing and then took a few steps back. "Now, how does it feel?"

Sihon began to move it around, "It feels... it feels, incredible!" But then he stopped and looked at Kedar with a renewed seriousness. "And what is it you want in return?"

"The lands of the north were my father's home and his heart has remained though he has moved on. Soon our kingdoms will meet. He does not wish for devastation to fall upon you, but neither can you be our enemy. Yet if you are to hold your borders and be our ally; you must also be strong for we will not allow any border connected to us to be weak." A look of concern was etched upon Sihon's face so Kedar continued, "Do you think we are the only ones with such weapons? Even now, a ruthless warlord tramples the Land Between the Seas and it is only a matter of time before he sets his sights further north."

"My father though, sick as he is, will never agree to this." Sihon admitted with some dejection.

"And will you, who sit upon the thrown, allow your rule to end with him?" Kedar stated this as a challenge and the eyes of the shield began to glow faintly red, though only he could discern that. A sudden surge of aggression came over Sihon that could immediately be seen in his eyes.

"No, I will not," he snarled resolutely.

"Then you are wise," Kedar smiled with approval. "With our help you will also be strong, strong enough to expand your own empire beyond the borders of your father."

"I will need some time to seize full control before you can return again to enter the city."

Kedar nodded as if this was expected, saying, "And we will await word of your success in the forests. Your envoys need only look for us and we will find them." Sihon looked down at the shield, hoping Kedar would not ask for it back.

"Keep it," Kedar said. "I can see that we have an understanding, and take the sword as well. But use it sparingly until you are properly trained in its use."

Sihon pulled the sword from the ground and Kedar handed him the cloths that covered the weapons. "Be strong young prince. Do what must be done to preserve your future and do it quickly." Sihon nodded in agreement and the two men parted their separate ways.

Gannim and Melek agreed to enter the city alone though not unarmed. They followed King Arioch to his large war chamber and, after a servant set out some strong wine, those permitted to remain were left to themselves.

Arioch began to pour drinks into metal goblets saying, "This is Maris and Wolf, my most trusted advisors. They will also hear your words firsthand. So then, tell me what I can gain through an alliance with you."

"You mean along with your life?" Gannim was quick to remind the king of the reality of his situation, but Arioch only smiled with feigned amusement. "The land between the seas will be conquered. It is only a question of by whom. Roar will not seek an alliance. It is he who overthrew the mountain of legend and if an alliance were an option then the survivors would not have fled."

"You know of the survivors?" Arioch asked, raising his brow in surprise as he offered them their drinks.

"Yes," Gannim answered, "but they do not wish to join us. It is a decision they will regret."

The king sighed, "They have not allied themselves to me either, but I have not given up. In fact, even now I am working to secure their aid. It sounds though, that an alliance with you will mean an end to my reign."

Gannim smiled, saying, "Not at all, but you will rule under the banner of an even greater empire. Our enemies will be your enemies and you would provide some level of aid be it food or soldiers when necessary..."

"And in return?" Arioch interrupted bluntly.

"And in return you not only be allowed to retain your reign, but will be given authority over more than this little piece of dirt now belonging to you. If worthy you may even be learned in the ways of real power."

"The lands of Baen, the king south of me... I want them, I always have."

Gannim laughed almost mockingly, "If that is what you require then so be it."

"How long until you require my answer?" Arioch asked.

"I require your answer now king," Gannim snapped. "For the days of doom are at hand and if you are not ready to fight alongside us then we will search for those who are. And you will meet your end when the Scourge arrives to raze your city to the ground." Having said this Gannim smiled.

Maris stepped forward, "If I may my..."

"No you may not!" Arioch cut him off sharply. "I desire land and I desire the power they possess. If his master will give me what I want then I will gladly rule under his banner!"

Gannim smiled, "Then it's settled. But we haven't much time, for if they are not already on their way, then they soon will be. We must bait them into our trap. What my personal army lacks in size it boasts in skill and power. And Melek commands more than two thousand warriors. What strength have you?"

"I have more than two thousand soldiers at hand as well. More than three thousand if you count the common man that can be armed. And hundreds of which can be mounted on horseback and of course there is the protection of the city in which you stand."

"And a resourceful knowledge of the terrain," Wolf added.

"Do you have any allies who would also join us?" Melek asked.

Arioch stroked his beard, "If the east is indeed overrun then we must look to the west. Nearby there are the islanders and their kin along the east coastlands of the West Sea. They are resourceful and have even tamed a breed of flying draak on which they ride. These men will not join any alliance, but they will fight for wealth."

"Good, then waste no time. Send for them tonight," Gannim admonished, "for the Scourge also boasts a band of fighters who scour the air. We will plot against them a plan of surprise." Gannim slapped his hands together and smiled with glee, declaring, "The Scourge will think they are going to lay siege to yet another helpless city only to find themselves assaulted by many unexpected adversaries.

"But in the meantime," he motioned to Melek, "our armies must await in the forest in hiding, for the Scourge mustn't know we are here. I trust you can conjure a way to summon us should there be any sign of their approach."

"We will blow horns," Arioch answered.

"Good. Then we will come again to you tomorrow. But be vigilant King Arioch, for though the Scourge may yet be days away, your men must be ready at all times ever alert for their flying scouts."

Hagen and Lyon lay awake within the eldest's room which was illuminated by the moonlight shining through the large open windows. "If I were but a bit older it would be me catching the eye of beautiful Feryn, not this forest dweller," Hagen muttered to his brother with resentful pride.

"Why torture yourself with such thoughts brother? If she is not already spoken for then surely she will soon be."

Hagen scowled at this, "Arioch has no sons and if I were to have her then I would be the heir of two kingdoms." Realizing how greedy he sounded he looked at his brother and said, "Or I would be able to give one to you."

Lyon laughed saying, "I know you brother and you spoke your heart when you claimed the two for yourself." Lyon laid his head back on his pillow, relaxing and enjoying the cool breeze. "Things are changing in these lands, but I have a good feeling about it. This man who speaks for the Highest Spirit, his words ring true, and I like our new neighbors as well."

With this the conversation grew still for though Lyon was cheerful and at peace, his brother did not share his optimism. Hagen had a mind for more and his ambition dictated that he would acquire a way to achieve it, by whatever means necessary.

Chapter 18
Waning Moments of Peace

By morning the Port City was engulfed in a whirl of movement as the Scourge began to mobilize for their westward march. Commander found Roar observing some of his soldiers training the new men who were to become a part of their army. Coming up beside him, Commander observed, "Un has proven helpful, but are you sure you want to leave him in charge of so many things while we're away?"

Without looking at him Roar answered, "We will leave three hundred of our number here to continue training new soldiers. That allows us to still march out more than a thousand strong.

"The city is subjugated. There is no hope of casting off our yoke, and even if they could, deep down they know we would only return to take it back again... with a vengeance."

Commander shrugged, "Just thought I would ask."

"So Commander, with Achaia holding the mountain shall I entrust the future of this city to you or Bashan?"

"Hmm," Commander considered the possibility then said, "how about I decide after seeing what's left of the other cities once we've taken them?"

"Whatever," Roar said indifferently. "Now then, enough of this talk and daydream nonsense. Get them outside the city's walls and ready, for it is time to move!"

Not finding Feryn within the king's dining hall, Gaius discovered her taking a walk outside in the king's gardens. She smiled when she saw him approaching, but waited for him to speak first. "I, that is, uh... we... my friends and I will return with you to meet with your father."

Her smile grew wide, "Thank you Gaius, my father will be most pleased. He is no doubt anxiously waiting. How soon can we depart?"

"As soon as we can all be ready," Gaius answered. "I will gather my friends and meet you and your guardians at the front of the city." Feryn nodded and squeezed his hand before she departed, and yet Gaius's joy in making her happy was tainted by the equally strong anxiety he felt at the thought of returning to Arioch.

In the north the sun was beginning to peak out from behind the gloom that was moving south. Kedar was leaning over to drink from the frigid waters of a stream when he noticed the reflection of one of his companions. He turned to find the man all tensed up with his eyes rolled back. As Kedar stood the man began to speak, "It goes well my son," the witcher whispered slowly the words of Mizrahim. "Even now they say the eldest son of Iomar erodes the confidence the younger has in his father."

Kedar stood, "This Sihon is a bold one. I think he would have stood his ground and died last night rather than flee to preserve his life! He may prove difficult to control."

"He has made his choice by accepting the weapons," his father replied. "For their spirits favor us. The bond of father and son is weak. You will see. Their father was foolish indeed in the way he dealt with me long ago; now he will reap bitter fruit. But I must go now, this vessel grows weak," and with the last being said, the witcher nearly fell as he suddenly regained control of his own body, and without a word Kedar returned his attention again to the stream.

Gannim and Melek came to Arioch while it was yet early. They plotted and planned late into the day while Gannim helped the king with the revision of his own map, so that he would know more concerning the places south of the Land Between the Seas. When their talks finally began to come to a close Gannim said, "My men have disguised themselves with the furs and such of Melek's people, and even then we are all trying to remain hidden in the forests just north of your city. However, as I said before, you must alert us concerning even the slightest inclination of anything large in the skies, for it could be the scouts of our enemies."

Arioch looked at Gannim and nodded in agreement, "My guards have been vigilant with horns at the ready, and will remain so day and night."

"The Scourge cannot know we are here; everything depends on this," Gannim emphasized, "for in there bold over confidence will lay our advantage. Our great number will mean nothing without surprise. They will attack you, and then Melek's men will attack from one position, and my skilled fighters will attack from yet another."

"They will not be able to ignore the threat of my men in particular and it is when they turn their attention to us that you, Arioch, must find your opportunity to strike."

"With or without the draak riders of the west, surely our victory is assured," Arioch declared triumphantly.

"We must finish them with relentless ferocity," Gannim's voice was emphatic, "or their leader will snatch victory from the jaws of defeat! The Scourge has never lost a battle, ever. They are not to be underestimated," Gannim's look changed from being grave to one of optimism, "but yes, with power, greater numbers, and a clever scheme, I resolve to be the first to defeat them in battle."

Shortly after the sun had set Gaius and his friends, along with Feryn and her guards, arrived at Arioch. Gaius glanced up at Ryn who seemed to grow tense as the gate opened for them. Gaius could not help but feel the same. Feryn took notice, "Worry not Gaius, I am certain that this time as an invited guest your time here will be much more pleasant than before. As soon as we enter, servants will be ready to take care of your horses."

The soldiers along the walls and just inside watched them quietly as they entered, being careful to give them space. "Do you feel it?" Colosso said to Ryn. "This place has a presence of evil about it." Ryn remained quiet, so Colosso added, "I can feel it."

He was right of course, though no one could see the truth. For many evil and deceiving spirits had come to Arioch for the purpose of manipulating and ruining men. One such spirit had already attached itself to the king in anticipation of his meeting with Gaius. It would secretly give him words to speak. A clever silver tongue meant to ensnare the young man for their kind had been prevented from harming him outright.

As they dismounted Maris approached them, saying, "Welcome home princess. Your father eagerly awaits a meeting with the man Gaius."

Gaius stepped forward, "Then let's not keep the king waiting." He then looked at his friends, "The king summons me now, but worry not my friends," he touched the hilt of his sword, "your strength is with me."

Ryn clenched his teeth, "Tell the king that if you do not return to us soon we will come find you," Gaius smiled in a vain attempt to lighten the moment and then turned to follow Maris.

Feryn looked at the giants and gestured for them to follow her. As they walked along, Colosso noticed a cloaked man passing nearby on his way to the gate.

Even with his hood up a few of his white locks could be seen in the flickering torchlight. For just a moment the man took notice of them as well and briefly locked eyes with him. The cloaked man gave a sinister grin as they passed one another. Colosso turned his head to continue watching him, but he could no longer see his face. There was something familiar about this hooded stranger and Colosso continued to contemplate this as they entered a wing of the king's palace where they would be able eat and relax while waiting for Gaius to return. However, it soon became apparent to those who were ready to wait on them that they were not in the least interested in food or drink.

An awkward silence followed as Feryn and the servants waited equally as quiet. "I know you can't understand me," she said to them. "But I am anxious to learn what my father wants as well."

Ryn looked at his friend and said, "This woman probably says we are great fools to have traveled here and will walk into a hail of arrows as soon as we leave the building."

Colosso began to laugh but stopped abruptly as his eyes grew wide. He had suddenly realized who the man was that they had passed along their way. "The hooded fellow who passed us as we walked along, he was the one who stood before our people only days ago, wishing to speak of an alliance!"

Ryn turned red faced with rage, "Are you certain of this?"

"Yes," Colosso did not hesitate.

Ryn quickly reigned in his emotions, "Let's calm ourselves and wait a bit longer for Gaius to return. I do not know the meaning of this man's presence, but if we make a disturbance now, any hope of leaving peacefully may be gone." The servants looked frozen with fright at this sudden display of raised voices and high emotion. Feryn looked at ease enough though she had managed to quietly remove herself to the far side of the room.

After traveling down a series of open halls and up a winding set of dimly lit stairs, Gaius was shown a large wooden door that was half opened. Inside Arioch stood within a well lit room looking up at them from over his newly revised map which was spread across a table.

"Ah, Gaius is it?" Arioch said, looking him over and struggling to recognize him in his new attire. "It would seem that having such friends as yours is rewarding."

Gaius glanced back as he heard Maris shut the door behind him. Now it was just the two of them and a look of amusement crossed the king's face. "I have not called for my daughter yet, but I trust the trip went well and that there were no signs of the enemies that are sure to come."

"We experienced no trouble at all," Gaius answered flatly.

Arioch strolled over to the stone window ledge and gazed out into the night, it seemed that there was much on this man's mind. He began with, "So you like my daughter don't you Gaius?"

Gaius did not expect this question and stammered a bit, "I, uh... I..." but no words seemed to come to him. The king turned and looked straight into his eyes, "Is she not lovely? Is she not fair? Is she not sweet, with a sharp mind to match her beauty?"

Suddenly words came to Gaius, "Yes, she is all these things and more. You have much to be thankful for."

"Ha! What I wanted was a son."

Gaius was quickly growing tired of this strange conversation, "Why have you called me here?" he nearly snapped.

"All right then boy, I'll get to it. I have seen this sign to the east. The enemy comes and yet your friends will not fight alongside us, but there are those who will."

"The exiled king of the south and the one called Gannim, who is the enemy of this Roar who leads the invasion; they have allied with me. But still, I would have more at my side, but you and your friends have seen to it that neither Baen nor Rhone will join us!"

"King Arioch," Gaius reasoned, "if you would only heed the words of the wise man Haran, then you will have no need to fight. This was the point of our coming!"

Their voices had grown loud, but Arioch now toned it down a bit, "The gods of my fathers have given me all that you see here. Am I now to just cast them aside on the word of strangers, strangers who will not so much as extend a hand in defense of my people? But my new allies promise me far more than I have even now." They stared at one another a long moment before the king broke the silence. "You know what I really want?" He asked, but Gaius waited for him to answer his own question.

"I want an heir. I don't know what I did to offend the gods that they would give me every trait I could want in a man, only to place them in, in, her... my daughter." His frustration seemed incomprehensible, unreasonable, and ungrateful to Gaius, yet he held his peace as Arioch continued. "My soldiers have brought to me more than a hundred girls of age and not one of them has been able to give me a second child!" Arioch smacked a metal goblet from a table that splattered wine against the wall.

"Perhaps it is not the maidens who have the problem, oh king," Gaius said, having heard enough and though he knew this was not a wise response, still he did not regret saying it.

Instantly Arioch had the look of a madman in his eyes, for never had he been so insulted; not even by an enemy, and for a moment Gaius thought the king might even attack him, but instead Arioch took a deep breath and composed himself.

"The king of the exiles assures me that his gods can give me a son, though it will require a sacrifice." Arioch offered a sinister grin as he continued. "And sacrifice I will, the flesh of my people's children if I must. I will even offer up my own daughter in exchange for a son." Having said this, the king smiled as though he were playing a game he had sabotaged to win.

Now Gaius was the one with a look of disbelief, "But why not just make Feryn your successor?" he pleaded. "You are king after all!"

"Because it's not what I want! And a king should have what he wants!" Arioch banged his fist upon the table with a shout.

"I can't help you," Gaius lamented, "even if I wanted too. My friends will not come to your aid."

Arioch grew quiet again before saying, "But you have power now, don't you boy? Come Gaius, show me your power. Give me just a little demonstration of what they've given you."

Without hesitation Gaius drew his sword and raised it high. It emanated a fantastic glow that made the king wince before he immediately returned it to its sheath, lest he lose control in his emotional state.

Arioch smiled being pleased with what he had just witnessed. "Remain here Gaius. Fight by my side! Do this and Feryn is yours," but Gaius looked away. He did not know how to answer him nor did he want to. "Fight not for me boy, do so for her. Or is she of so little value to you that you would just abandon her to her fate?"

Gaius raised his gaze to meet the king's, "I will do this so long as you allow my friends to escort her away from here. And once the fighting is over I will return to her."

"Very well, I care not," the king answered convincingly. He picked up a piece of leather parchment from the table and began to make an inscription. He rolled it up and after applying wax to bind it, he sealed it with his ring.

"Here," he tossed it at Gaius, "she's yours. Do with her what you will."

Gaius held it tight and turned to leave as the king added, "Fight for her Gaius. Fight for the life you will have together should you survive." Gaius did not reply as he exited the room and the king again strolled over to the window saying quietly to himself, "Your friends will not fight for me, but they may yet fight for you."

Maris had been waiting near the stairs to lead Gaius to where his friends were. Upon seeing him enter the room Ryn said, "We were nearly ready to rip this place apart to find you."

"No need, I'm safe," Gaius said dejectedly.

"Something is wrong," Ryn mused for it was plain for all to see.

"We have some things to discuss, but first I must speak with Feryn alone."

Ryn looked displeased with having to wait, but before he could protest Feryn spoke, "Can I show you to your rooms?" Having not yet seen her standing near the wall, Gaius was surprised to hear her voice. He nodded, thinking the walk would give him further time to consider his words, and they followed her out.

The walk was quiet and no one spoke to them as they passed. "I feel as though we have wandered into a funeral procession," Colosso murmured. Eventually they entered a large hallway that boasted rooms for them as large as those of Gull, but with not nearly as cheerful décor.

Ryn noticed Feryn waiting patiently out in the hall and said, "We will step away and keep to ourselves a moment while the two of you talk."

"Thank you my friends, I will try not to be long," Gaius answered and once they had exited Feryn peaked in. "You are expecting me to speak to you alone... in your room?" she said with amused suspicion.

Gaius was solemn as he held out the parchment, "Don't worry, your father will not mind." A look of curiosity filled her eyes as she took hold of the rolled message and broke the seal.

She began to read its brief content, but Gaius could tell by the way one of her hands reached up to cover her mouth that the message was clear. "I'm sorry if it's not what you wanted," he began. "It was your father's idea… he said that if I agreed, you could leave with my friends where you would be kept safe from the battle to come."

"Gaius, have you read the message yourself?"

"No." He answered her but as she began to hand it back to him he admitted, "I cannot read your words. I have never been taught."

"It simply says, in the hand of writing of my father that Feryn, daughter of Arioch is now the property of our ally Gaius."

Gaius turned away and kneeled down being overwhelmed by the confusion of emotions running through his mind. "I only meant to keep you safe, and once you are, I will not hold you to it. You may discard the agreement and live as you please."

Seeing that he could not bring himself to look at her, Feryn approached him and gently removed his helmet. With one hand she softly ran her fingers through his messy hair.

"Gaius, you have freed me from this kingdom of despair, and I will gladly leave with you… never to return to this place again. The meaning of father's inscription will matter not, for as I am yours, you are mine, and your God is now my God."

Hearing this Gaius was now willing to look up at her. He took her hands and stood tall. "Let us leave this very night!" She said, excited to be free from her father's whims and schemes.

But Gaius shook his head, saying, "You don't understand."

Her smile quickly faded as she said, "But of course he expects something in return. After all, he would not simply give me to you only for the sake of my safety."

"In exchange for you and the freedom to escort you from here with my friends," Gaius swallowed nervously, "I have agreed to remain here to fight alongside him when the invasion comes."

Feryn shook her head, seething with anger, saying, "Oh that man! And you Gaius, how could you agree to this? According to your own prophet this is a fight my people are destined to lose. What were you thinking?"

"I was thinking," he said, pausing a moment so as to contain his emotion. "I was thinking that you would be saved."

Immediately her anger melted as she stroked his face with a soft hand, saying, "In a world of dark, cold hearts, you are something altogether different."

Gaius looked sad as he began to lead her towards the door, saying, "There is little time to waste, for we know not when the invaders will come. Let me discuss the matter with my friends. They will not be altogether pleased, but neither will they refuse me."

"I will gather my things at once," she answered and headed for the door. Gaius watched her as she went. She looked back and gave him a little smile before disappearing down the hall.

Moments later his companions entered the room and Ryn wasted no time, "Why are we here Gaius? What does Arioch want?"

Gaius cleared his throat nervously, "I have a favor to ask of you, my friends, and you must not refuse me." They did not respond, but only waited for him to continue, "Arioch will not heed the words of Haran, but has instead secured alliances in preparation for the invaders. I have secured the safety of his daughter..."

"And in exchange," Ryn interrupted.

Gaius' tone grew quiet, "I will not be going with you."

"That's why the man Gannim is here!" Colosso nearly shouted.

"I'll crush this schemer," Ryn stated through clenched teeth.

"No you mustn't!" Gaius pleaded. "You must leave tonight and take Feryn with you. She has been given to me and should I survive the battle then she and I will be together. I do not fight for Arioch. I fight for her and what may be."

Ryn just shook his head, quietly saying, "Gaius," with quiet disappointment. He took a deep breath then continued, "We will be waiting for her near the gates, for I will remain no longer within this tomb."

"I will have the king's stewards prepare the horses for you immediately," Gaius replied with thankfulness in his eyes.

As they began to leave the room Colosso waited just long enough to look at his smaller friend with a chuckle saying, "You are a bold one Gaius," and then he too departed.

Feryn tracked her father down, finding him in the same room where Gaius had met him. He met her angry stare with the amused look of a boy who had been caught in mischief, "I see that you have learned about our arrangement."

"Father would you have me become a widow just as soon as you make me a bride?!"

"You're displeased," he said, pretending to be surprised.

"I beg you to allow him to escort me himself, if only to Gull."

Her father laughed mockingly, "You think me a fool girl? From whom did you gain your wiles, eh? If he goes with you now, then he will never return to me."

"He is a man of honor!" she protested.

"And this he will prove to me," he answered coldly. "Now be gone. I have important matters to tend to." As she turned to leave he added, "When the fighting has ceased I will send for you."

"When the fighting has ceased, "she began, "you will be dead." Having said this she rushed out lest he reply. Yet even as she hurried down the corridor she could hear him mock, "Ha!"

Within the hour Gaius waited near the front of the city along with his friends who were already mounted. Colosso was the first to see Feryn's approach, saying, "Here she comes."

Her horse was laden with some of her finer belongings with a second pony following behind, carrying even more. As she came near Feryn noticed them staring at all the stuff she was bringing. She looked at Gaius and shrugged, "I am a princess after all."

"Where shall they take you?" Gaius asked her.

"When the fighting ceases you will be able to reach me sooner if I remain at Gull," she answered.

"Then I will look for you there," Gaius smiled as though it were certain to happen.

He looked up at his friends, saying, "Take her to Baen on your way home. Be my life long, or short, you have changed it forever."

Ryn looked sad and remained silent, but Colosso answered, "Our people..." he started, but then thought it better to say, "Your people... will pray for you day and night."

Gaius turned back to Feryn and, after kissing her hand, he buried his face in her cloak and silent tears broke free from her eyes as she whispered, "I will watch for you Gaius." He squeezed her arm affectionately and turned away, heading toward the interior of the city without looking back.

"Feryn," Ryn said to break her trance as she watched him go. She looked up at him, offering an insincere smile but nodded, and the three of them trotted out the gate.

Gaius found his way back to his room where he wasted little time trying to lose himself in sleep, and yet sleep eluded him. As the night waned on, he lay awake a long time in his bed, his thoughts keeping him restless. He said many silent prayers, most of them having little to do with his plight and more to do with those for whom he felt great concern. Eventually sleep did overtake him and once it did his dream was one of a grim, disturbing nature, of things that seemed too real to be mere thoughts running wild.

Chapter 19
Skirmishes

Feryn and her new guardians made it safely to Gull before daybreak. The gate was closed, but it took those watching over the city little time to recognize who was approaching at such an hour, and so they did not even bother to wake the king before opening the gate. The giants allowed Feryn to enter first, but as the guards rushed to attend her, her companions did not dismount. They had decided along the way that they would not stay to rest, but would press on until they reached their own home.

Feryn looked back at them and could tell they were not going to stay. "Thank you for bringing me safely here," she said. They understood little of what she said, but the point was obvious, and they nodded in kind. Just as they were about to depart a guard rushed to them holding a rolled parchment.

He held it up as high as he could, as Ryn reached down to receive it, saying, "Haran." With the princess safe and the message in hand, the two turned their mounts and trotted off.

Gaius awoke shortly after daybreak to the screeching sound of what he could only perceive to be an animal. The sound, which seemed so close only moments ago, now seemed distant. More than curious, he popped out of bed and stepped out onto his roofed balcony. To his amazement, small men upon large featherless flying beasts with long beaks were gliding about and landing by the dozens. Rarely had he seen their kind and never mounted by men. They were the flying draaks, and in the wild the large ones could be nasty.

"More allies," he muttered to himself. As amazing a sight as this was, thoughts of Feryn and his friends began to grow within his mind. Gaius kneeled down saying, "El Shaddai... God of Haran, remember me here for I am more alone now than ever I was during my years in the forests."

Down below, Arioch met the new arrivals with the pomp of servants and guards to accompany his arrogant swagger. With arms open wide he greeted them with a smile to match. "Welcome to Arioch, Briain. You have arrived even before my emissaries could return with the good news of your coming."

Briain and his men, like the riders of the Scourge had to stay light, therefore they wore little in the way of armor. They did wear however, horned helmets that strapped beneath the chin along with furred, sleeveless shirts, bows, and spears. Their size and adornment made them all nearly look alike.

"They should arrive soon," Briain replied. "We passed them along the way. They spoke of riches and spoil in exchange for aid."

"That's right," the king answered. "There will be more than you can carry upon your beasts, should you do well. A hostile army known as the Scourge of…"

"We've heard of them," Briain interrupted. "Long is the reach of our ears with these creatures under our command," he patted his draak proudly. "We travel far and wide and it seems there is scarcely a large city that does not dread the threat of this warlord's coming."

Arioch did not like being interrupted, but tried not to seem bothered by the breach of etiquette. "In any case, my allies and I expect them to soon march against us. Should they succeed, in time they will reach your shores as well, for their ambition knows no bounds."

Briain looked at the sky as if deciding whether or not he was just going to turn around and head back home or not. "We will scout for them to start, find out what we are up against."

"You will find them to the east," Arioch assured.

"The east you say?" Briain repeated as if he were not surprised, but nor was he glad.

"So you too saw the sign of their coming," The king now seemed smug. "Be careful, for it is known that they have flying scouts of their own."

Briain nodded and then rallied his men, "To the eastern skies!" The beasts began to screech and cry out as the riders ushered them on. Arioch, and many others who had stopped to watch, looked on until they had all disappeared over the trees and out of sight.

Late in the morning Ryn and Colosso arrived home, immediately causing quite a stir. They were tired, and their beasts being even more so plodded heavy hooves through the entrance. Seeing their fatigue, some of the large men took the horses for them. "They need rest, food, everything," Ryn instructed. He sounded as though it was difficult for him to even speak.

Some women brought them water and receiving it, they sat where they were and began to drink. "You look unharmed," Argoes said as he and Haran approached. Seeing it was just the two of them he asked with concern, "Where is Gaius?"

The two men looked at each other as if neither one of them wanted to answer, but Ryn took it upon himself and said, "He has chosen to stay in Arioch for a time."

"Arioch," Argoes looked most displeased, "what do you mean he has chosen to stay in Arioch?"

Ryn sat his cup down and stood, "The girl's father offered her to him in exchange that he stay," Ryn breathed heavy before continuing, "for the battle."

"And he agreed?" Haran nearly shouted and the two nodded.

"You were sent so that nothing of this sort would happen!" Argoes rebuked sharply. "How could you let him do this?"

"I cannot order him about as if he were my slave!" Ryn countered nearly as loud and the gathering crowd began to step back and watch from a more respectful distance.

"But why? He knows that this cannot end well," Haran lamented.

"While spending time with him have you all heard nothing he's said?" Ryn asked. "He does not fight for Arioch, he fights for the girl. For he will not again abandon the innocent to their fate, or in this case her fate. By his choosing to stay we were allowed to transport her safely to Gull where she now awaits his return, as his wife."

"You mean she waits for a light to pierce the heavens declaring his death," Haran answered with harsh sarcasm.

Colosso now stood with them, "Which would be a pity indeed for there is love between them."

All were silent a moment, but then it was broken by Haran, "I must go to him."

"He is a man of honor, he will not leave," Ryn said looking sure. "Nor would that petty king allow it."

"Neither do I care," Haran snapped. "Open the gate!"

Ryn stepped out half blocking his march, "If you wish to go, I will take you. Only allow the horses... and me, a bit of rest."

"I'll not wait," Haran answered.

"Keep that gate closed," Argoes ordered from behind them and those in charge of it closed it fast.

Haran turned and looked at him with shock and anger, "You dare prevent my leave?!"

"Don't even pretend that the Lord of all has again ordered you into the woods," Argoes answered, his stubborn look equaling Haran's.

Colosso came and stood between them though they were not really near one another, "Come friends let us just wait a bit, pray... let calmer heads prevail."

Ryn again pleaded with Haran, "You will not get farther on foot then the horses can take you once they are rested."

He could see it in Haran's eyes that he knew he spoke the truth, "Then you will just have to pick me up once you've caught up to me."

Ryn folded his arms in resignation saying, "And I will."

"Open the gate!" Haran again ordered, and those operating it did not hesitate.

"Rest well," Argoes said to Ryn. "For I will wake you as soon as the horses look ready."

Briain and his warriors scoured the skies from high and low, north and south, as they searched eastward. By midday one of his men glided near him, pointing to three objects in the air a fair distance away. Briain raised one of his spears high, rallying his men and forcing his beast ahead of the others where all could see his lead. Soon his men began to form a wide, yet tighter formation.

Not far to the east of them Bashan and two others were searching the forests when they began to notice a large host of flying creatures approaching. They flew alongside each other just close enough to shout to one another, "Looks like the long beaks," Bashan called to them. "They may intend to group hunt. Fire some volleys into their midst and they'll scatter to the wind."

His warriors nodded and readied their orb bows, but as they prepared to fire, one of them shouted, "Riders!"

Immediately all three of them fired and the beasts did scatter, a few of them nearly colliding. Instead of fleeing they quickly regrouped and began to attack with spears and bows. The terrors of the Scourge began to click in order to better hear all that was happening. Knowing that they were surrounded they began to zigzag so hard and abrupt that if the men had not been hooked in they would have been tossed right off.

The draak were fast, and with so many soaring about, the chaos was proving too much even for the agile terrors. The Scourge riders found themselves maneuvering about so much they could scarcely return fire. Briain swooped in from a dive and pulled up just in time to hurl his spear at Bashan. He yanked his beast to the side, narrowly avoiding the point, but as the spear meant for him passed, it pierced a comrade who was following close behind.

As the injured Scourge rider slumped over with gnashing teeth, the enemy riders zeroed in. They finished off the beast and rider from every direction with a relentless assault of volleys.

Bashan blew his horn so as to garner the attention of his other comrade. He dove for the forests, knowing it would be their only chance of escape. The terrors were agile enough with their keen hearing to maneuver about the trees, but the long beaks needed much more space for their wide, gliding wingspan.

His comrade heard the call and followed, firing behind him as he dove. One orb connected, rendering a beast unconscious, taking its screaming rider along with it into a death plunge.

The trees were old and tall, but Bashan and his comrade burst through the upper foliage with so much speed they nearly hit the ground. A barrage from above rained down on them, but it had little success of breaking through the thick upper canopy.

The eyesight of the long beaks was keen, but could see little for the trees were still thick with leaves. Briain and his men continued to circle about searching, but soon they had lost the trail. Bashan and his comrade continued on, carefully navigating through the forests until they were well out of the reach of those pursuing them.

In Gull everyone was whispering about yet another unexpected visit from the princess of Arioch. Lyon found his brother watching her from his bedroom window as she walked outside and said to him, "Do not spread it about, but I have heard from father that the man Gaius has pledged to fight alongside Arioch in exchange for the hand of his daughter."

"Good, I hope he dies," Hagen answered him without looking.

"What do you mean... you hope he dies?" Lyon was incensed.

"If he falls then surely I will have her," Hagen explained.

Lyon stared at him from behind with disbelief and then tossed the contents of a goblet upon him. Hagen abruptly stood to learn why he was suddenly wet, "Are you mad?" Hagen nearly shouted in anger.

"No, but you speak the evil words of a petty... jealous... child," Lyon's words were not loud but blunt and deliberate.

"Get out of my room," Hagen demanded "or we'll come to blows!"

Lyon waved him off with a gesture of his hand and marched out. Hagen knew his brother spoke truly and yet he did not care. This commoner Gaius stood in the way of the things he wanted. He would eagerly await news concerning the outcome of the battle.

Argoes stood upon a ship's deck that gave him a high view northward. He had been there for some time alone when Honora came to stand behind him. "You are troubled," she said; her voice was quiet and concerned.

"I am at war within myself," he confirmed. "Believe me when I say you do not want to hear what's in my heart."

"Of course I do, and I don't have to hear you say anything, for I already know you fear for your friend. But you cannot change what will happen."

Turning to her he said with a sad and desperate frustration, "But I can. I just don't know if I should."

Honora took his hand as he looked out into the distance and said, "I would be lying if I were to say I wanted you to go. I want you to live and we cannot know what will happen should you interfere with what is to come."

Argoes's voice grew quiet, "I have asked the Creator for understanding in this matter, but He does not speak to me... not like he does Haran."

They stood there quietly but a little more than moments later a freedman rushed up to them saying with heavy breaths, "Haran asks for you at the gate."

Argoes and his wife looked at one another and then hurried down, running across the openness of the settlement and garnishing much attention. Some of the men followed him out, thinking there may be trouble. Ryn was among them for he had just gotten up. As more than a dozen men filed outside the gate Haran's eyes singled out Argoes, "I have a message for you."

Chapter 20
Standing before the Crossroads of Destiny

"Do what you will," Haran declared. He was looking at Argoes but the message was for all, and they all looked surprised by the old man's sudden return. "But do not fight alongside Arioch in an attempt to save the city, for his time has come. And do not presume you will live, for should you march against this enemy, then great will be your loss. Yet, in spite of all this, even greater will be the good that arises from one who lives."

Argoes's eyes grew wide as he considered what the prophecy might mean. "It's a bit of a riddle, is it not?" one of the men surmised. "Surely it speaks of Gaius," another suggested. This was indeed what Argoe's as well as the others were hoping.

Ryn came forward and looked at the men, "Hear well the words of our wise friend Haran, for some among you have families." He looked Argoes right in the eye when he said this, but then looked at the others as he continued, "But as for me, I have no such reservations. And it's because none call me father or husband, that I have already made my choice." And with that being said, Ryn placed his helmet on and began to check the gear that was on him as he reentered the city to fetch the rest of his armament.

It was clear to all that he was going to face this enemy no matter the outcome. Some of those standing there began to beat the butt of their spears into the ground. The sound of war chants grew also as most of them followed him to gather what they would need to fight. Everyone inside knew that these were the sounds of war and a concerned crowd quickly gathered to watch these warriors begin to gird themselves.

Honora saw the look in Argoes eyes and took him by the arm, "And you as well husband?"

Without an answer she knew what he was going to do, though there was some turmoil in his eyes. Still he would not leave his comrades to engage in this battle without him.

It did not take long for the warriors to become battle ready. Their loved ones lined up in two long, crowded rows, along the way to the gate. They embraced the warriors as they made their way out and Argoes kneeled down so that his wife, his sons, and daughters could all embrace him at once.

It was happening so fast that many were yet unaware as to why sorrowful cries had begun to arise among the crowd. After more than two hundred warriors filed out the gate, Argoes looked up to the crowd gathering along the wall and said to them, "Whatever may come of us, know that an even greater good follows; it has been foretold. Hold true to the better way we have all learned and He who has given us new life will continue to shelter you."

As the warriors followed him into the forest Ryn stopped Haran and handed him a message, "It is from Gull, I had not thought to give it to you when we arrived."

Haran opened it up and quietly read its contents, "Baen gives us his thanks, as well as that of Rhone, for warning them of those in the woods. The messengers of Gull could tell that a large host had passed northward but they encountered no enemies." Haran looked up at him and said, "Your presence here has made a great difference in the lives of many."

"And it sounds as though my death will do even more."

Haran's countenance grew sad and Ryn continued. "We are not afraid to die Haran."

The old man sighed as he began to walk, shaking his head and waving his arm, "I know," he said as if he didn't want to hear it.

From time to time Bashan and the other surviving rider would stop to have a peak at the skies. They returned to the air just as soon as they could no longer see their enemies, and just before dark they spotted the marching lines of their comrades. After landing a good ways ahead of the front; Bashan quickly dismounted and rushed toward Roar.

"Is it me or does he look alarmed," Roar asked sarcastically.

"No, something's happened to be sure," Commander agreed.

"Three of us were attacked by a large host of mounted long beak draak," Bashan reported fretfully.

"Will they outnumber you once the rest of your riders are gathered?" Roar asked.

"To be sure. They were skilled, I'll give them that. And neither did the power of our weapons unnerve them for long."

"Well blow your horns throughout the hills and summon those under your command," Roar exhorted. "I care not who hears or if they know we come. Indeed it seems they already know, doesn't it Bashan?"

"I do not believe it was a chance meeting," Bashan was confident of this. "Surely they were scouts."

"Keep your riders together and spy out this city by night, for the dark belongs to beasts such as yours. Fear not the numbers of these riders for we will come up with a clever remedy for the large chickens that have rattled you so."

Bashan had a look of displeasure over Roar's taunt, but said nothing as he returned to his beast to again take to the skies.

"How long, Commander, does Un's map suggest it will be before we reach this tyrant in the west?"

"I checked it not long ago and at the progression of our march, I'm thinking a day... maybe two, Bashan will soon know for sure."

"Good," Roar said, looking as though he were contemplating a new development. "I think we're walking into another trap."

By nightfall Arioch had called a meeting to discuss what he had learned from Briain's scouting efforts. From within the darkness of the large, hearth lit room, he, along with Maris, Wolf, Gannim, Melek, and Briain had gathered. He did not summon Gaius for he knew that the young man did not believe they would to be the victors. Arioch addressed Briain first, "Share with them all that you've told me."

"We fell upon some unsuspecting scouts riding winged creatures. Their weapons were strange to us, like magic, but still we easily prevailed with our surpassing numbers."

Arioch looked at Gannim as if desiring confirmation. "Yes, this would be them," Gannim admitted indifferently.

"Further," Briain continued, "after we fanned out to find those who had escaped, one of my riders who had taken to the heights saw a well organized force marching westward."

"How many?" Gannim asked.

"He remained very high so as not to be seen, but still he believed there were no less than a thousand."

"Well done Briain," Arioch commended. "So then," he continued smugly, "having already bested them in our first encounter, we may well outnumber them five or even six to one."

"And we will need to," Gannim assured, annoyed by the king's optimism. He looked at Briain, "Tell me draak rider, how many of the enemy did you surprise and kill?"

"There were but three and only one was slain," he hated to admit. "Though he was killed easily and the outcome would have been the same had there been twenty," he added defensively.

"You say," Gannim answered, looking unimpressed. "When the battle comes, you may very well outnumber them. However, you must be the first to strike their riders if we are to own the skies during the battle. We must surprise them wave after relentless wave, until they know not which way to press."

"Indeed," a voice hissed from the shadows and all those with weapons drew them, save Gannim, for he knew the identity of this new addition to their meeting. As they searched the shadows intently one of Gannim's remaining witchers emerged.

"Fear not lord of Arioch," Gannim said, growing smug. "It seems that you will now speak to Lord Mizrahim himself through this vessel."

The men stepped back warily as the hooded medium entered their midst saying, "Our allies among the spirits tell me the Scourge of Roar is spread thin. Only half its strength marches against you. Although do not be careless, for our adversary is worthy of his infamy."

"You have done well my son," upon hearing this Gannim's eyes grew wide. "You are now poised to sever this dead branch. Their leader will set upon the city boldly, just as he always does. Heed the words of my son, for he knows the enemy well. The witcher began to moan as the connection faded and suddenly it was apparent that the witcher's mind was once again his own.

Gannim faced them all and smiled, "The moment is upon us and should we prevail... the world is ours."

Gaius tried to keep to himself as much as possible but having received permission to send a letter to Feryn, he had spent most of the evening with a servant girl. She inscribed his words as he struggled to find them, much to his embarrassment.

She was quite beautiful, which he surmised was a deplorable ploy of Arioch's in order to entice him further into his favor. Fortunately Gaius was not the base and carnal type the king surrounded himself with. So, though polite enough, he hardly looked at her.

"That will be all," he said feeling relieved to have such an awkward experience over with. He approached her so as to take the message, adding, "I will deliver this to the messenger myself."

The girl did not immediately release it saying, "Is there anything else you desire sir?" Her look was warm and seductive and Gaius swallowed uncomfortably saying, "No, that will be all. Thank you for your help." With a tilt of her head she slowly left the room as if giving him plenty of opportunity to change his mind. She had an uncanny resemblance to Feryn. It was not just her clothing, but even her appearance that was similar. Gaius concluded that she must be some kind relative of Feryn's, perhaps a cousin.

He held tight the letter praying, "Lord of all, the king is more clever than I. Rescue me from becoming as he, be it through my life or death." He could not believe he uttered the words at the last, but he meant them. He waited long enough so not to encounter the scribe girl again, and then leaving the room he sought out the means to which his love would receive the words of his heart.

Well into the night, the servants of King Baen knocked upon his chamber door alerting him to the arrival of numerous armed Nimerian's. He quickly dressed and rushed to the gate to find his guards watching nervously the sight of the giants girded for battle. Talon was waiting for him at the foot of the wall and as the king drew near he asked, "Have they been here long?"

"No my king they have just arrived, I have yet to even speak with their wise man... assuming he is among them."

Baen rushed to the top of the wall and called out, "Haran my friend, are you among those girded for battle?"

The old man's little frame emerged from the crowd and approached the gate, "Do not be alarmed, I am here."

"Is everything well?" Baen was at a loss as to what was going on; but in the back of their minds, they all feared that they had come to lay claim to their city.

"It is well for you... but it is complicated for us right now," Haran admitted. "We are passing by but hoped it would be all right if we encamped near the city along our way."

"But of course," Baen assured.

"On behalf of all my friends, I offer you our most sincere thanks," Haran said with a respectful bow of his head.

"I will join you in a bit, with uh... um... some bread and drink!" Baen added.

"Your kindness is even more than could be expected and it will be most appreciated," Haran replied.

The word of their coming began to spread about the city and soon the king saw Feryn approaching with her gaze set on him. "Oh dear," he mumbled under his breath. "Feryn my dear, what has aroused you?"

She looked at him so as to reveal the absurdity of his question. "Is the one they call Haran among them?"

"He is," Baen confirmed.

"Then I wish to speak with him."

"I'd really rather you not my dear; after all you are under my prot..." Her look stopped him before he could even finish and the king sighed in resignation, "Very well you may accompany me. But it will be a while yet; for I will not go out to meet them empty handed."

"I'll wait for you beside the gate," she said looking happy to be getting her way.

The Scourge had decided to bed down for some rest as well. Commander returned to the front to report to Roar after having given instructions to the men. "I told the men that there could be no fires tonight for we are nearing the place of battle," he said to Roar who sat a good way out so as to be alone. His back was to the men and his head looked toward the stars.

"And the demeanor of my warriors," Roar asked without looking.

"They are happy to eat and rest but there is nervousness about them. This is uncharted territory for them. Our numbers are down, their siege master waits at the mountain, the enemies are known and unknown...."

"Shut up," Roar interrupted, though he did not actually sound irritated.

"Are you sure that we want to walk right into another trap?" Commander asked.

But Roar continued to gaze up with indifference, "When we crossed some highlands earlier in the day, I saw rainclouds from the north pushing towards us. I think we could be in for a cold wet fight." "And I am sure that 'we' do not want to attack, however I do, for I will not allow my enemies to gain anymore footing here." They both remained silent a moment before Roar began again, "You know, my mother told me that all the ancients said that He who made us destroyed nearly all of our ancestors because of their violence."

"I am a violent man Commander and yet I cannot fathom that the Ruler of all would choose the foul animal Gannim to triumph over us. That is... assuming He even cares what happens upon the earth."

"I think we have all heard that story," Commander replied. "It is even said that one of the survivors yet walks among the living. I would like to meet him."

"As would I," Roar admitted to his surprise.

"Well then," Commander said, "let us hope that our violence is of a sort that does not garner the Maker's attention." Roar remained silent and neither did Commander know what else to say. And so it would be the last either of them spoke to each other until morning.

Feryn walked alongside the king while dozens of servants followed behind them. They carried bread and wine which they quickly began to distribute. Haran was about to spread his own cloak upon the ground for Baen and Feryn to sit upon but the king stopped him, "No, it's all right; mine will do."

Haran smiled appreciatively as they sat down and Baen asked him, "So what might I ask, is the meaning of this fierce procession?"

Haran looked down as if troubled before saying, "My friends are determined to engage the mysterious enemy and return Gaius safely home."

"He is in danger?" Baen asked, looking surprised.

"Then the daughter of Arioch has not told you?" Haran stated, looking directly at Feryn who would not meet their gaze.

"No, she has mostly kept to herself since her arrival," Baen confirmed. "I know only that she has come to remain safe with us when trouble arrives in her homeland."

"Will you give him a message for me?" Feryn interjected, changing the subject. Haran nodded and she removed her hooded cloak saying, "Give this to him. Tell him I'll be waiting to receive it back from his own hand." She stood as the tears she could no longer hold back began to stream down her cheeks. "I must go. Thank you for going to his aid." They watched her as she departed and then Baen looked at Haran with confusion.

"You see," Haran began, "Gaius has stayed behind to fight in exchange for her hand as well as to ensure her early departure to find safety behind the your walls."

There was a sudden look of understanding in Baen's expression, "Then he will not be disappointed, for safe she will remain."

"I can see her love for him is genuine," Haran admitted. "Tell her I am sorry, I should have never doubted. We will carry on our way early, but I cannot thank you enough for both your wisdom and friendship."

King Baen held a cup up saying, "To a safe return." Haran repeated the words loud enough for the Nimerians to join in. The words were repeated throughout the camp for it was a sentiment shared by all.

Chapter 21
Marching Northward

By sunrise Haran and his friends were ready to depart again. A sizeable crowd had gathered along the walls of Gull to watch them go and wish them well. It was a beautiful day, yet despite this the procession was rather solemn. A wary quiet had settled upon the city of Gull like a thick blanket for the reason of their march had cast a shadow upon all.

Within Arioch, Gaius was awakening to the sound of a man's voice, "Wake up, wake up, wake up," he calmly repeated over and over again. Gaius opened his eyes and saw a man leaning against a column upon the balcony, "I've been eager to meet you," Gannim said with a grin.

Gaius immediately began scrambling for his sword and, seeing this Gannim held his arms out as if to gesture that he was not a threat, "Calmness, calmness, I am clearly not here for your head or otherwise you would already be dead, right?"

"Who are you?" Gaius demanded with a troubled brow.

"I am Gannim and I hear that you are a friend of the Nimerians. In fact, by the look of your cloths and that fancy sword over there I'm quite sure of it." Gaius looked as though he were about to speak, but Gannim continued, "So then, the next question of course is, what do I want?"

Gaius did not respond as Gannim began to stroll about the balcony playfully. "If we are to all survive, then we need to help one another. How would you like me to help you wield that fancy sword of yours, hmm?"

"I wield it well enough."

"Really?" Gannim answered, looking as though he were amused and unconvinced. "Come on then boy, show me the way out." There was an unmistakable sharpness to his tone and Gaius knew that this man wanted him to use force.

He rolled out of bed while reaching for his sword at the same time. Gaius stood battle ready with the blade raised beside his head.

"I'm waiting," Gannim taunted loudly. Gaius stepped forward with a down slash of the glowing blade, releasing a forceful blast. Gannim held his arms wide open as if to embrace the attack and was pushed back, but he used this force to propel his leap backwards over the balcony, throwing his whip around a rail. It held fast and he swiftly lowered himself to the ground.

"Come on down lad. I want to see more," he called out. Gaius looked over the balcony, searching for a safe way down. Gannim laughed, "I see you do not know how to lighten your fall."

Gaius ignored the taunt and spied a stair well on the balcony to the right. He would have to jump several feet to reach it, but he didn't hesitate. He darted toward it and with a step from the ledge, lunged over to the next side, stepping down from the rail smoothly enough.

He made his way down the adjoining steps and found Gannim waiting in the open, but now he held his twin stars down at his sides.

"What is the point of this?" Gaius asked as he noticed the startled onlookers shuffling away.

"Just play a bit longer," Gannim answered him.

Gaius ran forward and down slashed again, but Gannim stepped right through the blast with an upswing of one of his stars. "Can you at least unleash an orb?" he heckled.

A look of uncertainty crept across Gaius's face, "I have not yet learned."

"Feel it in the hilt and let it grow. Once you're ready, give a swing... let it free." Gaius looked down at the hilt and he focused. He could see the imbalance of power within the weapon as the hilt grew brighter than the rest.

"It will help if you target me when you attack," Gannim shouted.

Gaius took a step and lurched the sword forward as if he were going to throw a knife, only he held it tight. The power surged along the blade and erupted from the end, soaring at Gannim who countered it with an underhand throw of his own. His weapon buzzed right through the glowing sphere; seizing all the orb's power within itself. The spinning blade stopped not more than an arm's length from Gaius's face, giving him quite a scare. Gannim walked purposely over to him and grabbed it out of the air saying, "Your giant friends are not the only ones who offer power. If you should survive the battle then you would do well to seek me out."

Having said this, Gannim walked away to leave Gaius to his thoughts. Though he did not intend to volunteer his answer, Gaius had already made up his mind as to what his answer would be should he be pressed for one; it was no.

As the giants marched toward the top of a wooded hill, a rider suddenly emerged but seeing them he brought his horse to an immediate stop. Clearly he was more than startled at the sight of these men so armed. All the Nimerian warriors fixed their eyes on him; remaining quiet though they were not scared in the least. As the man began to turn his mount around Haran looked up at Argoes, "He is from Arioch. Do not let him escape!"

Immediately one of the warriors hurled his spear and it ran the horse through. The animal toppled like a felled tree and the man quickly arose in an effort to scurry away. Several warriors broke off in a sprint after him provoking Haran to desperately call, "No need to kill him!"

It took just seconds for the giant's great strides to overtake him and the first one to reach him grabbed him up right off his feet as if he were a child. The warrior carried him back to Haran and being terrified he almost screamed, "I merely carry a letter to Gull from your friend Gaius!" "Set him down," Haran said and the warrior did so. "We are not marching to attack your city, if that's why you were trying to flee. Although, now that you've seen us you cannot be allowed to return. Your city is doomed soldier of Arioch and so I offer you but one choice, continue on to Gull and remain there so that you may return to God and live. For if we catch you trying to return to your homeland," Haran shook his head in warning, "then you're a dead man."

As night fell, Ryn, having already been to Arioch twice now announced, "We are close. It is little more than a short walk from here."

"I will go to Gaius alone," Haran said to them. He could see the protest already welling up in Argoes's eyes, "You heard the message Argoes. You cannot protect this city and should the attack come while I'm there, then what would you do?"

"He's right," Ryn added.

"Is the battle near Haran?" Argoes asked.

The old man was quiet a moment before answering, "It is and you will know when it is time; not only by the sounds of battle, but also by the stirring in your hearts."

Argoes came down to one knee and set a hand on his little friend's shoulder saying, "You have rescued us Haran. Whatever may come, know that my people survive because of you."

Haran patted the large hand, "Pray often while I'm gone and I will hope to return to you before the fighting begins, but if you do not see my return then fear not for me."

Haran departed into the woods, and after what seemed like a rather short walk through the darkness along a well traveled route, he found himself within view of the city. The guards were alert and took notice of him right away, but it was not until he came close that they recognized him.

"I am here to speak with the man Gaius," Haran called to those in charge of the gate. The men began to speak to one another, though he could not hear what they were saying. He waited patiently and soon Arioch himself appeared upon the wall. "What business do you have with my young champion? You have not come to steal him away have you?"

"My business is my own and I do not presume that I will be allowed to take him anywhere," Haran answered sharply but Arioch just stared down at him a moment with a look of annoyance. "Perhaps you do not want me to speak to him because you hold him against his will. His friends will hear of this at once," Haran turned as though he were leaving.

"Bah, speak to him if you like, I care not," Arioch relented bitterly. He had hoped for Haran to offer up more favorable diplomacy, but the old man was as wise as the king was crafty. The gate opened just enough for him to squeeze in and the king met him at the base of the stairwell leading to the ramparts. "By yourself are we?" Arioch asked.

"I am never alone for my Lord is ever with me." Upon hearing this, a look of disdain immediately crept over the king's face, but he said nothing.

"Follow me," Arioch barked.

Soon they entered a sturdy stone building and after ascending a spiraled staircase Arioch pointed toward a door, then immediately departed. Haran tugged on its circular metal handle and when the door opened Gaius looked up to see who it was. "Haran!" he nearly shouted. "What are you doing here my friend?"

Coming in he replied, "I have come to check on you lad, to see for myself this trouble you find yourself in." He handed him the cloak that Feryn had given him, "A gift of love from your beautiful wife."

Gaius took hold of it with both hands and held it close, "It smells like her... like lavender." Her cloak made him smile, but it quickly faded as he looked Haran in the eyes, "I've disappointed you, haven't I?"

"Things have not remained as simple as I had hoped," Haran admitted, "and I would be lying if I said I agreed with your choice, but the choice has been made. I know that you have done this knowing full well that it may prove to be her life in exchange for your own, and there is honor in that."

The look on Gaius's face grew serious, "Do you think we will all die?"

Haran considered his words carefully before answering, "Yes we will all die, if not here and now, then on another day." Gaius smiled knowing that his friend knew that it was not the answer he was looking for; but there was wisdom in it nonetheless.

"I had a dream the other night that seemed more than a dream," said Gaius.

"Oh," Haran's voice carried sincere interest, hoping that it was a message from the Highest.

"Yes, well, there was this bold and hateful man that stood boasting before the city, but just as he began to signal the attack that of the army behind him... he fell lifelessly to the ground. Dark spirits that had conspired against him swirled about his body before gathering to a city far to the north. Then, from the north a dire shadow hand reached down and engulfed all the land in darkness." The look on Gaius's face made it apparent that he could remember the dream vividly.

There was a stirring inside of Haran that could be seen by the troubled look on his face. "What's wrong Haran?" Gaius asked. "What does it mean?"

Haran looked down a moment and then said sharply, "Nothing. It means nothing," but Gaius knew this was a lie. Haran abruptly stood and marched for the door.

"Where are you going?" Gaius asked, but without looking the old man only shook his head and waved his hand, continuing on without responding. He made his way straight for the city's front gate, which was opened promptly. Haran pressed onward toward the east to see for himself what he had never seen before.

Morning came and the Scourge marched toward a peculiar sight. Standing in the middle of the road was what looked to be a weary traveler leaning upon his staff. "What do you make of that?" Commander asked Roar.

Roar held up a fist and the march came to an immediate halt. He stared at the old man in the road a moment and then raised his brow in surprise saying, "Isn't it obvious?"

Commander threw his hands up and guessed, "What? Is it the next person you're going to kill?"

Roar gave him a glare of contempt that quickly faded, "Perhaps. Wait here and I will go see." Dismounting he walked casually over to the man with his axe resting upon his shoulder. The distance took him out of the hearing of his men who began to whisper among themselves; guessing as to what was going on.

Roar stopped just a few paces away from the old man and said, "I know who you are; bold, staff in hand... old. Are you not he that goes before us to announce the end of those who cannot escape, robbing them of their last restful night?"

"But some have escaped," Haran countered confidently. "Nor did I warn the city along the coast, for things have changed."

Roar glared at him spitefully, "And why do you now stand before me? Do you dream of being trampled by the murderous ranks just behind me?"

"I wanted to see for myself who the Creator of heaven and earth has aroused to execute justice. Besides, it has long been my custom to announce the end to those whose time has come."

Roar almost growled his disdain, "Perhaps it is your time that has come. How weary you must grow of being the bearer of ill news." Roar held out his axe, "Would you like for me to ease your suffering?"

"Many have tried bitter and hateful one." Having said this, the old man turned and began to walk away adding with a glance, "but alas, I cannot die unless He who watches over me allows it."

Roar stomped back to the front, "Give me a bow and arrow," he ordered to no one in particular and accepted the first that was extended to him. Turning around he looked at the old man and drew the bow string back. Foom! The arrow soared, closing the gap between he and Haran in the blink of an eye only to bury itself into the head of the seer's wooden staff. Haran slowed down just long enough to glance at the arrow sticking out both ends before continuing on.

"Why were you trying to scare him?" Commander asked.

"I wasn't," Roar growled with his eyes still fixed upon his would be victim. "I was aiming for his head."

Chapter 22
The Siege of Arioch

The day crawled slowly for all those waiting for what was to come, and by nightfall the cold north winds had brought clouds that blotted out the stars of the night sky. Bashan and his riders approached from behind the infantry. The men under his command landed at the rear, while he continued on to the front. He brought his beast to a stop alongside Roar who was back on his horse. "So," Roar said to him, "what news?"

"From a great height we examined the city. It's just ahead and it is apparent from the amount of torch light and soldiers along the walls that they are indeed expecting a fight."

"And they will not be disappointed," Roar stated as a matter of fact. "What of the draak riders which bested you the other day?"

"They perch about the city's heights."

"Good," Roar replied. "Then they will die first... but from above."

"As you wish," Bashan answered, knowing the attack he had in mind.

Roar turned his horse around so that he could address the troops His armor stretched around his face to enhance voice as he declared, "The battle is at hand Scourge of Roar. We may yet have a real fight on our hands; prepare yourselves." Activity and enthusiasm erupted among his men as they prepared themselves.

Roar looked at Commander and said, "The road is too narrow and there could be those who spy about. From here until the walls are within sight I want the artillery to level the surrounding forest."

"Understood," Commander assured and then departed to see it done.

Roar then looked at Bashan, "I will address these people as usual, only you will execute your attack as soon as I do so. Cause as much havoc as you're able on the opposite side of the city and we will do the rest."

"I will watch for the glow of your armor from the sky," Bashan answered before urging his beast into flight.

Haran was returning to where the Nimerian's were hiding out in the woods when a large figure suddenly snatched him up. "Unhand me," he snapped and the warrior immediately set him down.

"It's only Haran," he announced to the others standing guard.

Everyone took notice of him as he passed, curious as to what he had learned. "Did you speak with Gaius?" Ryn asked.

"Yes, and I also spoke to the man you're about to fight."

Those who heard him say this looked as though they were filled with questions, but Argoes's expression was defiant as he asked, "And what do you think of this man who leads them?"

"He is a killer," Haran answered without hesitation. Just then they began to feel the ground begin to rumble and hear the sounds of blasts echoing in the distance.

"It has begun," Ryn announced resolutely.

The men began to stand, but Haran wanted to council them, "Patience brave warriors. Do not approach them at their full strength. Let them weary themselves a bit first. And remember it will do you no good to attack if the reign of Arioch does not come to an end."

Ryn looked at Argoes, "He's right. I am eager to fight, but we should give ourselves every advantage to prevail."

"Tell us of Gaius," Argoes changed the subject, addressing Haran again.

"He is ready to give his life for the one he loves, as ready as one can be I suppose." He could see the warriors who heard this contemplating the significance of his words. "Why don't we take a moment to pray together?" Haran suggested and as he knelt down on his knees, all the warriors dropped to one knee as well.

"God of our father's, the victory is yours and to those you give it. I thank you for the bond of friendship between us here, and that I am able to know such men of courage. You have promised that good will rise from this adversity and we believe you... that it will be just as you say. Strengthen these men for the task at hand."

With this being said, Haran arose to his feet and began to touch the heads of the men as he passed. He was saying things too quietly for them to hear, but they knew it was for their benefit. Afterwards he once again disappeared into the woods.

The artillery of the Scourge began leveling the ancient forest. The trees along their approach snapped and shattered ahead of them. Those within the city watched with a fearful expectation that grew with each enormous timber that crashed and shook the earth. Arioch joined the guard on top of the gate, with Wolf to his right and Gaius to his left. Briain's riders struggled to calm their mounts at the rear of the city while Gannim stood alongside Melek from hiding places within the forests.

A chant began to ring out from the approaching invaders, "Die! Die! Die! Die! Die!" Over and over this was repeated until the last few obstructing trees were blown apart, revealing the formidable front line of artillery bore by armored beasts. Roar and Commander rode just ahead of the army and as Roar was about to address the city Commander murmured, "Here we go again."

"It seems that everyone here speaks the dialect of the south," Roar mused. "You best get yourself out of harm's way Commander. That wall is lined with archers." Roar ushered his horse ahead and his armor molded around him defensively. Once he was half way between the city and his artillery he addressed them, "Greetings filth... or should I say those who are about to die. I am Roar of the Scourge and we have come to rid the world of your vile disease."

"Then what are you waiting for?" Arioch shouted. He was intimidated, but pridefully indignant. "Bring on the attack!" He challenged.

"We already have," Roar answered coldly before turning his horse and trotting off. He dismounted as soon as he joined the ranks of the siege artillery.

"What is this nonsense?" the king said to those near him. No sooner had the words left his mouth than shouts and screams began to resound from the rear of the city. Bashan and his riders had dived hard from high above, firing volleys that targeted the enemy riders where they had perched in waiting.

The Scourge riders were able to get a few volleys in before they had to pull up, sweeping about the heights of the city. Their terrors would snatch men up by the face, ripping them from their mounts only to drop them from the heights as they ascended once again.

"Fire," Commander ordered the artillery in the front; taking full advantage of the distraction. A relentless barrage ensued that began to pound the city's front wall, gate, and towers. Wolf forced the king to the floor as Gaius ducked behind his shield, backing his way down nearby steps. Many of the warriors began to flee the wall as the exploding orbs destroyed stone and launched men from their posts.

"Halt the bombardment," Roar shouted and it quickly ceased. Commander looked at him for an explanation and he pointed toward the heights of the city. "Bashan leads his men this way." The terrors glided over the heads of troops cowering along the wall, followed closely by Briain and his riders.

"He baits them into our net," Roar surmised.

Knowing he was right Commander addressed the infantry saying, "Look to the sky but await my command!" Moments later Bashan and his men came soaring over their ranks with the draak riders eager to overtake them. "Strike them down!" Commander shouted and his men filled the air with a hail of arrows and orbs.

Gannim who was watching the battle unfold in secret knew that slaughter would befall his allies. "No fools... what are you doing?" he lamented in frustration.

The barrage quickly overwhelmed the enemy riders who began to scatter and crash, barreling into the trees and lines of soldiers. Some men were able to create a defensive aura in time to save their lives, but others were crushed or impaled by the crashing beasts. Few of the draak riders escaped, Briain was not among them. Those who did survive however disappeared over the forests. Having tasted a fuller measure of their enemies power, the draak riders would not return. Gannim raced back to rejoin his allies to prepare them for the attack. "How goes the battle?" Melek asked upon seeing him reemerge.

Gannim wore a look of irritation, "Difficult, like we all knew it would be. The invaders will resume their assault upon the city at any moment. My men and I will blow horns at the rear of their ranks before revealing ourselves. That is your signal to attack, and once they fix their eyes on you, we will tear into them from the rear; understood?" Melek nodded and Gannim led his men away.

The attack against the city resumed and the echo of its pounding resounded throughout the forests. Argoes looked at Ryn who nodded in agreement for he knew what was on his friend's mind. "It is time," Argoes announced to them all.

"You will lead the left," he directed Ryn and then looked at Colosso saying, "And you the right." They both rushed to opposite ends as he continued to address the rest of the warriors, "Wall formation and no one reveals their power until I reveal mine. They must not see us before we strike." With a deep breath and a grim look of determination, Argoe's began to lead the march.

Chapter 23
Rise of the Nimerians

Within Gull the solemn quiet continued as people anxiously awaited news concerning the outcome of the conflict. Faint rumblings could be heard, and some light could be seen flashing on the distant horizon. Some believed it was an approaching storm, but others countered that the color was like that of the giant's weapons when they had practiced in the nearby field.

Feryn stood atop the balcony of the hall where she had first spoken to Gaius. She looked northward and held the scroll the messenger from Arioch had faithfully delivered. She had yet to read it and none was willing to ask her what it said.

Roar smiled confidently as the bombardment began to break down the city's front walls, crumbling their defenses. Those who had survived the initial shock of the Scourge's ferocity had pulled back further into the interior. Arioch paced nervously while his men stood poised for his orders, though rattled. Amongst all this chaos, Gaius alone stood as if it were all of no surprise to him at.

"We cannot rush headlong into that attack and expect anything less than death," Wolf pleaded with the king. "And we haven't long before our wall is pounded to dust."

"Might I suggest a hasty retreat through the rear of...?" Maris began to council but was silenced with a look of his king.

"We must hold out as long as we can for our allies to attack," Arioch snapped with impatience. "We must give them more time before we attempt any dramatic change in strategy."

"That is, if your other allies have not fled like the winged riders, oh king," Gaius interjected with a deliberate sting.

Arioch glared at him with disdain, but then turned his attention back to Wolf saying, "Our cavalry will remain at the ready, able to charge should the opportunity present itself. I will remain here to direct the archers to whatever new position the battle demands." He looked at Gaius, "And you my boy will lead the charge of the infantry just as soon as I give the command."

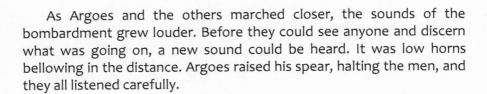

As Argoes and the others marched closer, the sounds of the bombardment grew louder. Before they could see anyone and discern what was going on, a new sound could be heard. It was low horns bellowing in the distance. Argoes raised his spear, halting the men, and they all listened carefully.

"For your glory, men of the south," Melek shouted and his men cried out, charging for the clearing where the enemy stood. Roar's warriors began to search the dark tree line for the source of these noises. "What now?" Roar exclaimed to Commander, looking rather annoyed.

"Hold your positions," Commander shouted. "Raise your defense to the sides!" The men began to split their lines almost in half with space enough for him to pass between them as he raced down the length of the ranks repeating the order. As he approached the rear, Melek and his numerous warriors poured out of the forest just north of their position, throwing themselves into the front half of the invading ranks with abandon.

"Defend the heavy artillery," Roar shouted! "Take aim on those warriors," he ordered a few of the siege men in the front. Knowing it was going to take precious time for them to reposition, he ran several steps and leaped over the heads of his troops. As he descended he dragged his axe from above and smashed it down from behind his head into the midst of at least fifty of the enemy warriors.

Immediately the power released on impact blew them away from him with a flash in every direction. Now, with there being at least twenty long strides between him and the next living adversary, Roar began to rotate his blade hand over hand. Spheres erupted one after another from his weapon. They hammered devastatingly the assailants and trees from which they continued to emerge.

He continued this attack until he could see the artillery firing from behind him. Suddenly, Commander returned looking alarmed exclaiming, "Gannim attacks the rear. Nearly half of Bashan's riders were slain before they were able to escape to the skies. The rear flank is holding their ground, but the fighting there is fierce."

"Bring the signal to the front Commander," Roar ordered sharply. His most trusted general looked bewildered by this request, but did not hesitate to turn around to fulfill the order.

Melek was losing the battle at the front nearly as soon as it had started. His men were being pushed back everywhere they had engaged in battle. The Scourge's superior skill and weapons were increasingly hacking and blowing them apart, but the stakes were high for them, and they had yet to fall back in full retreat.

Gannim's men were keeping the battle at the rear competitive, but he could tell his ally's flank was faltering. He blew the horn all the more in hopes of renewing their spirits, but it was of little use.

"Yes," Roar caused his voice to echo throughout the battle field. "Yes, look upon the fate of your dead and ruined brothers. Know that this too is your end. Death is all that awaits you now."

The attempt at intimidation looked as though it was taking a toll, that Gannim's allies would be routed at any moment when suddenly hundreds of turquoise orbs exploded into Roar's army from the south. He and his men looked on in disbelief as a glowing line of enormous men began to emerge from the trees south of them. "I don't believe it," Roar declared angrily as he realized from whom this vicious attack had come.

The giants prepared to fire again at range, giving the ranks of Roar's men just enough time to reset defensively. "Fire upon those warriors," he commanded the artillery men near him. Ryn's end began to focus their fire on the armored beasts at the front, making their masters struggle to control them. As one beast panicked and resisted, its driver was fatally blasted off.

Roar rushed over and grabbed the beast by its bit; yanking it to face the giant lines. He returned to its rear and with a few heavy slashes, severed the wagon end that bound it to the artillery. Then, with the flat of his axe, he swatted the hind quarters of the beast hard. Frightened, it charged frantically into the Nimerian line, causing many of the determined warriors to break their concentration and scatter lest they be trampled.

Those inside the city were beginning to notice that the bombardment against them had stopped. A guard rushed down from a tower breathlessly confirming this to the king, stating, "The giants have come and now the invaders give all their attention to them!"

The king looked at Gaius and grinned as if it were all a part of his brilliant scheme. And though he had hoped as much, it was as much of a surprise to him as any. "Ready the charge," he ordered Wolf. Then he looked at Gaius, "Lead the foot soldiers through that break near the south corner of the wall. We will meet them head on with two frontal assaults."

Gaius drew his sword which immediately emanated a brilliant glow. Without a word he headed for the gap with a thousand foot soldiers following him from behind.

Commander drove the beast bound to the signal hard in his haste to return to the front. He avoided the heavy fighting on the south flank, but trampled as many of Gannim's allies as he possibly could along the way.

"At last," Roar said to Commander as he approached alongside him, turning the beast pulling the signal around so that the cart was facing the city. At that moment the damaged front gate doors were forced slowly open, revealing a large host of mounted warriors preparing to ride out. Simultaneously, to the south of them, soldiers began to pour out of the broken wall, led by a warrior with a magnificent glowing sword.

Roar looked back at the line of giants which engaged his men in fierce combat and then back at the masses who now approached, weighing carefully his next move. He growled in anger before slashing the axle on the side facing the city. The wagon's bed hit the ground causing the signal apparatus to slide out and tilt at an angle.

"Back the beast up," he ordered and Commander did so until he heard Roar say, "Hold steady." Roar grabbed hold of the signal which was now forced on its side causing it to glow fiercely. Stabilizing it onto its side he called out, "Prepare to fire!"

Commander understood now what Roar intended to do and so he began to crank the signal. The infantry was closing in and the riders were now trotting into a run, but the signal was not fully prepared. Roar was out of time. "Fire!" he shouted.

Commander released the lever and dove out of the way as the fury of the beam was unleashed straight into the oncoming riders. Those in its path were annihilated on impact. The beam penetrated all the way through the back of the ranks, hitting some of the buildings behind.

Roar yelled as he struggled to wrench it along the angle of the infantry who had all but frozen in their steps in the wake of this destructive power. The beam ripped through the wall and the other structures it touched. Arioch had ducked down, along with Maris, in an effort to save themselves, but as a nearby tower was undercut, the structure began to collapse. Arioch and all those near to him peaked up just in time to see their end come crashing down upon them.

Gaius and some others outside had dove to the ground as the beam passed, but those who tried to flee were obliterated. Just as Roar angled the beam enough to sever through the southern front corner of the city, its surging power dwindled to a halt.

Commander looked over at his exhausted leader who was no longer illuminated and said, "So much for them." No sooner had the words left his mouth, then his eyes grew wide. Seeing this, Roar knew that danger was just behind him. He snatched up his axe and spun into a bold shockwave slash which surprised the giant who was just a step or two away. He followed this with a half turn and a thrust of his short sword which he had unsheathed with a reverse grip.

The blade ran his adversary through, severing his spine, and the determined look of the attacker was quickly replaced with the vacant stare of the dead. He collapsed and Roar rushed to stand atop one of the artillery wagons to get a better view of the battle. His air mounts, led by Bashan, swooped about taking opportunistic shots, while Melek having already lost half army, retreated to the forest edge. Taking cover there the king of the exiles wavered on the precipice of attack or flight.

Despite this, it was apparent that his men were barely hanging on against the combined might of Gannim at the rear and the giants to the south. The surprise attack of the Nimerian's had killed hundreds of his men in a matter of seconds and it looked as though the losses were proving too much to recover from.

Suddenly an orb came soaring straight at him. Roar swatted it away with his short sword as if it were but an annoyance before hopping down alongside the cover the beast provided. "Direct the artillery Commander," he said. "I have to deal a heavy blow to those giants or all will be lost." He rushed out into the open field between his army and the fragmented city, aligning himself with the ranks of the Nimerian's.

He prepared to hurl his axe down their line with the intention of cutting as many of them in half as would be possible before their defensive aura would be able to stop his mighty weapons momentum. His axe began to glow bright and just before he committed to the throw he noticed the quiet, but deliberate approach, of an armored warrior.

Gaius raised his glowing sword high and heaved it down with all his might. An orb erupted from the blade, but Roar simply thrust his axe forward severing orb and dispersing its power harmlessly away from himself. Roar quickly closed the distance between them with several strides, and the two men's weapons clashed with enough force to send them both recoiling back a few paces. As soon as Roar regained his footing, he again dashed at his enemy with a combination of attacks. Gaius quickly found himself on the defensive, stepping backward as he countered so as not to be overwhelmed.

Roar drove Gaius's sword down with a powerful swing of his axe and then rammed a shoulder into his enemy's chest. As Gaius stumbled back Roar's next swing just nicked the brim of his helmet. He smoothly followed the swing through with a reverse blast that hurled Gaius right off his feet. Gaius crashed helplessly to his back and Roar closed in for the kill, only to be forced to defend against an approaching orb.

He stepped and weaved just out of its path as it soared by to erupt a safe distance away. Marching toward him with determination was Ryn. His attack had given Gaius just enough time to struggle to his feet. Roar swung his axe in a figure eight, releasing volleys of orbs at them both. While Gaius dodged, Ryn powered through the attack with his shield held high.

The giant warrior came within range and thrust his spear forward, but Roar dashed toward his shield side with a drag swing that Ryn was just able to defend as the axe scrapped along the breadth of his shield. Roar immediately followed the attack with a reverse swing, which Ryn easily defended, but before he could counter thrust, Roar had already stepped out of range.

Gaius heaved his sword down unleashing a shockwave, but without even looking, Roar raised a glowing gauntlet, thwarting the momentum of the gust as if it were nothing. The three of them stared at one another, each waiting for the other to make a move. Roar took this opportunity to draw his short sword with his left hand. As the three of them stared at one another a moment longer, a third figure approached... it was Argoes.

Roar took several steps back so as to give himself more room to work. "You're outmanned invader," Gaius declared to him. "Arioch is little more than a heap now. Why not cease this fighting? Why must any more of us die?"

"Bah! Who among you deserves to live?" Roar hissed before hurling his axe into a swift rotating arc. Argoes raised his shield just in time to block, as did Ryn, while Gaius boldly deflected it with his sword. Roar kept his eyes on the giants as the weapon returned and without breaking his stare he snatched it out of the sky.

Argoes ran forward and lunged with what looked to be a thrust, but it was a trick and an orb was released. Roar weaved as he stepped out of its path, but the orb erupted just a few strides behind him. The blast pushed him forward and Ryn took this opportunity to attempt to run him through.

Roar smacked the head of the spear with the flat of his axe blade. There was a flash of light at the impact, and Roar slipped between Ryn's legs in order to roll out of the way of a thrust by Argoes.

He stood fast with a bold swing that unleashed a powerful shockwave, but the giants were quick to brace themselves with their shields. Gaius heaved another orb at him and, as Roar leaned back to allow it to pass by, the giants took this opportunity to make a combined offensive.

They pressed forward, jabbing with their spears, and though it did not seem like a struggle for Roar to parry the attacks, he was still being forced to step back. He noticed Gaius circling behind him so as to cut him off completely. The war lord wasted no time, dashing between the giants with a blinding illumination of his armor. Once past them he gave a wide arching reverse swing. Being to Roar's right, Ryn took a hit to the side while the attack grazed Argoes's shield.

Ryn's armor kept the hit from being deep, but as soon as they both turned to face their foe, he was already stepping into another attack. The heavy down swing hit the shaft of Ryn's spear wrenching it from his grip. He continued this one smooth swing up to parry Argoes's attack, causing his spear arm to recoil high.

Roar immediately down slashed through the gap the deflection had provided and the heavy strike hit both Argoes's chest and thigh. Instead of reaching down for his spear, Ryn gave him a shield blast, but as soon as Roar tumbled to the ground he just as quickly rolled back up to his feet.

"I have no time for this," he growled before lunging into the air. Being surprised by this bold move, both of the Nimerian warriors raised their shields defensively. He slammed the axe down just in front of them, blasting both men to their backs. Gaius hurled another orb at him, but Roar countered it with one of his own, and another to follow it. The balls of light collided between the giants who were trying to get up only to be forced back down again by the blast, while the second orb soared through the haze catching Gaius by surprise. All he could do was wince as it erupted into his chest piece, hurling him to the ground.

As soon as Ryn rolled to all fours he looked up to catch a strike to his helm. Roar immediately gave a reverse swing, which caught the dazed warrior just at the neck. He face planted into the ground as the few brief moments of life he had left drifted away.

Argoes had stood up just in time to see his comrade collapse. He rushed at Roar with a shout and released a blast from his shield which was immediately followed by an orb volley from his thrusting spear. Roar could not easily dodge them both so he thrust his axe forward splitting through the shield wave and then thrust his sword out to meet the sphere racing toward him.

The orb traveled along the shaft of the blade, to the hilt, and then along Roar's arm. He weaved and funneled the energy along his chest into his right arm, channeling its power with the throw of his axe. The spiraling weapon split right through the top of Argoes's shield, smashing into his face mask and chest.

Roar dashed forward and snatched his weapon out of the air before either it or Argoes could hit the ground. Roar leaped over the giant as he collapsed and raced back to the front for the Nimerian formation had changed as they began to collapse the defense of his men. As soon as he reached his chaotic siege line, he climbed atop an artillery wagon in order to get a clear view.

He knew he had lost valuable time and, as he surveyed the battle it was clear, the three warriors had preoccupied him long enough to prevent him from enacting the counter attack that would have turned the tide. His troops had all but faltered, but Roar would not be denied.

He spotted Commander who was nearby still directing artillery and rushed to him. His leading general looked relieved to see him, saying, "It looks bad for us this time."

"But the Scourge must live on Commander," Roar answered gravely. "Sound the retreat."

"We have no horn for retreat," Commander shouted!

"You don't understand Commander; I'm going to kill everyone," Roar said empathically before walking back toward the signal. He raised his axe high saying with his long reaching voice, "Hear me men of the Scourge. Anyone who does not wish to die should now flee for their lives for this is the end."

The raised axe began to illuminate brilliantly and Commander now understood what was about to happen. He grabbed the reigns of the beast that pulled his cart and whipped it into a gallop. "Clear a path for our comrades," he shouted to those who were in control of the beasts bearing the siege weapons.

Roar plunged his axe deep into the signal and wrenched the metal side to side in an effort to pry it open and reveal its core. Not all of the men heard the warning in the heat of the battle, but many of those who did tried to break free of the fighting as Commander shouted, "With me men of the Scourge, with me!" Some men fought on, while others climbed aboard the wagons as they came by. Then there were some who grasped the situation in time to follow as fast as they could on foot.

They charged along blasting and trampling a path with the help of Bashan and his men, who did not fully understand what was happening, yet they tried to distract their enemies from above. The wagons attempted to encircle the men who were trying to keep up, but those who fell behind were quickly overwhelmed by their pursuing enemies.

The beasts pulling the wagons smashed through Gannim's lines at the rear, but Gannim's men were able to pick a few riders off as they passed. In spite of this the retreat had been executed savagely well. "Should we give chase?" a warrior asked Gannim.

He considered his options a moment before answering, "This can only mean their leader has fallen. These men nearest me and I will give chase, while the rest of you finish those left behind."

"Make peace with the giants if your able, if not, we will fight them another day." Gannim quickly selected around fifty of the men closest to his position and then sprinted off into the darkness, while on the far side of the battlefield Roar had exposed his prize.

It was a large chunk of one of the very rocks that had fallen from the skies so many years ago. Roar gripped it with his free hand until it grew so bright he could hardly look. He drew his axe back with a protective aura and prepared to release the rock's catastrophic potential. As he exhaled for the swing an orb erupted into his side. The blast hurled him several feet away from the signal before he crashed into the ground.

Argoes had made the hit, but just as quickly crumpled to all fours, barely clinging to life. Gaius, who had just stood in time to see the hit, stumbled alongside his friend and asked, "What can I do?"

"Finish," Argoes said weakly as blood flowed from the wounds in his face and chest. Gaius looked up to find Roar already struggling back to his feet. Though he himself was also still dazed from the hit he had taken shortly before, he charged forward. Roar looked up and met his gaze only to be blasted back again and again by a series of the wind attacks from Gaius's sword. Seeing that his enemy was disoriented and reeling, Gaius raced to close the distance between them and slammed the blade down with both hands as soon as he was within range.

Roar raised his armored forearms up just in time to block the blow, yet Gaius used his momentum to keep pushing him back. Roar could tell that he was being forced further and further away from his prize. He allowed this to continue until his head cleared, and then he unexpectedly side stepped, causing Gaius to stumble right passed him. Gaius then turned into a reverse swing, but his enemy ducked. The blade just passed over the top of Roar's head while he drew his short sword out from his belt holster into a wide swing that slashed Gaius along his armored side and chest. He then immediately stepped in close and drove the blade hard into his opposite side and this time the armor was pierced.

Gaius cried out and began striking him desperately with the hilt of his sword. Roar released his grip on his own sword to grab hold of his enemy's chest piece with both hands. He hoisted Gaius above his head saying, "Nice try boy." Suddenly even the tainted armor that Gaius wore began to glow as Roar took a heavy step toward the signal and hurled him toward it as if he were a small stone.

Gaius crashed into the ground with his sword still gripped in his hand and the enemy's still wedged into his side. Despite searing pain he struggled back to his knees to see Roar reaching out a glowing gauntlet. His axe which had dropped near the signal when he was blindsided returned to his grip.

"Gaius!" Argoe's shouted as he hurled his spear toward him before collapsing again. The spear landed just barely within reach of his friend, and as the young man laid hold of it with his free hand, Roar noticed that the giants were now beginning to head their way, having overran what was left of his army.

He swung the axe around his head and then into an under swing releasing an orb in the direction of Gaius who raised both weapons the best he could in an effort to block the attack, yet it wasn't meant for him. He watched helplessly as it curved right passed him with a hum toward the glowing rock within the signal. "At last," Roar shouted, "the end has come!"

Unexpectedly the image of this very man dying within his dream flooded Gaius's mind and in an instant he understood what it meant... what Haran was unwilling to admit to him. "Not yet," he shouted back as he turned to face the signal, and as the orb connected with the rock core Gaius sunk both weapons into the earth, conjuring all of the defense he could from the two weapons.

"No," Roar whispered as the rock erupted with a thunderous boom emitting a shockwave that shattered men, trees, and whatever else was in its path. Gaius held on to the embedded weapons just long enough for the blast to pass by, but it still had nearly ripped him free of his grip. Those with Colosso were pressing into a melee with a defensive aura when the shockwave hit. Their distance, along with their defense, kept them alive, but still they were hammered to the ground senseless.

Everyone else anywhere near the blast site was dead. All that had remained of the Scourge and Gannim's horde, Melek and his warriors who had fallen back to the tree line, and all those of Arioch who had taken cover within the front of the city.

The large flash was witnessed from the house of Rhone all the way to Gull. Those who beheld this enigma gasped in fear and wonder as to what it could mean. Gannim and those with him were close enough to hear the blast and feel the faint push of its waning power. They stopped their pursuit just long enough to discuss among themselves what it could have been.

They who fled with Commander pressed on at his urging for he knew full well what the sound had came from. Seeing the flash from the sky, Bashan turned back to see for himself the source of the light. Gaius leaned against the weapons which we're now the only things still holding him up. The defensive aura had been large and strong enough to protect Roar, which was exactly what he had intended, yet he was to weak to even turn over and see the outcome for himself.

All was suddenly quiet. Roar's expression of disbelief was quickly replaced with one of outrage as he stomped over to Gaius and turned him around snarling, "No one saves me! Why?" he demanded.

Gaius's eyes were glazing over but he managed to utter in a hushed tone, "You must live... for us to live."

Roar again grabbed him up by his chest piece and hoisted him high, "I didn't come here so that you could live! I came here to destroy you!" Yet it was too late for any more answers from Gaius, for he was dead and Roar now stood alone. He released the body which dropped limply to the ground and turned his gaze to the devastation surrounding him.

All seemed surreal, even to one who had seen so much death. Soon the silence was broken as the sound of distant cries began to echo from deep within the interior of the city. With the fighting having ended, people were now beginning to experience the woe of the battle's aftermath. There was scarcely a child whose father had not died or a woman who had not become a widow.

Their heartbroken wails grew in number as more and more discovered their loss. Roar bowed his head and winced at the sound. He gnashed his teeth, shut his eyes tight, and clenched both fists near his face as if resisting whatever was going on inside of himself. Unable to tolerate the cries any longer he covered his ears in a desperate attempt to block the sounds out all together.

Deep within his mind, memories of the screams from his own village began to rise up again to the forefront of his mind. Abruptly he opened his eyes and knelt down, wrenching his sword free of the dead man's side. He then retrieved his axe and began to run, seeking to escape the sounds from the city which were haunting him so. Roar fled from these cries, and the memories they conjured, disappearing into the darkness of the forest.

Chapter 24
Someone to Hate

"Colosso... Colosso my friend, can you hear me?" Haran repeated, looking down at him. Though his eyes had opened, the warrior still looked out of sorts.

"Either I've lost part of my hearing or the fighting is over," he replied.

Some of his comrades began to help him up. "Have a look for yourself," Arnost said to him.

As soon as he stood upright he was immediately astonished by the sight of all his fallen comrades. "Then we lost," he stated with disappointment.

"I don't think so," Haran answered. You are the only ones I've seen standing, though if you listen carefully you will hear the cries of those who now find themselves widows and orphans. I was praying in the woods a short distance from here when I heard a great noise. The earth shook and then all was quiet. When I arrived, it was only those among you who were showing signs of life."

"We were grouped defensively," Colosso replied, "But pressing forward for the finish as many of the enemy had begun to flee." Suddenly alarm crept across his brow, "What of Ryn... what of Argoes?"

Haran looked just as concerned admitting, "I don't know but let us search for them."

"Check all of our brothers for life," Colosso ordered the small band of twenty who stood beside him. They searched body after body, checking for signs of life and trying to determine who the mangled remains once belonged too. It was a grim exercise of bitter sadness which increased in melancholy with the confirmation of each lifeless shell.

As they neared the blast sight, the bodies were scattered far, many in pieces. Though they could not identify them all, they attempted to confirm their findings by number until all but two were accounted for.

"It's Gaius!" Arnost shouted and all rushed to where he stood. His body lay there face up with a blank stare. The warrior who had found him knelt down and felt the wound at his side. He raised his hand showing his comrades the blood of the fatal wound.

Haran looked furious. He stepped away and gazed towards the sky a moment composing himself until his anger over the loss of his friend was replaced with grief. He too kneeled down beside the body and placed a gentle hand on it saying, "Gaius... brave lad, we will meet again."

"Is this not the sword that Argoes gave him and is this not Argoes's spear also?" Arnost gestured to the weapons still protruding from the ground.

"Indeed they are," one of the warriors confirmed.

"There!" Arnost exclaimed, pointing to a few bodies that lay between them and what remained of the city front. They all rushed over to get a good look at them and in spite of the horror that had been wreaked upon the remains; there was no doubt as to their identity. Some of the armor was intact and there were only two men unaccounted for; these were indeed the remains of their champions.

"Double-check the fallen," Colosso said to the others. "So few of us remain we will not be returning the bodies home. Nor will they be buried now, but retrieve all the sky metal you are able to carry."

The men hesitated for they were inwardly conflicted so Colosso said to them, "This is not easy for me either, but our people eagerly await the return of the living. We only have so much food and the journey will not be so easy in our weary condition. I intend that no more of us die between now and then." With that being said they held their peace and carried out the orders.

Bashan stopped a short distance in front of Commander who still led the way for the hundred or so who had escaped. Commander brought them all to a stop and Bashan announced, "All are dead at the place of battle, but it looks as though a band of perhaps fifty are following after you."

"Are they ours?" Commander asked.

"I was high, but even in the dark I would say not."

"Gannim was nipping at our heels as we departed. This can only be him," Commander declared, looking a bit disturbed at the thought of being stalked.

"What happened back there?" Bashan asked.

Commander sighed, "Roar saw that we were being overrun and decided that the only way to win would be for everyone to lose. We have no time to discuss it now. Your riders are no doubt far ahead of us, racing for the Port City. I do not want to fight Gannim unless I have to, or else you've returned to us with fresh soldiers."

Without a word Bashan ushered his beast back into the air and raced eastward shouting, "Be careful until I've returned!"

Feryn had not even attempted to find rest, but had kept watch late into the night. Finally she decided to break the seal on the message she had received from Gaius, and she began to read.

My dearest Feryn, your father has been very busy building alliances, but I know that victory will not be found in them. I hope to return to you soon, though I know I can promise nothing. I do not regret my choice to remain so that you could leave. If the cost of your safety is my life then so be it; I will gladly give it.

As I await what is to come, I find myself often wondering why men rage in pursuit of what belongs to others? Surely the accumulation of wealth cannot make one any happier than I am when walking by your side.

I only wish that my life solely consisted of such peaceful moments. Whatever happens, remain true to He who gave me the means of securing your rescue. Know that I carry you in my heart always, Gaius.

A call rang out, breaking her concentration. "The giants return!" The news resounded again and again all over the city. Feryn rushed down from the balcony on which she stood and made her way towards the gates. By the time she came near the front of the city, the crowds had already gathered to the point where she could see little, yet she could hear the crowd saying things like, "There are so few." and, "Could they have lost the battle?"

Soon there were gasps as the crowd began to part, allowing the weary warriors to enter. Haran led the procession, and just behind him two of the giants carried a fallen warrior upon one of their large shields.

From his size and the sad look in Haran's eyes Feryn knew immediately the identity of this man. With her heart broken, the favored daughter of Arioch who seemed ever composed, dropped to her knees and wailed.

By dawn, fatigue had all but swallowed Commander and those with him. They stopped along a shallow ford that sat in the open in order to drink and rest a moment. "Stay alert, we will not stay long," he admonished his men.

Though they had been defeated, the men were confident that they could handle things if those following were to catch up to them. This they reasoned, because Bashan had told them their numbers were greater. However, Commander was uneasy for he understood full well that Gannim was indeed a very crafty warlord.

He was just about to get them moving again when he noticed some birds fleeing out of the forest as if startled. "That'll do boys. Let's get moving," he called out, but only moments later Gannim and his men came into view along the path leading to them.

All the men scrambled in readiness for a fight, "Calmness... calmness," Gannim urged them lightheartedly. "I have not come seeking your lives. I have come to restore you to the fold. After all, your leader is dead, is he not?"

Commander and his men said nothing, but watched their enemies closely for any trickery. Gannim began to meet the gazes of the men as he sought to assure them, saying, "Return to your true master Mizrahim, and all will be forgiven. This land is within our grasp, soon it will be ours!" He sounded optimistic but those with Commander remained stoic.

"Really?" Commander chided having heard enough. "We hold the mountain and the port as well. Not to mention Roar took your army with him."

Gannim grinned, but there was a dangerous look of annoyance in his gaze. "Ah, Roar's favorite lackey. I had forgotten you were there. I suddenly have a grand proposition. You and I will duel and if you should kill me then you will return to what's left of your rabble and celebrate your greatness. But if I should kill you, and I will kill you," Gannim assured, "then your men may still return to tell the rest of their comrades of my most gracious offer. The Scourge or Roar will not cease to be, it will simply be led by me now."

Commander knew he was being set up, but he was angry. He thought about his friend and leader's willingness to die in order to preserve their survival. Roar had done so with the intent that they put an end to the rule of men such as Gannim.

"Very well," Commander announced resolutely as he drew his short sword. Instead of a shield, he accepted an identical sword from one of his men. He looked at them and said, "Whatever happens, remember what courage looks like. Remember that Roar of the Scourge died so that we could put an end to the likes of him." He motioned toward Gannim who looked bored as he waited for him to stop talking. "That is the message we are taking back to Bashan and Achaia."

He turned to face Gannim who was smiling wide with his tri stars at his sides. "Come on with it then," Commander shouted at his enemy harshly as his swords began to glow. Gannim nodded and hurled one of his blades. It hummed as it raced at Commander who side stepped and swatted it with a clang, but its twin was already on its way. Commander reversed his swing with the same arm and sent the star arcing high only to have it return to its owner. The blades kept coming one after the other and Commander kept parrying effectively. Gannim halted a moment, looking annoyed.

"This aint my first fight lackey of Mizrahim, or did you think I became Roar's right hand because of my good looks?" Commander taunted. Gannim spit in disgust and tossed his blade underhanded with bad intentions. The blade curved up and dropped suddenly toward Commander's face. He had just enough time to dive for the dirt as the blade embedded itself in the ground behind him.

Commander scrambled quickly to his feet with a swing releasing an orb, but Gannim spun out of its way hurling his other star when he turned to face him again. Commander crossed his blades and blocked the powerful attack. As the blade was returning to Gannim, Commander charged.

With both swords in hand and seeing that Gannim was recalling only one star, Commander figured that now was the moment to make a strong offence. As he neared, Gannim caught the star with one hand and reached behind his back with the other.

Commander was several strides away when Gannim pulled his whip from behind his back and snapped it just in front of his enemy's face. The blast unleashed brought Commander to an immediate and dazed stop. Gannim's blade immediately followed the snap and it slammed into Commander's chest.

He fell backwards, gasping and gurgling the last remaining moments of life. Gannim watched him a moment with great satisfaction before raising a hand. The blade wiggled within the dead man's chest and then ripped out to return to his grip. Gannim met the angry stares of the men he desired to win over, but they looked half ready to fight. "Tell your leaders the kindness and the severity that is weighing upon their decision." He gestured toward Commander's body continuing, "Tell them there is but one choice or this man's punishment will also be yours!"

Sihon stood upon an outcrop of the Tower of the Iron Gate looking down at the witchers who stood stoically just outside the city. His new shield was slung to his back and the word bound to his waste. Standing at the front of them was Kedar who gave the bold prince a nod. Sihon returned the gesture with a steely glare before abruptly turning away to head into the interior of the city. His steps carried determination and his demeanor was grim.

Secret plans had been made since the arrival of the hooded strangers from the south. Those who knew what was about to happen watched him quietly and stayed far out of his way as he marched into the palace of his father.

His brother stood just inside and looked as though he had something he wanted to say, but relented to do so. Still his countenance was grieved. As Sihon began to ascend the steps that would lead to his father's room Drakon finally spoke up, "Are you sure brother?" Sihon's step slowed just a moment, but he did not reply, and neither did he look back before marching on.

As he neared the doors to his father's room he drew out the sword called Wrath and those standing guard quietly stepped out of the way. Sihon opened one of the dark wooden doors and entered in. "Who pays me a visit?" King Iomar asked from a large chair facing a window overlooking the city. "Is it you my sons?" The king could not see behind him from where he sat, and being very sick he did not even attempt to stand.

"It is your eldest son, Sihon, my king."

"Ah, son of my strength. It is good to hear your voice. You have not come to me for a few days now. What news do you bring of these strangers from the south? Do they have anything more to say?"

The eyes of Wrath grew bright, though Sihon was unaware. The prince clenched his teeth before answering, "Yes, father." He stepped just behind the king's chair and raised the sword high, "They say long live the king!'" and with one merciless stroke Sihon slashed through the heavy wooden chair his father sat upon, severing his spine and following through until the end of the blade was imbedded into the cold stone floor.

He winced a moment as the reality of what he had just done washed over him. He swallowed hard as feelings of confusion and grief began to well up inside, but then he noticed that the blood upon his sword was not running toward the ground. He watched in near disbelief as instead, it was drawn toward the vile guard until it pooled into the mouth of the skull.

Soon the blood vanished, appearing as though it had been devoured by the weapon itself. Sihon held the sword out at arm's length. Looking the skull in the eyes he asked, "What are you?"

In the warmth of a clear sunny day, a pretty young maiden took hold of the cool end of the branch which she had earlier leaned upon the edge of a cooking fire. The end that had been in the flames still smoked profusely just as she had intended, for she intended to use it to frighten bees. Branch in hand she hurried out of her village toward a tree on a nearby hill that was surrounded by wild flowers. There was a grin on her face and a bounce in her step that only faded long enough for her to chase what she considered buzzing pests out of her path.

Resting beneath the shade of the tree was a young man. She crept towards him silently and plopped herself down beside him, her long wavy braid dangling over her shoulder. He knew she was there but did not open his eyes.

"Talal... do the bees not bother you?" she asked.

"No, for I am not sweet," he answered, still keeping his eyes closed. "But even though you are my dear, they will not bother you either so long as you do not step on them."

She smiled wide and spotted an ant marching along the trunk of the tree. "What about the ants then? Do they bother you?"

"No," he answered. "For though I am not large, I am much larger than they."

She cheerfully laid her head upon his chest and listened to his heart beat. They remained there enjoying one another in the quiet a moment before she declared, "I have something to tell you."

"And what is that my love?" he asked.

She leaned in close to his ear and whispered, "I carry your child..."

Roar opened his eyes and jumped to his feet. He was alone in the dark on a rocky hillside overlooking the forest. Something did not feel right; then he realized he was not holding his axe which scarcely left his grip even when he slept. He spied it lying on the ground just beside the place he had been sleeping and dreaming.

He stretched out his hand and the axe came to him. He looked to the moonlit horizon and spotted a large pine in the distance. His axe suddenly began to illuminate and with a few angry strides he hurled it with a shout. The weapon soared furiously until it severed the top off of the massive tree which slowly tilted until it crashed into the forest below, hitting the ground with a thud.

He had thrown the weapon so hard and far that he was not at all sure if it would even return to him, but at that moment he didn't care. Roar turned his back to the wooded hills and stood in silence. To his surprise he began to hear the growing sound of his weapon spiraling toward him. He turned around just in time to see it pass him by and imbed itself into a nearby rock. This seemed very unusual indeed for he had not summoned it.

He cast his gaze into the clear night sky and said, "So El Shaddai, God of my wife, once again you've taken everything away from me. And it matters not if I am a man of peace or of war. But why?" he asked with frustration. "Why do I garner your attention so, and why has death eluded me once again? I would have gladly died on the same day of my people." Roar looked down, his anger replaced with a look of disappointment on the brink of despair. "I can only imagine that now more than ever I stand before you as someone to hate."

The Tale to Come

And so, no sooner had the Scourge of Mizrahim became the Scourge of Roar it fell against the might of its combined enemies; but on that fateful night truly no man was the victor.

The landscape of the Land Between the Seas was changing. The plans of those seen and unseen were both taking shape. A storm was coming, but not a storm composed simply of the elements. It would be a mighty torrent of swords, spirits, and the strength of men.

As for Roar, though his army was spread thin and much of its strength shattered, he remained the mightiest of warriors. Great would be the disappointment of his enemies who would soon learn that the pronouncements of his demise were declared far too soon, but that is a story for another time.

16839477R00120

Made in the USA
Lexington, KY
13 August 2012